TOUGH CITY, TOUGHER WOMAN

RICHARD E. RIEGEL

Black Rose Writing

www.blackrosewriting.com

First printing

ISBN: 978-1-61296-203-0

PUBLISHED BY BLACK ROSE WRITING

www.blackrosewriting.com

Printed in the United States of America

Tough City, Tougher Woman is printed in Minion Pro

For Marianne
For every woman
For every man

TOUGH CITY,
TOUGHER WOMAN

CHAPTER 1

One o'clock in the morning in the big city is a betwixt and between zone.

It was betwixt and between gettin' drunk at the local dive and getting that dreaded "last call for alcohol," between 2 and 2:30 a.m.

At that half hour, the cross section of the male of the species was daunting. Pimps, whoremongers, drunkards, criminals, out-and-out freaks.

Linda Avery had seen them all.

As the cigarette girl at the Club Festival in Portland, Oregon, she knew her way around all sorts of drunken, foolish men.

The life of a cigarette girl.

Hawking cigarettes, breath mints and the occasional condom wasn't actually the end-all and be-all job occupation for Linda.

But without a high school diploma, and a sincere lack of interest in what some would consider a career, she knew her options were limited in today's society.

Oh, no, here at the Club Festival, ethics and morality were only gauged as highly as the limits of an individual's cash in the wallet.

Money, honey, that made things move all about her.

Linda Avery was a city girl, born and bred.

She was born in the big city of Portland, Oregon, and although raised in a small town a few miles away, came to the big city for excitement. She came to the city both with her parents as a child and as an adolescent on her own. She remembered that back in the day, coming into Portland with her parents was a matter of finding the main drag, Burnside Street, that connected the west side with the east side; now there's more than one freeway route through town.

As an adolescent, Linda was adept at hitchhiking back and forth between the big city and the small town. Her parents, for whatever reason, had no compunction about allowing her to hitchhike, as it was common in her day. Linda grew so adept at hitchhiking that she felt she could write a book on the subject. Her most unique technique was to point at a driver passing her by, feigning recognition; the technique worked on occasion, but usually it was a matter of sticking out the thumb and looking nonthreatening.

As an adult, she would move to the big city and make it her home.

She was in her element walking the concrete sidewalks, listening to the buzz of traffic and the hum of city life. One reason was because as a child she lived in the old downtown of the small town, where the movie theater, the bank, several restaurants and most of city's government structure was located. As a child she'd seen empty wine bottles and empty snuff boxes littering the streets on Sunday morning.

In the big city, as an adult, one aspect she never tired of was listening to the homeless men chatter incoherently to themselves. Some of them were quiet and reserved, others loud and abrasive. It didn't matter to her, it was harmless, and she pitied the men more than anything. She looked down on them, as an average citizen might, as the waste and refuse of human existence.

Linda felt as if some of the homeless were on the streets because of bad luck and no better choice, but she'd come to the conclusion over the years that a big percentage of the street folks are hardcore homeless, and are on the streets because that's the lifestyle they've chosen.

"Spare a quarter for some food?" an out-of-doors person would ask.

"Sorry," was all Linda would say. She knew you didn't want to get into a conversation with any of them, and you certainly didn't want to get confrontational. She also didn't want to give any money to them for concern over what they'd do with the cash, like spend it on alcohol.

She tried getting confrontational with a homeless person one day, and she nearly paid the price. That price would have been bodily harm.

As she walked out of a supermarket in the middle of the city one day, a row of shabbily-dressed men lined the bench outside the entrance. One of them pleaded with her.

"Spare some change, lady?" a disheveled old bum asked her.

Instead of her usual, "Sorry," she decided she'd give the old guy some backtalk.

"No, I can't spare any change," she barked back. "Why don't you get a job?"

That snapped it for the old guy. He began yelling at her, incoherent gibberish, but at the top of his lungs.

"You bitch," he yelled. "Fuck you!"

When she tried walking away, the old guy got up and started following, yelling as he pursued her.

She picked up the pace, and was nearly at a trot as she rounded the corner. A few quick steps and she was out of the vagrant's sight.

Close call.

That rude encounter taught her a lesson, a lesson she already knew, but now was positively entrenched. The city offers challenges, but she'd been lucky to never have had a gun or knife pointed at her on the street.

She knew that much of the violence and insanity that occurs doesn't happen between strangers. It happens between people who know each other. Violent, abusive partners seem to be the most prevalent combination. Violence and insanity between friends, lovers, relatives.

On the street, if you minded your own business, and didn't mouth off to the beggars and panhandlers, you survived. Play it straight was the lesson learned.

In the main, Linda had enough self-esteem and enough confidence to be able to deal with the street people in a tactful manner. Her encounter with the angry homeless man taught her a lifelong lesson: Leave well enough alone.

But she truly enjoyed walking the streets, taking in the cityscape and all its blasé sameness or bright wonders. To her, the city was a place where the humans lived, loved and laughed, and to deny the city its inherent wonderment was to deny life. She knew the city had its share of "bad people," but in her short, sweet life she'd learned no matter where you go, be it the middle of the city or the middle of nowhere, people were basically the same, either good or bad, or a combination of the two. You didn't have to travel to a big city to get ripped off, beat up or killed.

She loved and respected the city and its inhabitants. She avoided trouble if she could, but when push came to shove, she felt she could give it as good as she got it.

Knocking off after a slow weekday night at the Club Festival, cigarette girl Linda Avery headed home to her apartment in the same quadrant of the city. Not owning an automobile or motorcycle made it more of a challenge to get around, but she could easily navigate the city by foot, by bicycle and by mass transit. Portland's vast mass transit system covered three counties, with Portland in the middle. Multnomah, Washington and Clackamas counties are covered by TriMet, and although the cost of traveling on the bus and light rail system was increasing year by year, it was still one of the best systems in the nation.

Linda didn't mind paying for the cost of traveling the mass transit system, and felt that those who use the system must pay their way. She also knew that many citizens felt entitled to cheap transportation, entitled to the many benefits that had been increasing in American society over the decades. She didn't feel the same way; she felt that the benefits accrued by citizens were a gift not automatically endowed. She had some sort of crazy idea that benefits needed to be earned by citizens, not given out like free candy. That was her opinion, of course, and not the opinion of all.

It was cold outside, but not raining. She'd dressed appropriately, preparing earlier in the day for whatever may come her way. She always carried an umbrella, and wore shoes practical for walking. She kept a dressier pair of shoes, with supportive soles, at the workplace. She was a practical, pragmatic woman raised by parents who had lived through the Great Depression, so there was a hint of that mindset in everything she did. She was frugal to the maximum, and hated to see anything go to waste.

What she learned from her parents, survivors of the Great Depression, was that you adapted to live without those items you could, well, live without. You learned not to waste food. You learned to eat good food, certainly, but nothing extravagant. You learned to buy only what you needed, and to make sure you didn't pay too much for it. It was almost a game to her parents to see how much they could save on any particular item. At the same time, you made sure what you bought were of good, decent quality. You also learned to repair something if it could be repaired, like an article of clothing or a piece of furniture. You didn't live like a pauper, but you didn't live like a king. You lived within your means.

As she walked the city streets on the way to her apartment, she noticed as the years went on more and more waste on the sidewalks of her city. People too lazy either to take reusable furniture, clothing and household items to a charity or to have a charity organization pick them up would place those items on the sidewalks in front of their apartments, condos and homes for others to rifle. Linda herself had found a few good items, but stayed away from furniture and clothing, for fear of bringing vermin and virus into her apartment. Unfortunately, all it took was an overnight rain to soak any usable items on the street and make them generally worthless.

Walking home after midnight, in the first few hours of the day, was possibly a risky thing to do, but Linda knew the city, knew her limits and knew how to handle the usual rabble that populated the streets. But she also wished she knew more about self defense, maybe some martial art. She didn't believe in carrying a gun, figuring that's a good way to get the damned thing taken away from you and used on you, or some other person in the future.

As she approached her apartment building, she noticed a man loitering at the outside entrance to the three-story brick complex. Built in the early 1900s, it was known in the commercial rental business as a secure entry facility. Renters needed one key to get into the bottom-floor entrance, which opened into a lobby; those same renters needed another key to open their own individual apartments.

Typical of all such buildings, there was also a dedicated telephone system located at the entrance to allow visitors access to the inside. Visitors would ring to an apartment, and would be allowed access by the apartment dweller inside pushing a button that remotely unlocked the front door.

Instead of heading right to the entrance, Linda decided to diffuse a possibly risky situation by walking around the block once. She figured if the fellow knew someone inside, and had used the access system, he'd be inside by the time she came back around the block. City blocks in Portland were smaller in size than in larger cities like New York and Chicago, so it wouldn't necessarily take that long to go around the block. If the person wasn't home, the visitor would hopefully wander away. Any other person hanging around the outside of a secure building gave rise to suspicion best noticed.

Linda walked around the block, and when she returned to near the front of the building, the person, a medium-height, medium-build white man, remained at the entrance. Linda did not like to be confrontational, but if she needed to be assertive, she could be.

Not willing to avoid the situation, and wanting to get into her apartment, she approached the front entrance cautiously.

"Excuse me," Linda said as she walked up the three steps to the entrance and to the front security door.

"Oh, sorry," the man said.

As Linda put the key in the front door lock, the man made a move to follow her inside. Linda hesitated with the door open only two or three inches.

"Excuse me," Linda said, "but do you live here?"

It was then that Linda noticed the man's breath smelled of alcohol. He didn't appear homeless, and was dressed in the mode of the day.

"No," he said, sounding somewhat indignant that Linda was questioning him. "I'm visiting a friend."

"Well," Linda said, "you have to get let in by your friend." Linda positioned herself between the stranger and the slightly opened door, barring his entrance.

"Can't you let me in?" he asked, now sounding both indignant and put off by the whole scene.

"No, I can't," she said. "I'm sorry." She opened the door enough to begin sliding inside, using her body to fill the gap between the door and the door jam.

"Come on," he pleaded, sounding more childish than anything else, "let me in."

"No," she said, firmly yet politely, trying to keep the conversation civil. "You'll have to wait for your friend to let you in." Linda knew the score. If he was lying, she didn't need him wandering the halls of her apartment complex, and neither did the management or the residents.

She had a keen sense of civic responsibility for her fellow apartment renters.

As Linda said the last few words, she let the door close between her on the inside and the stranger on the outside.

"Well, that's fucked!" he yelled at her through the door. The front door had a large plate glass window, and she could see the stranger's face turn instantly red, his countenance full of anger.

"Sorry," was all she could say as she turned her back on the man and proceeded to her apartment. She'd done the right thing by not letting the man inside and she knew it was very possible she'd prevented a burglary or a rape.

"You never can be too careful," she thought to herself as she entered her own apartment.

The Club Festival was no Cheers bar. In fact, it was a place where no one knew your name, and that was just as well. Regulars kept their lives to themselves, and waitresses understood that unless someone was forthcoming with an identity, they didn't ask customers for names, dates and locations.

It wasn't a private club, and as a matter of course tourists and unknowing Portlanders wandered in off the dirty street to become part of the huddled masses in the club. The club didn't advertise in the local media. It didn't have to advertise.

Club Festival was one of those places where only insiders knew the score. Tourists, military and conventioneers who had the guts could ask a cab driver where to go in town for excitement. At first the wise cabby would feign ignorance. You'd have to press the driver for the right information, know somebody or provide a little cash incentive to get the scoop on where to find the action.

The club was exclusive among the cadre of other seedy dives in the City of Roses. It dealt in one line of excitement and made damned sure it stuck to that vein.

"Where's a fella gotta go to get laid in this town?" asked one of the three sailors jammed into the backseat of the Radio Cab as it zoomed out of Portland International Airport one dark and rainy Saturday evening.

"Sir, I do not know what you are talking about," said the cabbie, a black man who recently moved to the United States from Angola.

"Come on, dude," the young man said, "you know, wine, women, song, where's the best hangout in this berg?"

"I'm sorry, sir," the man politely replied in a heavy Angolan accent, "I'm not sure what you mean."

There was an uncomfortable silence for a few seconds. The three sailors whispered among themselves in the backseat.

"Where can I take you fellows?" the cabbie asked.

"Downtown," another said. "Just take us the fuck downtown."

Once in downtown Portland, near the old and new hotels, strangers wouldn't be in much better shape to find out where "the action" was located. Portlanders are an unusually friendly lot, for certain, unlike bigger cities. Need directions to an address? No problem. Need a recommendation for a good restaurant? Ask anyone on the street, man or woman, and for the most part you'll get a straight answer. But try to find out where to go if you want to run the whores or snort a decent line of cocaine, and lips are sealed. You've got to know somebody. Even those "somebody" types won't necessarily know about the half dozen truly wicked bars and clubs. Sure, places with throngs of people, bass-thumping music and crazy-drunk women are everywhere. Anybody can see them, hear them, find them.

But to the regulars at the Club Festival, it was OK to them that the bar wasn't jammed with tony young men and women, gang bangers and hep young people. The kind of people that hung out at the Club Festival kept to themselves.

This atmosphere of secrecy and the hidden agenda kept the club's clientele anonymous, but the tension created by such covert activity made for an odd mix of alcoholics, stoned-out potheads and introverted weirdoes. That couldn't be helped. It also couldn't be helped that the continued repression tended to cause more than the usual altercations and fistfights. It went with the territory.

Maybe calling the Club Festival a dive would be a bit harsh, but right away the name of the place was deceiving. It wasn't as if the place had some sort of tropical motif to the interior, or that there was a truly festive feeling about it. Because the club was so purposely hard to describe as having any sort of look or feel to it, anyone who wandered off the street usually didn't return for a second helping of the hospitality. It was off-putting enough to deter the uninitiated, and that was fine with the staff and management.

Probably the only thing unusual about the club was the old-fashioned accouterments, like having a coat checkroom and employing a cigarette girl. There were no couches and no drinks with umbrellas. Again, as in the demeanor of all Oregonians, the waitresses were friendly enough, on the outside. But ask about hooking up with a hooker or scoring some weed, you'd get the cold shoulder on the first go around.

Linda Avery, cigarette girl, was the bastion of propriety at the club. Ask her for anything she's carrying in her tray and you received a pleasant response. Ask for something you didn't see, something you couldn't get at home or at the store, and it was a different matter.

"Hey, baby, tell me a story," the customer said as Linda walked by him.

"What sort of story, sir?"

"Oh, come on, loosen up," he said. "I'm in the mood for a story."

"How about a story," she piped up, looking over the head of the customer, "about a man named Jed?"

"Funny girl," he said back.

"You know," she continued, "he was a poor mountaineer, barely kept his family fed."

"OK, OK, cut the bullshit," the man replied, instantly tired of her feint humor. It was fortunate for him that he asked her to halt her dissembling line of claptrap. Linda knew pretty much the entire words to the theme song to The Beverly Hillbillies, and would have continued if not stopped.

"I got a different story in mind," he continued to press.

"What might that be, sir?" she said in her best aloof tone.

"How about you get the hell out of my face?"

"Fine," she responded curtly, and slinked away to help other customers.

CHAPTER 2

Linda's mind drifted freely, unhinged, as it were, from its moorings.

"Now we're talkin' my lingo," yelled the drunken drunk man outside of Linda's second floor apartment, waking her from her daydreaming. "Damned drunks," she thought to herself.

Drink, drank, drunk. This is also the tawdry scene at the nearby Club Festival.

The men gather at the Club Festival to drown their sorrows, check their integrity at the door and try to put the make on some suspecting woman.

In a bar, early in the evening, men would attempt some reserved ice-breaking conversation.

"Come here often?" or "Can I buy you a drink?" were common to the sober man.

"What's your name, sweetie pie?" or "What's a good lookin' gal like you doin' in a place like this?" from men a little later on in the evening, with a few drinks under their belts.

By the end of night, men had either given up trying or were too damned drunk to care. Then they'd stumble out of the Club Festival to a local strip club or to a cheesier bar to "run the whores."

This is the environment in which Linda plied her wares. The rough trade, the sophisticated lothario and the prowling eye.

She knew men, had dated many men and had interacted literally with hundreds of men over her lifetime. Now in her 50s, she'd seen her share of Sad Sacks, losers and crumbs. She'd also known a handful of good men, men she could trust, men with whom she felt comfortable.

But the majority of men Linda had known weren't the most sterling examples of the male of the species. She often wondered if it were her bad luck that she'd mostly run into unfit or unstable men. Was it how the cards were stacked in her life? Sometimes she felt as if the preponderance of men were born under a bad sign, that bad luck was the only kind of luck they had. Again, though, there were good men, few and far between.

As her life unfolded, she also saw a good share of bad women. Women who had not much going for themselves, not much more than their good looks and conniving minds. She'd known scheming women, women who had no more moral scruples than the lowest man. She'd known women who enjoyed teasing, taunting and tormenting men.

What would come out of this stew, this brew of bad devices, would be a tale of revenge turned into revulsion transformed into redemption. The moral of the story. That moral would be at the hand of a scorned woman. A woman out for revenge. At least that's how it started.

Our story features Linda Avery, the hard-working cigarette girl at the Club Festival, who begins to plot revenge against one of the most cruel womanizers, and ends up forgiving Tail Gunner, the most notorious user and abuser of women in town.

Given the opportunity to act like all the men she'd known, she opted to take the higher moral road and apply forgiveness as opposed to retribution. But taking the high road isn't always the road to redemption. Sometimes evil gets in the way.

It wasn't as if Linda hated men.

Growing up, her stepfather was strict yet fair with the children. He was by far much stricter with her brother Joe than with her. Mom kept the daughter in line, Pop kept the boy on the straight and narrow.

But as she blossomed into womanhood, boys were turning into young men. Young men with raging hormones, Roman hands and

Russian fingers. There aren't any demographic statistics to prove the concept, but Linda was convinced every boy in her hometown walked around with a permanent hard-on. Catcalls, wolf whistles and indecent proposals were the norm in her Pacific Northwest town.

"Let's get naked!" was a typical catcall out the car window from the guys who cruised the boulevard in her hometown. It was probably the same in New England or in the Deep South. For Linda, the struggle to keep the male of the species in line and off of her back began early and never let up.

As she left the teenage years, young men's curiosity turned into obsession with "getting some," as the crude types would put it. She'd tolerated males for years, and sometimes enjoyed their company. Again, she didn't hate men, she hated the chauvinism and sexism many displayed.

But what put the icing on the cake for her was the man who menaced her after she had one date with him. He seemed like a nice guy, but that's always a danger in the beginning of any relationship. Courtship history, at least in America, has shown repeatedly that a man will place his best face forward in the beginning of a relationship, and then, when he's finally landed his catch, the façade comes down and the real man is exposed.

For Linda, one date with the man was enough. At first he was too nice, too accommodating, too willing to please; then the ugly side of his psyche appeared.

"How would you like me to take you out to a movie sometime?" he asked her after their initial dinner date.

Linda was taken aback that the man would ask her out for another date right away. The man had driven her home from the restaurant, and the two were sitting in his car in front of her apartment.

"We'll see," she said hesitantly.

"Crap on a cracker," he said, testily, "it's not as if I'm asking you to marry me."

"I said we'll see," she said firmly and with a bit of frustration playing on her vocal cords.

But in her mind, the first date would be the last date. She wanted to avoid any further argument with an argumentative man. Still, he persisted.

"Listen," he started right away, "I picked you up, brought you to a nice place for dinner and paid..."

"Wait a minute, buster," she said, interrupting him. "Do you really think that because you did all those things for me that you deserve to have me indebted to you in some way? Is that the way you think?"

"Hey, come on, give it a rest. I was just saying..."

"I know what you were saying. You were trying to make me feel guilty for taking advantage of poor, pitiful you."

"Calm down, calm down."

Linda stifled herself and stopped giving the guy any further ammunition. The two sat in uncomfortable speechlessness. A car driving by honked the horn, which broke the monotony of silence.

"I'd better get going," she said.

"OK," he said. "Thanks for a nice night."

Linda exited the car, shut the door and headed to her apartment. Like a gentleman, the man waited until she was inside the building to drive away.

"Fuckin' bitch," he said to himself as he motored off.

He tried to call for another date. She cautiously and purposely did not answer the phone for several days following the date. Linda was careful not to answer her phone for those few days, so put off by his syrupy-sweet passive-aggressive behavior. She thought he was too tightly wound; conversely, she thought he also had a screw loose. He called once a day for several days, then apparently threw in the towel and gave up.

When she thought it was over, after about two weeks, she got an odd phone call. A man called and said he was interested in an escort, and asked if she was available. Upon further querying the man, she found out that her name and phone number were listed in a local alternative newspaper's want ads, under Escort Services.

She called the newspaper and found out that the ad was placed by a person with the same first name as the fellow she'd dated recently. She asked that the ad not run again with her name and phone number. Thankfully, it was another woman whom she dealt with at the newspaper, and that woman was sympathetic to Linda's plight. The ad never appeared again. Linda called the police to complain, but there wasn't much they could do. They did request she come down to the station and file an official complaint, to get the incident on record in case the man escalated his behavior.

She continued to get phone calls from strangers seeking an "escort," maybe another half dozen, but the whole thing blew over within a week or two. Still, it left a bad taste in her mouth. She was young, and it was the first time in her life that some had become borderline threatening to her. It made her a bit cold to men she'd meet in the future, but it didn't put out the flame of passion and desire. She was resilient and forgiving.

Other men would test her faith by their pestering and peskiness, and some seemed too overly aggressive when it came to finding a date or a mate.

Later in life, when she thought of some of her past women friends, who'd taken "The Love Boat to the Isle of Lesbos," as Linda comically stated becoming lesbian, she wondered why she hadn't completely given up on men herself.

Still, she kept hope alive that somewhere out there might be a decent man, a man who wasn't a womanizer, a woman user or, worse than anything, a woman abuser. She'd known all types and discovered that 95 percent of guys were plain losers. She knew that most of the women friends she'd had over the years possessed steady jobs and were paying mortgages on houses or condos. The same couldn't be said for the men she'd known, since most were lazy drifters with no roots.

"Men," she thought to herself. "Can't live with 'em, can't live without 'em."

Linda was daydreaming.

"I'm out of my mind," Linda admitted to herself, half awake, half asleep. Did she really say that, out loud? "Is anyone there?" she pleaded in the inky darkness of the night.

She didn't go to bed alone, but alone she was now. Living like she did, alone and all, was the common denominator that you never get used to, but you adapt to it in a subtle way. You know that at the very least, it's a common occurrence, nothing to worry about, women, men die alone all the time.

She imagined herself dying in a hospital, with a relative by her side, maybe a friend or two. Who knew? Who cared?

"If I only knew who to blame," she said aloud, on purpose and for the world to hear. She knew this was going to be a great day, because she had revenge planned, sweet revenge. As "revenge is a dish best served cold," Linda liked to think of serving someone up a "cold bowl of hate." She may have gotten the phrase wrong, but she was on the right track as to how to treat human beings. Treat every human being with respect and dignity. Up until the time they begin to act like animals, then treat them like that. If someone barks at you, bark back. If they try to bite, show them your fangs. If they make actual physical contact, give 'em a punch in the jaw. If a man acts like a rabid dog, he needs to be restrained. If a man acts like a predatory wolf, he needs to be penned up. The man/animal analogy could be made endlessly.

So it was that Tail Gunner was going to get his, all right, he was going to pay and pay and pay for all that he'd done to her, all he'd done to every woman. He'd meted out plenty. Disrespect. Verbal abuse. Physical abuse. Men who take advantage of women are low, but just as low as any manipulator, any criminal bent on ripping you off. It's the common criminal that brings the whole human condition down to the gutter.

Tail Gunner was the worst of the male species. Sure, men should be given equal opportunity to live, to breath, to exist, but so many are like Tail Gunner, out to put the screws to another guy or put the root to some misbegotten woman.

Women should steer clear of anything to do with men, it's that simple. Men are slime balls, ask any streetwise woman. Ask Linda Avery.

"I am so totally fed up with how men treat women," Linda told a woman friend of hers once. "I'm tired of the way they look at us, how they treat us, how they take us for granted."

The odd contradiction for Linda was that she worked among some of the most amoral men in the city of Portland. Those men who frequented the Club Festival represented not a cross section of the residents of the city, but a distillation of all the worst homo sapiens that could ever be gathered in one locale.

The sheer volume of bizarre behavior and strange happenings could have earned it a reputation with local media and law enforcement. Within its walls ranged a wide spectrum of human behavior. Its denizens amounted to a borderline bedlam; to be sure, the residents of an insane asylum at least had some manner of supervision. Club Festival was a place where the worst proclivities of mankind found succor. A man's worst habits were nurtured there on a nightly basis.

By 2010, the Club Festival could have been Portland, Oregon's most notorious dive. But that wasn't so. Although the scum of the earth congregated at the club, word of the goings on within the walls of the seemly club never usually traveled far.

If it weren't for the cooperation of both the management and the patrons, a virtual posse of newspaper hacks, loud-mouthed radio talk show hosts and overly nosey TV reporters would have caught wind of several – maybe by rough count dozens – of scofflaw incidents.

But the patrons at the Club Festival knew a good thing – or maybe more correctly a bad thing – when they saw it, and for whatever reason – self-preservation, greed, denial, smarts – made a conscious decision to keep their collective mouths shut about this goose that laid the golden egg.

Portland, Oregon was and is no New York City. Portland didn't have the tourist draw, the nightlife or the glittery attractions of the City That Never Sleeps. But sleepy didn't mean dopey, and Portlanders all knew a good thing when they had it. That went triple for the Club Festival patrons.

Owner/manager Lou Brodsky and his lean staff at the Club Festival also had enough insight into how modern society worked always to keep appearances slightly kosher. New customers were always welcome with open arms, but favors were hard earned, not easily handed out. Illicit drugs were always available from any of the helpful staff, but new customers were never serviced on the premises, and deniability was factored into any transaction.

Flesh peddling was not encouraged at the club. It was a social necessity but a societal stigma. Lou saw no percentage in it. He had easier ways to earn money. Besides, attracting prostitution always presented myriad issues, resulting in headache and heartache. Lou didn't need and didn't want the headache of dealing with prostitutes and their requisite pimps. He didn't need the heartache of watching a woman sell herself and her soul.

Lou may not have had a heart of gold, but neither did he believe that gold, or money, ruled the world. Early in his adult life he saw what happened to friends and relatives who fixated on the almighty dollar. He didn't believe much in religion, and didn't believe that money was the root of all evil. He knew that men and women created the evil on this earth, and that for some of those people, it was enough to cause havoc and chaos.

"I don't believe that hate is the only thing that lasts," he told his cigarette girl one night. He was quoting a line from the movie Barfly, based on the life of barroom sage poet Charles Bukowski.

Cigarette girl Linda Avery was beginning to get to know her boss after procuring her position at the Club Festival. He was an odd duck, but not mean spirited or evil. If nothing else, he was, as he described himself, a "goofy fuck" who took life as it came.

"I really think the thing that lasts is caring for one another," he said, tenderly.

Linda looked at him and wondered what motivated a man such as himself.

"Lou," she said, "I think you're a deep man. I'm not bullshitting you, really."

Brodsky looked at his cigarette girl and began to tear up.

"What is it, Lou?"

He wiped the moisture from his eyes.

"Don't even ask."

"But…" she was about to add. Lou cut her off.

"I've seen a lot of pain, a lot of suffering in my life. I've watched friends die off or go insane. So don't ask me anything more. I don't know why I started talking."

Linda knew. She knew that there was a connection between the two. They were both in their late 50s, which meant they grew up in the 1960s, and saw the promise of the Love Generation turned to greed and avarice. Both were mute witnesses to the Kennedy brothers cut down by assassins, to men like Malcolm X and Martin Luther King, Jr. dying the same way. Both Linda and Lou were around when America lost its first war, the Vietnam War.

An abiding sense of sadness permeated their very existence. Somehow, some way, both would have to find happiness in the midst of the sadness. Somehow both of them would live to tell the tale.

CHAPTER 3

The bedroom reeked of stale perfume, cigarette butts and condom lubricant.

She knew she was lowering her standards and principles by going to bed with the man who sold brushes door to door.

But, what the hell, he was willin'. And soon enough, as far as she knew, they'd both be usin' penicillin. That may be an old joke, but mixing sex with anything was dangerous enough. In the world of whores, pimps and drug dealers, what, are you outta your mind?

Linda had for her entire adult life been aware of the dangers of unprotected sex. It had been drilled into people from before she was born.

The human immunodeficiency virus/acquired immune deficiency syndrome (HIV/AIDS) crisis that began in the '80s really wasn't a wakeup call for Linda. She already well knew of the proclivities and antics of the human animal. Humans were simply animals. The desire for sex wells up, bubbles up from a burning cauldron deep within every creature, male or female. It's instinctive. It's raw to the core.

But with the human, there was so much to work with, so many deviations from the norm. So many deviants. Perverts. Weirdoes. Freaks of nature.

Sometimes we are hard pressed as people to be able to divine whether the person with whom you are sharing a drink is a complete psycho, a nutcase ready to go off in your face. But you have to trust, you have to take a chance, so chances are taken, strangers are met, spit is swapped, body fluids are exchanged at the high rate of consumption.

Thereby lays the twist of the tale, the odd ending that catches you off guard.

"You've got genital warts," the doctor says, and like a dumbass all you can say is, "So what do we do now?"

Linda had been lectured all her life, from the moment she could comprehend, before becoming a teenager, that sex with anyone could result in a wide variety of frightening and dangerous outcomes. Of course, the main danger was getting pregnant.

But since she'd heard early on that there wasn't anything like getting "a little" pregnant, keeping the life-rich substance known as sperm away from her reproductive organs was the number one concern.

She remembered the frightening World War II posters, warning servicemen of the dangers of the "woman with the deadly disease," venereal disease, syphilis, gonorrhea, hell, it was a world of sexual disease.

Hurting to pee was a sign of a sexual disease, and you heard about it as a child on the playground, with off color jokes and puns.

Venereal disease was portrayed as something that could render you sterile, disfigured, or just plain dead.

Linda remembered some of the jokes from her brother's Playboy magazine, the jokes that were placed literally on the back of the precious fold out, the Playboy Bunny of the Month, a two-foot tall homage to womanly breasts filled with life-giving milk and luscious hips filled with venal mystery and muff-dive.

Linda never had a serious disease, she thought. She remembered getting penicillin shots when someone she knew came up with signs of syphilis, but she was never positive she had the disease.

She had genital warts, but those were easily cured with applications of wart removal medicine. The burning sensation of the harsh chemical wasn't that painful, more of an annoyance.

She did remember avoiding sex with one customer who admitted to her that he had herpes. She was highly appreciative of the honesty of that person. It was a frustrating situation for the ever-amorous Linda, having to stop groping and pleading and basically getting in rut like a wild animal.

Sex.

She knew that men wanted it. Bad. Always.

Beverley Beech, Linda's friend, also knew the score when it came to men. Talking with her friend Bev, Linda waxed philosophic on several topics.

The two were sharing a drink and a sandwich during the noon hour at the Club Festival. The club was a seedy, down-in-the-mouth sort of place when the sun went down, but during the daylight, Linda enjoyed the food. The head cook, who'd been working there for several years, was top notch. An older fellow with long hair, he'd picked up cooking tips and techniques while working at various good restaurants around town. He was in charge of a rotating group of part-time cooks who worked the various shifts at the Club Festival.

"You know what I like about catching a cold and getting sick?" Linda asked her friend.

"No, honey, tell me," Bev replied.

"It's great when it's over. That's what I look forward to when I get sick. I look forward to being normal. It makes you appreciate all the things you lost, like being able to breath, not having snot run down your upper lip, that sort of thing."

"OK, OK, I get it," Bev said, in a disgusted tone. "Let's not get too graphic, I'm trying to eat here."

"I'm sorry," Linda answered, sheepishly.

The two continued to eat. The club was quiet, and the music played softly. It was Miles Davis, from his work with Gil Evans on Porgy and Bess. Quiet, flowing jazz.

For Linda, being healthy was part of being happy. She had always taken care of her health, made sure that if there was any problem, she'd go to the doctor and have him or her check it out.

"I'm so glad for doctors," Linda said to Bev, out of the blue.

Bev, a nurse, had her own take on doctors.

"Doctors can be such losers," she told Linda. "You see, in my world, nurses really run the hospital. Doctors are only there 9 to 5, while nurses are there around the clock, taking care of patients on an ongoing basis."

"I get it," Linda replied. "Still, I like doctors. It's the doctor who prescribes medications and has the patient's overall health in mind.

"Doctors are like lawyers," Linda told her friend. "You go see them when something's wrong, with some amount of fear and trepidation. But, for the most part, both fix the problem. At no small cost, maybe, but the problem's usually always fixed. You go in scared, and walk away with everything fixed. That's always been my experience."

"It sounds like you've had good experiences with doctors and lawyers," Bev commented. "Unfortunately, working with doctors has taught me a few things that aren't so positive.

"For one," Bev continued, "again, nurses are at the hospital around the clock. A doctor will come in, maybe see each patient for two minutes, maybe not even that, maybe look at the patient's chart, write a few orders and take off.

"So if someone is truly taking care of the patients," Bev explained, "it's the nurse."

"Girlfriend," Linda said to Bev, "I never knew this kind of stuff. Go on."

"It's a dance between the doctors and the nurses," Bev continued. "For an experienced nurse, with the background and training, you're with the patient consistently, and you know XYZ, you know what the patient needs.

"You also know that if there's something important that needs to be done, or an order that needs to be changed, you know you have to call a doctor if there's an issue. But if you want the patient to get the right treatment, before you call the doctor, you have already formulated in your mind the question. You know what the patient needs, you know what they need for the order, but you need to get the OK from the doctor.

"Of course," Bev continued, "the long and short of it is that if there's some diagnostic indicator that's missed, the doctor's gonna take the hit for it. But you know pretty much what's needed."

Linda stared at Bev, fascinated by the inner workings of the hospital setting.

"It's a total crazy dance," Bev said.

"Wow," Linda said, "it sounds like it."

"There are standing orders," Bev went on, "stuff that's already agreed up. Stuff like if a patient can get out of bed on their own, or if they need assistance, those are orders you need to get from a doctor.

"But when a doctor shows up at the hospital," Bev explained, "there's only a minute and a half for them to make the diagnosis. Then there's the case of the doctor who's on call, who doesn't know the patient, and has no real intimate knowledge of the patient. It's nuts."

"You must have to really jump through hoops with the doctors," Linda said.

"Yeah," Bev said, "and that's not the half of it. I called a doctor once to change an order on a patient, and I could hear by the background noise he was in a bar. It also only took a few seconds listening to the doctor ramble on to realize that he was as drunk as a skunk. Wild stuff."

Later, the two women drove the short distance to Linda's apartment to hang out and finish the day. It was getting dark in the city.

"I love the sound of a trumpet on a stereo while a police siren goes off in the background, on the street," Linda said to Bev as the two relaxed in Linda's apartment. It was a small studio apartment, all that Linda could afford, but comfy and homey enough for her. A few pieces of art on the wall, a few books, a stereo and a TV adorned the Spartan digs. She enjoyed living the barebones existence; she had no use for the clutter of an abode filled wall to wall with bric-a-brac and knickknacks. In life, she traveled light.

Linda's friend nodded off reading the Reader's Encyclopedia from 1948, half listening as Linda droned on about life in the city.

The conversation from Linda trailed off.

"Wha…?" Bev responded, sleepily.

"Never mind, wasn't important," Linda said.

"What time is it?" Bev asked.

"Well, I could say it's now, but that wouldn't be much help, would it?" Linda sparred vocally.

"No, not really. Come on, tell me what time it is."

"Around 7 p.m. I was listening to the jazz and the cop car siren outside."

"Nice," Bev said.

"I was commenting that I liked the sound of the two. They go together."

Sunday night at Linda Avery's apartment wasn't exactly a hoedown, but at least there was some life.

"I've always hated Sunday nights," Linda said, "you know, 'cause that's the night before school or work." She mulled over her own statement. "Of course, now, workin' at the club, well, every day is a holiday, every meal a cause for celebration," she said, wryly.

"You're in a mood, aren't you?" Bev queried the odd-acting Linda.

"No, no mood. Just sort of melancholy, wondering what's coming next, wondering how things are all gonna turn out."

"Melancholy? That sounds melodramatic. Are you sad, sweetie?" Bev asked.

"No, not exactly," Linda said. "I'm not down. I'm not up. I guess I'm neutral."

"Well, neutral can be good. 'Throw the mind in neutral,' like the underground comic said," Bev retorted.

Bev sat there and pondered Linda's words for a few minutes, then became a bit philosophical herself.

"I think you're right," Bev said. "I think there's a great deal of value in stopping the world and taking it all in. Too many people stay busy doing chores and other tasks, and then blur their minds with TV or pulp fiction novels. I don't think that people take enough time to sit in silence and contemplate the world. There's too much activity."

Linda thought about what Bev said.

"It's too easy these days to fill your time with entertainment," Linda said. "I agree, TV, movies, books, they're all great, but I think that sitting there and thinking about stuff has been highly underrated. You've got to slow down and take it in. I like doing what a friend of mine advised: At the end of the day, go over what happened during the day and take some mental notes. I've been able to keep my mind sharp by simply reviewing the day's activities."

The conversation lapsed at that point. Linda and Bev sat quietly and took in the world. Their ennui was interrupted by a loud crash of metal against metal outside on the street.

Startled, the two bolted upright at the same instant. At once they both dashed to the window. What they saw on the street shocked them.

Two cars were sitting in the street, steam and smoke coming out of both of them. It was obviously a rear end collision, with the second car plowing into the first car.

"Dial 9-1-1," Bev said, instinctively. She turned around and headed out to the street. Linda grabbed her cell phone and called for an ambulance.

By the time Bev reached the street, the driver of the car in front was already out of the car and lying on the street, face down. That driver had occupied an older Oldsmobile, a 1970s sedan, without air bags. The driver of that car had a severe head injury and was bleeding profusely. His blood ran in the street as he lay motionless.

Bev ran to the driver's side of the second car and tried to open the door. It was jammed. She pulled again, this time harder, and the door creaked open, but only inches. She put her foot on the car frame, and tried to wrench the door open. It opened another couple of feet, enough for her to reach in, push the airbag forward and through the smoke and steam surrounding the car, undo the driver's seatbelt.

She pulled the woman out of the car before the front end burst into flames. Putting her arms underneath the woman's armpits, Bev extracted the unconscious victim from the quickly rising flames. She dragged the woman to the sidewalk, and laid her down.

Although only seconds had passed, not even a minute, an ambulance, sirens screaming and lights flashing, pulled up to the scene.

The ambulance driver acted fast. He and his partner rushed to the cars to see if anyone else was in them. No one else was involved. The ambulance driver, a trained emergency medical technician, went immediately to the driver of the first car, still lying in the street.

The other EMT rushed to see what needed to be done for the woman that Bev had dragged to the sidewalk.

"Were you in the car?" the EMT asked Bev.

"No," Bev blurted out. "I saw the accident and came to help. I'm a nurse."

"Good," the EMT said. "You can help."

Days later, the two best friends, better friends now, shared thoughts and feelings. Their talk was free and loose; they were ensconced in the privacy of Linda's apartment.

Bev was commenting on how some '60s rock star was all "burned out on drugs," as she put it.

"Drugs make you a burn out," Bev said.

"No, that's not it," Linda said in response.

"Oh, so I guess you know," Bev said.

"Well, maybe I have experimented once or twice with drugs," Linda said, "but it's what I observed that really counts."

"Go on," Bev said, patiently.

"It's not the drugs, really," Linda said. "It's the type of person and what they do with the drugs.

"Take PCP, for example," Linda continued. "I tried it three times: once I smoked it, another time I snorted it, and the third time I took a pill. When I took the pill, I downed it with some beer. That was a bit of a mistake, but I recovered.

"What I'm talking about is some blockhead who takes not only too much of the drug, but takes it day after day in quantity. That's what kills the mind, deadens the spirit. I've seen it. I saw this young guy I knew take so much PCP, I remember hearing about him diving in the Columbia River in the middle of winter, not feeling a thing.

"But that display of insanity doesn't explain why some folks take too much of one drug and it affects their minds, it affects their personalities. I've seen it with folks who took too much cocaine, too much alcohol, hell, too many pain pills. It's not good for you."

"Makes sense, I guess," said Bev.

"Makes plenty o' sense, girlfriend," Linda replied. "Abuse of these drugs is the problem. It's not the experimentation, that's harmless, maybe beneficial. But abusing the drugs, taking them day in and day out, that's where the damage occurs. You've got to let the mind have a break from the crazy places you take it.

"It's like I heard Alan Watts say one time, and I'm paraphrasing here," Linda said. "He said, 'Once you get the answer, hang up the phone.' He said that with regard to drug experimentation. I think he was talking about LSD, in fact."

"When you have to deal with death," Bev said, "it wakes you up to how people take for granted the toughness of the human body and its ability to bounce back from adversity. Carting a body to the hospital morgue is not pleasurable."

"The hospital morgue?" Linda questioned. "I hadn't thought of that before. So hospitals have morgues?"

"Oh course," said Bev, who'd worked in more than one hospital in her life. "I mean, that's the reality of the situation. Of course, it's not something that a hospital advertises."

The two sat in silence for a few seconds.

"I never thought about it," Linda told her friend, "but I guess it makes sense."

"Sure," Bev said. "Again, though, it's not something hospitals advertise. When I was a young nurse, one of my most memorable experiences was trying to cart a dead patient from the Intensive Care Unit to the basement where the morgue was located.

"It was kind of touchy," Bev continued. "I didn't want any of the patients or visitors to see the body, so I waited quite a while for an empty elevator. People don't think of what happens when a person dies in the hospital, but that's the way it is."

Linda did know one thing she liked about hospitals: The food. She loved visiting her friend Bev at the hospital Bev worked, and eating in the hospital cafeteria. She always loved institutional food, and although some of what patients get is necessarily bland, there's always two different entrees, along with other tasty, healthy items. There was always Jello.

Linda also knew, in a humorous sense, that if she got sick while eating the food in a hospital, for whatever reason, be it instant ptomaine or a heart attack, at least she was right there for quick treatment.

Hospitals were an oasis of good people, with helpful nurses and doctors. It was usually calm and quiet. There was also the added benefit of always having some security personnel around to police the area.

Linda got to know the hospital where Bev worked, and got to know a little bit of the inner workings of the hospital.

CHAPTER 4

The bar was nearly empty.

Except for Squint Eye, passed out at a table near the bathrooms, the place was pretty much the domain of the bartender of the moment, Emily Lou Resnick. The girl was large and in charge, and she knew it. It was around 2:15 a.m., time for the bartender to announce, "Last call for alcohol." In Oregon, the law said absolutely no alcohol served after 2:30 a.m.

Surely some stranger, some idiot, will come in past last call and try to order something to drink.

Then it was a matter of sizing up whether or not the person making the request was a bona fide customer or a representative from the Oregon Liquor Control Commission. Of course, the difference would be vital. It could mean a few bucks earned from the common citizenry versus being closed down for two weeks for an infraction, in this case customers quaffing after 2:30.

Cigarette girl and part time waitress, Linda Avery eyed the situation.

"God," she thought to herself, "what a waste of humanity."

But, she'll be patient. Purveyors of mixology must be patient while the fly comes to the spider, the thirsty man to the trough, the Sad Sack with the tale to lament.

Bar life was sad, yet as the last stop on humanity's trip through human companionship, it fills a role, a much-needed role. That of confessor, brother, sister, mother, father.

The bar.

Oh, what an interesting, stimulating concept.

The Club Festival was the best bar.

It gave you everything you ever wanted, and more, so very much more.

Linda was wary of men like Tail Gunner, for sure. But she was also wary of a world filled with a web of lies and misinformation.

"Listen to that great big liar," she told her fellow employee at the Club Festival, Emily Lou Resnick, nodding towards the loudspeaker at the end of the bar.

Emanating from the loudspeaker was the deep, authoritative voice of a man hawking his wares on the radio. What Linda was referring to was the line the man announced, saying, "You have a friend in the auto business."

"I can't believe the crap that comes over that speaker," she said. "He said, 'You have a friend in the auto business.' What a load of crap. That guy's no friend of mine. He's saying that so he can get you onto the lot to rip you off."

"I know," Emily Lou replied. "I guess he's appealing to the dopes out there who'll believe anything anyone says."

The women agreed on that point. Linda was only getting started.

"The stuff that people say," she says, "on the radio, on TV, on those commercials before a movie, it's a bunch of stuff made to make people feel comfortable, to get them softened up for the sales pitch.

"I've always been a big believer in checking things out before believing something," Linda continued. "Books, magazines, newspapers, all of them need to be questioned. It's so sad that we live in an age where people are so easily taken in."

The two lingered a moment at the bar. Linda Avery, cigarette girl, and Emily Lou Resnick, barkeep, were old enough to know better. They'd been around the block a time or two.

"Man," Linda mused, "it's like the old saying. 'Believe none of what you hear and half of what you see.' That's so true."

"I think it's worse than that," Emily Lou responded. "Not only are there lies, but advertising tries to get you to believe that you need the best of everything, that you need the latest shiny bauble, to be 'cool' or 'hip.' It's a lifetime of deception and lies, stacked up like cordwood. Lies stacked upon lies."

"It's incredible," Linda said, "the total amount of bullshit we put up with these days."

With the radio advert over, smooth jazz was crooning from the loudspeaker.

"But I don't know if this is something that's all that new," Emily Lou commented. "From what I can tell, men have been lying and manipulating other men for ages."

"How's that?" Linda asked.

"Well, I think about the old snake oil salesman in the Wild West," Emily Lou said. "The newspaper ads from the 1800s and 1900s that promised everything under the sun, cures for every known disease and ailment. It's been going on for centuries. Men and women have been lying to other men and women for as long as there's been a language."

"You're right," Linda said, pausing to scratch her ankle.

"I think there's more to it than that," Emily Lou added. "For any young person, or really anyone in our society, seeing all these movies and commercials and magazines with rich, Hollywood movie stars and Internet tycoons, seeing all that affluence makes those people want that lifestyle, too, or at least feel they deserve it.

"It creates a false sense of what life is all about," Emily Lou continued. "I mean, when you see people in nice houses and big cars, you think to yourself, 'I want that, too.' It doesn't do any good for poor people. It reminds me of watching the movie Scarface with Al Pacino: Kids see that and say to themselves, 'If I deal drugs, I can make a lot of money and live the good life.' That sort of thing is turning this nation into a nation of mobsters and gangsters."

"I agree," Linda replied. "Why can't people be happy with themselves and live the simple life? I think the best thing we can do is to help each other, not gather up a bunch of material goods. It's like I said…"

Out of the blue, customer Squint Eye barked out a drink order to no one in particular.

"I'm dry," he said. "I need drink, bad."

"Be right with you, buddy," said Linda, who filled drink orders when needed. "What'll it be? This will be the last drink I can get you."

"Dewar's," he said, "and make it a double."

"Comin' right up," Linda said.

Linda had lived on the edge of society for so long, it was as if she was born on a high wire.

It was as natural for her to have no money and no job as it was for other folks to have cash in the bank and a steady source of income.

As she aged, her self confidence, self assurance and self esteem seemed to grow. She never worried about finding work, getting work and losing work.

"Don't worry too much about it," a friend once told her when she was unemployed and out on the streets looking for work. "Work is always there, don't worry about that. You'll always be able to find work."

She'd done every kind of work imaginable, from manual labor to desk work. She'd worked pouring concrete, as a carpet measurer and as a receptionist. She'd worked for below minimum wage to as much as $50 an hour.

From her perspective, there was always work, if you were willing to do the work. That attitude kept her alive over the years.

As she reached middle age, she looked back on her work career and was fairly amazed. She was always able to stay one step ahead of living on the street. In fact, living on the street never crossed her mind. She knew that somehow, some way, she'd always find something to do.

She motivated herself to find better work by accepting the fact that, if nothing else, she could work in a convenience store or at a fast food restaurant. She'd worked retail once or twice, and knew that occupation was all a matter of attitude.

She didn't have any respect for people who say there's no work out there, even during the recessions that seem to hit the American employment scene in cycles. During the recession of the early 1980s, she remembers being told that a recession was as good as any other time to get a job; you just had to work a little harder at finding work.

No smart ass smarty pants college graduate, she nonetheless could read. During her life she'd read many books from the library on the subject of looking for work. She felt as if she'd read every book on the subject, starting with that old beginner's book on the subject, What Color Is Your Parachute? She'd borrowed a lengthy expose on the subject of searching for a job from a scholarly man from India she'd run into. She couldn't remember the man's name, and unfortunately could only remember the moniker she'd given him: The Ovulation Man.

One of the first things she discovered in her self-education on job search techniques was that a huge majority of jobs are not advertised. Something like 90 percent of the jobs offered and taken were not placed in the help wanted sections of newspapers and, later, on the Internet. She discovered a big chunk of jobs are filled by people inside the company. But another source of filling job vacancies comes from the pool of prospective employees who actively circulate either regionally or nationally. Resourceful people use networking techniques to keep their names out in front of the decision makers who do the hiring. People who influence the hiring include bottom rung employees who know about a job opening before it happens; people who are thinking of leaving a job, who can tell you about a position before it opens; and human resource people and executives who do the hiring.

Linda learned early that the way to be in the know about job openings isn't to wait until the job comes open and is advertised for every other woman or man to see, it was to be ahead of the curve, to anticipate the next job opening, and to have your name on the lips of those hiring early in the process, not in the middle of the process.

The best example for Linda on how to be there ahead of the curve came with a job as a saleswoman for a newspaper advertising supplement.

She'd been circulating her name around the Portland area, including all the suburbs and towns surrounding the bigger city. She'd found a man, an associate publisher at a local newspaper, who later became her mentor. She arranged a personal interview with him, although there was no job being offered. She'd impressed him with her savvy of the sales business, and her knowledge of the work that salespeople accomplish.

The fact that she neither owned a car nor actually had a driver's license was of no matter; she knew how to make sales from the inside, from a desk, and knew that working potential customers was a matter of skill.

She'd been networking actively among all the major businesses in Portland when one day she received a phone call at home from her associate publisher mentor. He'd heard some news that morning that Linda might be interested in hearing.

The associate publisher had heard that a salesman had died at one of the local newspapers, a salesman who worked on one of its advertising supplements. Since Linda had already been circulating her name among local newspapers, she knew who the associate publisher was talking about. She had interviewed at that newspaper a month or two prior, and was told at that time there were no job openings.

With the death of a salesman, there was quite obviously a job opening.

Linda immediately called the woman with whom she'd been in contact at the newspaper, and said she'd heard about the demise of one their employees.

"I'm so sorry to hear about his passing," she said to the human resources contact. "He was a great salesman." Without missing a beat, Linda continued. "I am sorry about his passing, but I'd like to remind you that I'm still out here looking for work, and I'd be glad to help you out by interviewing for the position."

Linda got the job interview, and received an offer of employment.

Linda's lifestyle also gave her an edge on staying on the edge and not falling over into the abyss. She'd never lived an extravagant lifestyle, mainly because her life was not filled with the acquisition of possessions. She didn't own a car, didn't own a house and didn't have any desire to fill her life with material possessions.

She lived simply, and spent money only on necessary clothes and food. What else do you need in life?

Never without a rented room, apartment or house to call home, Linda felt at ease in the West, the land of the cowboy, the logger, the fisherman. She felt that as long as she had her health, she could always find productive work to bring in the money.

She also knew that if she didn't like a particular job, if the boss was an asswipe or the position so boring or demeaning as to be intolerable, she could always quit. In her attitude, there's always going to be another job somewhere else.

Like everything else in her life, she gave her best when she was there. She also took her time off from work as seriously as she took her work. She lived life to its fullest, and approached life head on, with no hesitation.

She remembered in the '70s watching old black and white samurai films from Japan, and recognized herself in the roles the ronin, or unattached samurai, played. They were like gunslingers for hire, and Linda felt like she was a gunslinger for hire, ready to do any work for any pay. The tougher the work, the higher the pay.

When you'd lived on the edge for so long, you got used to the view.

There wasn't much that got by Lou Brodsky. His Club Festival did not appear especially modern or updated. The interior was plain and almost drab. It was dark inside and out. But looks can be deceiving.

Lou was too "old school" to go into the latest service industry fashions, like TVs in bars or the legalized gambling provided by the state of Oregon. But he had taken certain precautions that no one except himself knew about.

Both inside and out, the entire establishment was wired for video. One camera would catch you on the way in, from over the front door. Two cameras, covering different angles, watched the only cash register in the joint. Club Festival faced the main street, and had a side exit in an alley. Another camera kept vigil near the exit door, while two others aimed at the adjacent parking lot.

The system was modernized and digital. The signals were electronically transmitted via airwaves to a storage system located in Lou's office. Lou had the device re-designed to look like an old fashioned video cassette recorder hooked up to the only TV in the club, a small set sitting next to his desk.

The location and design of the cameras were also carefully thought out. Lou had an ex-convict acquaintance of his properly scout the interior and exterior of the club for weaknesses in surveillance. His ex-con buddy knew about robbery, since that was what he'd been popped for enumerable times. One weakness in operation that constantly bothered Lou's buddy was how far away the cameras were located; another weakness was the graininess of the images.

He solved one problem by locating all the cameras at about seven-foot high. That way, faces were easier to photograph. The other problem was merely one of lighting and camera precision. He advised Lou to place strategic lighting near the cameras, and to invest in video reproduction of the highest quality. Lou was outraged at the price tag for the system, but was convinced by his jailbird friend that the investment would be worth it, and that it would be a one-time major purchase. He did tell Lou that upgrades would be available and advisable in the future.

Another clever aspect was disguising the cameras so no one would know they were present. Camouflaging was easy conceptually, difficult in execution. Instead of having the entire camera visible, only the lens surface was exposed; the lens was then covered with a dark mirrored surface, and further camouflaged with various design elements. To pull off doing the construction without anyone noticing, Lou told the curious a lie.

"Oh, those guys? They're doing a couple of things. Checking for radon, and checking for vermin. Don't mind them, they'll be done in a jiffy."

Lou kept the system a secret from his employees, knowing that "loose lips sink ships." So none of the staff, including waitresses, cooks, coat checker and cigarette girl, knew that Lou had created a complete spy system.

During the many years Lou had owned and operated his Club Festival, he was only robbed twice, once during daylight and another right before closing. Both times the equipment he had for surveillance, updated frequently to state-of-the-art quality, caught images of the perpetrators electronically. In both cases arrests were easily made from the clear, close-up photographs of the criminals involved.

CHAPTER 5

She was never really lonely.

Randi Obvitz remembered the joke from high school: A woman without a man is like a fish without a bicycle.

I mean, girls had it made, really. All they need to do is sit around waiting for the men to flock about. Well, it doesn't always work that way. Sometimes it pays to advertise, if not in a subtle degree. Randi was spare in her advertising.

Tall, dark and fetching for a well-aged 43, Randi Obvitz knew that she was attractive to men. It was a matter of finding someone high quality, but not so high quality that he's full of himself. Think about it: The losers keep losing and the winners keep winning. What's left? Those potential winners, men that need women to make more of them, to promote them, to champion them.

Or to use them.

Use them like a shop rag, then tossed off with no care.

The sad, sad bottom end of humanity is the user. The man who uses a woman. The woman who uses a man.

But when two users of the opposite gender meet, shouldn't they get what they deserve? Shouldn't two users use each other, call it even and walk away?

Men and women who use each other are a highlight of the low side of town. Is it a victimless crime? Is it a crime at all?

Bartender Randi Obvitz was taking a break in the action by having a Coke at the bar.

"What's the haps, honey?" asked the fellow sliding in next to

Randi. Randi was working, wearing the bar apron with "Club Festival" emblazoned on it. She was staring straight ahead, lost in thought. The salutation woke her from her daydream.

"Nothin' much, sweetheart," was her snappy, if automatic, reply.

"I just got into town, noticed you sitting alone, thought I'd take a chance," he said.

"Chances," she replied, "don't take chances." Randi was feeling good, so she elaborated. "Stick with me, fella, I'll show you the ropes."

Ropes, he thought to himself. Ropes. "Funny thing for a girl to say," he thought to himself.

"Yeah," Randi continued. "I've been part of the scene around here for quite some time," she announced to her newfound friend. "Been part of the scene for quite some time."

"That's sweet, baby, I like the sound of that," he responded. He immediately warmed up to Randi, and enjoyed her lingo.

The two freshly-minted sweethearts passed some witty banter between them for a few minutes, and then he got down to brass tacks.

"Where's a dude supposed to score some weed around here?" he asked out of the blue and in a low voice. "You know, enough for the weekend."

"Hang on to your horses, stud, we'll get you fixed up," she said.

"I've got cash enough for maybe $50 worth, how's that sound?" he told her.

"Sounds good," she said, and Randi O. was off and running, taking a little trip around the block, to the secret location where she kept her stash for sale. There was money to be made and dope to be smoked. Randi was no prostitute, yet she knew how to use her good looks and charms to their best ability. She was a black woman with an innate sense of right and wrong, good and evil. She was wary of strangers, but knew how to handle herself.

"It's going to be a good night after all," Randi thought to herself. A very good night.

“Not a bad night after all,” she said aloud, walking down the street, turning up her collar, realizing it was the middle of the damned winter, and damned cold.

When she returned, she had told the man to wait outside, in his car. She knew better than to let the deal go down within the Club Festival.

Randi had experiences with marijuana. Buying, selling, using and abusing.

Although she waited until her junior year in high school to experiment with smoking pot, she enjoyed a wide variety of experiences after that point.

It seems that nowadays marijuana is available everywhere, from all manner of sources. But when Randi was a teenager, decades ago, the situation wasn’t so fluid. So as a teenager without connections, there was only one way to score: You had to buy the stuff on the street, from a street dealer. It was a chance that had to be taken.

In her small hometown in downstate New Jersey, it wasn’t easy to obtain the illegal drug. It was not readily available in her berg. So she went to the big, big city. New York City.

Once in the big city, she and a couple of friends didn’t really know where to buy it on the streets. So they went to a retail outlet that sold drug paraphernalia.

The three of them hemmed and hawed, shuffling about the store, not knowing what to do next. Randi took the bull by the horns.

She walked up to the fellow behind the counter.

“Where does someone go to buy pot?” she whispered to the long-haired gentleman behind the counter.

“Go up to the fountain in the park,” he said, “someone will come up to you.”

The three adventurous teenagers strolled lazily up to the park, and within minutes of loitering around, as the man said, someone came up to them and offered them pot to buy. They scored the weed and off they went.

It was like that for several months, until people in the small town finally began buying larger quantities and selling to friends.

Buying pot got easier in a sense, but never completely easy.

When she was younger, she'd go to great lengths to score weed. One time she and another woman drove 150 miles to Washington, D.C., to the Foggy Bottom neighborhood, to buy the green stuff.

It was a harrowing trip, made late at night, and to the home of a stranger. The whole scene was full of danger, considering she was handing money over to someone who could just as well take her money and kill her.

But that's way too dramatic. For Randi, the worst part of the trip was her friend's horrible driving skills, displayed in all their glory in the trip there and the trip back. Maybe the journey back was worse, since the two young women were both stoned out of their ever lovin' gourds.

When they arrived in D.C. at the address they were given, it was rather drab from the outside, but inside was a different story. The resident, a soulful black man, was playing soothing music from gigantic speakers. The interior was decorated tastefully. The black man knew Randi's friend.

"Have a seat," the man told the two women. "Relax."

The two women were tired from the long drive; relaxing was easy.

Another black man came out of one of the rooms carrying a satchel.

"Hey, girls," he said. "I've got some fine product for you here."

"Sweet," was all Randi could say. "Sweetness," her friend said.

The man with the satchel opened it up to display a variety of different bags, filled with different quantities of what was apparently marijuana in a range of quality.

"How much do you girls want?" he asked.

"Just an ounce," said Randi's friend.

"That's too bad," he said, immediately causing alarm in the girls. "I have so much of this stuff, and I can't seem to get rid of it. People are too paranoid, too worried about the cops. So, an ounce, OK, try this."

He got out one of the bags, took some pot from the bag and placed it on the table. He took a pack of cigarette papers out of his shirt pocket and began expertly to roll a joint for his guests.

Once lit and passed around between the four people, the girls truly relaxed.

"Well?" asked the man with the satchel. "What do you girls think?"

"I'm high," said Randi. "Me, too," said her girlfriend.

"It sells itself," the dealer said. "Are you sure you don't want anything else?" he asked Randi in particular. "I've got speed, acid, anything you'd want."

Staying on task, Randi and her girlfriend declined the offer.

"How much do we owe you?" Randi's girlfriend asked the dealer.

"That'll be $45," he said.

The girls were not shocked at the price, and had come prepared to pay as much as $100. Randi's girlfriend doled out the cash to the dealer; the two stood up, and made their exit.

Stoned to the bone, the drive back was a bit of a trial, but Randi and her friend made it out alive.

In the rear of the bar, huddled near the back wall next to the restrooms, a customer who had way too much to drink had passed out. It was a peaceful yet slightly disturbing scene.

"Can't say I know him," was the only response from one of the strangers surrounding the man, as the drunkard lay prostrate in the back, a perfect sight of the fetal position. No one in the pub seemed to recognize the stranger, whoever he was. So he lay there, breathing smoothly and evenly, more at home than if he'd actually been at home.

After a few minutes, waitress Randi spotted the man, and went to see if there was anything she could do.

"Sir? Sir?" she asked in a medium loud voice, trying to wake the man. She was afraid to touch him, afraid he might wake up in a sour mood and start some physical altercation.

Randi went to the manager's office and retrieved Lou.

Lou was chagrinned to find a customer passed out on the floor in his bar. It wasn't the kind of publicity he needed. Randi stood next to Lou, hands on her hips, lips pursed.

"Hey, buddy, wake up," Lou said in his husky voice. "Hey! Buddy! Get up!" Lou repeated. He nudged the man with his foot, pushing against the soles of the man's shoes.

No response.

It had been a long day at the Club Festival, and Lou wasn't really in the mood to play games. He asked Randi to go fetch a glass of cold water.

"Make it a plastic glass," he added as she walked back to the kitchen.

"Here you go, boss," she said, returning with the requisite water, and as requested, in a plastic cup.

Lou took the cup of water and splashed it in the man's face. That did the trick.

"What?" he said, groggily, as he bolted to a sitting position. "What happened?"

"You passed out, buddy," said Lou. "Are you OK?"

The man shook his head side to side to shake off the water, and wiped his face with his hands.

"Yeah, I'm OK," he said. "What time is it?"

"It's time to go," said Lou.

"I get it," the man snidely replied. "Time to hit the road."

"You got it," said Lou.

The man rose to his feet by initially getting on his hands and knees, then slowly, with the help of Lou and Randi, to his feet. The two helpers guided him out the backdoor into the night.

"Another good night," said Lou, laughing.

For somewhere between one year and two years Randi shared a house with an older woman and her two daughters, a woman Randi had met while dating another man. Ultimately, the woman would date Randi's man, but that was another story.

The woman, Concertina Fluke, had a reputation as a tough cookie. She was from rural New Jersey, the Garden State, and her girls were cut from the same pattern. Each one owned a different kind of gun, one a shotgun, another a handgun, and everyone in the house, except for Randi, was armed.

Randi never liked guns, and would tell her friends that she thought guns ought to be done away with entirely. Except for maybe controlling a wild animal, or protecting yourself from a bear attack in the wilds, there really wasn't any use for the damned things, she thought.

But with every woman in the house - again, excepting Randi - owning a gun, strangely enough Randi felt safe. Everyone in the house liked her, and she figured if there was some sort of squabble, at least she was on the side with the most ammunition.

The Fluke family had quite a few acquaintances and friends, some of whom would end up living at the house with Concertina and her girls. Some were drifters, others outright criminals. It was a strange living situation, but it was cheap for Randi, and she somehow felt at home with the motley crew.

When she first ran into Concertina, she was visiting the house before she moved in. Randi was over on a Saturday morning, and before she entered the house, she could smell something cooking in the kitchen. It was breakfast time.

"Can I scorch you up a couple of eggs?" Concertina asked Randi, in a friendly tone.

Randi thought about the way Concertina put the question, and quickly answered. Scorched eggs sounded disgusting to Randi.

"No, thanks," Randi said. "I'm fine."

From that point on, she thought of a private nickname for Concertina: "Scorch An Egg."

In fact, after she moved into the house with Concertina and her daughters, Randi called the abode The House of the Scorched Egg. She also liked to try to translate the name into Spanish: Casa del Huevo Quemada.

One of the many drifters and semi-criminals to live on a temporary basis in the house was a rough, tough stocky woman named Nicolette Love, an old family friend of Concertina's. Over the months that Nicolette lived there, Randi found out that she'd spent some time in jail. Nicolette warmed up to Randi right away, and the two shared beers, joints and a few stories.

What Randi especially liked about Nicolette were her stories of self defense in and out of the prison system. Although Randi had no desire to spend any time in prison, she enjoyed the stories of the other tough monkeys in the slammer, and felt there were lessons to be learned.

"I'm telling you now," Nicolette told Randi, "if I hadn't told you before, prison's a place where you learn how to defend yourself. Either that or end up with a shiv jammed up your ass."

"Sounds super icky," Randi said, making a grimaced face.

"It was no beauty pageant," Nicolette explained, "but I did learn a few things about self defense."

The two were sitting around in the middle of the afternoon, in the middle of the week; Randi was working part time as a Kelly Girl doing odd jobs, and Nicolette, well, she seemed never really to have a job. Nicolette appeared to make money through attorneys and numerous lawsuits.

"Two things you gotta keep in mind," Nicolette further explained. "In a fight, you've got to be able to use anything at your disposal.

"One time," Nicolette said, "I was in a traffic accident, nothing too serious, but the other driver had gotten out of his car, and was all jacked up, freaked out about the whole scene. He was about to come charging at me, to attack me, when I noticed a loose roadway sign post nearby. As the loony came running my way, I grabbed the signpost and took a swing at the guy. Hit him right square in the jaw."

"Ouch!" Randi said. "That's gotta hurt."

"Oh, yeah," Nicolette said, "that knocked him on his ass. That's the other part of how to defend yourself: Catch your attacker off guard by being the first one to throw a punch. Don't wait to get attacked, go on the offensive right away."

Randi enjoyed living at The House of the Scorched Egg because of people like Nicolette, and others, who shared what they had. What Randi didn't enjoy was the fact that Concertina's daughters would get high as kites on excellent bud marijuana, and then raid the fridge and pantry for anything instantly edible. That included Randi's food, which she clearly marked with her name. That didn't seem to slow down the occupants of the house. On drugs, they turned into ravenous beasts.

One day, she went to use her peanut butter, and noticed what appeared to be the tracings of fingers in the jar.

"Hey," she said to the two daughters, "what the hell is going on here? Who's been into my peanut butter with their bare fingers?"

The daughters looked at Randi, then each other.

"I don't know," one said. "Couldn't be us," said the other. From that point on, Randi kept what food she could in her bedroom. It was the price you paid for living with people who smoke pot like it's going out of style.

Not that the smoking situation was a bad thing, from Randi's perspective. It meant that she had others to get high with, and a secure place to purchase dope if she wanted. It was better than having to buy the stuff on the street from strangers. Randi had done that, in New Jersey and New York City, and that was always a risky situation. Not so much risky from the standpoint of violence, but Randi had heard plenty of stories from friends who'd purchased poor quality dope. If it wasn't poor quality, it was something altogether not marijuana. In one instance, a friend had purchased a baggie full of toilet paper.

So Randi enjoyed buying and smoking with the mother and her wayward daughters.

One night, Randi smoked a big joint of some heady stuff with the daughters. The stuff was so potent, it brought on an instant coughing jag.

"Shit!" Randi said, coughing and choking, barely getting words out between the convulsions. "This is some potent shit!" After the big joint, Randi went upstairs to her room.

She came back down an hour later with a tale to tell the other girls.

"I just had a unique experience," Randi said to Concertina's daughters. The daughters looked up from watching TV, in rapt attention. "I went upstairs," Randi continued, "and watched a great program on my little TV."

"That's cool," said one of the daughters, absently.

"The only problem was," Randi continued, "the TV set wasn't turned on! That dope you girls fed me was so intense, I was hallucinating freely, and without the set being turned on at all. I sat there and imagined some sort of elaborate plot on TV!"

The girls fell about the place laughing, thoroughly amused by Randi's imaginary adventure.

CHAPTER 6

Being a cigarette girl has its ups and downs. Mostly downs.

The usual cigarette and matches transaction. The occasional, "The wife's wise to me, what covers up the smell of perfume?" and the rare, "Where can a guy score some good weed around here?"

It wasn't like that in the '70s, Linda recalled. A little hanky panky was OK, but she always thought the drug trade should remain on the street, where it belonged, then disappear altogether. She'd tried a few things, weed, a couple of downers, a few more uppers, but that's it, a little experimental thing. She'd seen what dope did to people. Still, she wasn't immune to the fascinating draw of some drugs, especially marijuana. She wasn't an addict, a "mariholic," but she occasionally would come back to the drug. But not all of its effects were in the mind; for some steady users, the consequences were obvious to outsiders.

What did it do? It made you silly, made you make poor decisions. It was a slow bleed on the pocketbook, something that had you living in a rented apartment when you could just as well have been in a condominium. A condo you were buying, not renting. Dope.

Then there were the less obvious detriments. Like getting the "munchies" and eating everything in sight. Linda remembered one choice evening eating raspberry jam right out of the jar.

But the weed was popular among a certain crowd.

Selling weed at the Club Festival had its risks, but there were ways to assure a smooth transaction. Caution and common sense, for instance.

Linda realized that after a while you start to give in to the pleadings to buy marijuana, the demand was so heavy. What the hell, it was only a harmless weed. “The weed with its roots in hell,” she thought to herself, remembering the cornball poster to Reefer Madness.

In the “getting some on you” area, also known as getting laid, there was always the sale of condoms.

She prided herself in carrying two sizes. Regular size Trojans and Sheiks, along with Trojan’s Magnum, meant for the better-endowed man. She never put the man on the spot by asking him for a preference, because, after all, it’s something a man asked for by name if he’s in the know. A man knows his own penis size.

Quite a sundry assortment of goods and goodies, she knew that. Everything for the man. Except, of course, Linda. She wasn’t for sale. Not at all.

Some idiot customer, full of drink and himself, began complaining to Linda about the education system in America. Linda had heard it all before, and was tired of listening to boneheads with nothing of intelligence to add to the conversation. Having had enough of the bullshit, Linda snapped.

“What the hell are you talking about?” she said, in a loud voice. “When I went to school, sure, I was restless and untamed and didn’t want to go sometimes, but when I started to get a bit smart, as a teenager, I realized there was much to learn at school, many books to read, and if I didn’t like the education I was getting, it wasn’t the teachers’ or curriculum’s fault, it was me, no one else, that could make a public school education relevant to me as an individual.”

She was on a tear, but not on a high horse, trying to relate a little of the wisdom she’d picked up over the years. She wasn’t trying to tell her customer how to think, but she wasn’t shy about expressing herself.

"I'm not saying I know it all," she continued. "In fact, I don't like know-it-all people. Most of them are men. They get to a certain point in life, usually after high school, when they marry and have a kid or two, and then they think they've figured it all out, that they have all the answers.

"The person who says he has all the answers," she said, "is actually the kind of person who is the very opposite: They don't have any answers. Life is a mystery; there are no rule books; there is no operator's or owner's manual to life. Sure, we can learn things, we can add to our wealth of knowledge, but to say that you have all the answers, well, that to me means you are totally ignorant, totally full of yourself and your dogmatic bullshit."

The customer was dumbfounded, stunned, floored. He'd never heard such intense philosophizing from what he assumed was an ordinary cigarette girl. His face was contorted with a puzzled look, his eyes staring straight at Linda.

"Where did you come up with all this bullshit?" he asked.

"I came up with this bullshit young, buster," she retorted, "in high school. I had teachers who believed in me and believed me, because they, too, sensed that no one person had all the answers, and that life is an experiment, meant to be carried out scientifically."

"Well, aren't you the smarty pants," he quipped.

"Again, fella," she said, "I don't have all the answers. I've learned from my teenage years forward that the man or woman who says they have all the answers doesn't. They don't know shit. They want you to think they do, they want you to be like them, to be full of the answers. It's a quality shared by people who are ignorant.

"I'm tired of people putting down the educational system," she continued, "whether it is here or in Europe. The education system in the United States is peachy. It's the people getting the education who need to wake up and realize they are in charge of their own schooling, and to work with teachers and schools to get something valuable from their education."

"Again, who the hell are you?" the customer asked, beginning to realize he had bitten off more than he could chew.

"I'm Linda, I work here, I live in this world right alongside the senators and congressmen and the president of the United States.

"Those people are no different than you and me," she said. "We all have the same capability of becoming educated and aware. Only some of us limit ourselves. Some of us feel that because you've got a degree or a certificate or some sort of award, you're smarter and better than the rest of mankind. That's crap. It's up to the individual to figure out what is right and wrong and go from there."

Linda knew how to use her mind. She exercised it like an athlete, constantly proving that a little common sense and a lot of street smarts can take you far.

Her occupation as cigarette girl at the Club Festival is an excellent example of how to use common sense and street smarts.

The position of cigarette girl at the club did not exist before Linda created it.

She'd gotten to know the owner and manager Lou Brodsky at the Club Festival over a period of several months, while dropping in for the occasional rye and ginger ale. She and Lou hit it off, on a professional and personal basis, because both had done what needed to be done to survive in the world of work and both were middle aged.

"Anything for money," Linda used to say to her friends.

But of late, work for her was not as steady, and she was tired of her previous job. She was eager to expand her horizons. She thought that maybe she could create a job for herself at the Club Festival. She carefully thought about what kind of a job she'd like to be doing, and at what kind of a place she'd like to work. She conceptualized, conjured and connived.

Then one day, she popped the question to Lou. She waited until the club was quiet and subdued.

"Lou," she said on a lazy, drizzly Tuesday, "I got something I'd like to talk to you about."

"Fire away," he said.

"I've got an idea for a position I'd like to create here at your club," she said.

Lou at first was perplexed. He immediately thought that instead of being a casual customer, she was turning out to be a prostitute, and that her proposition would be lewd.

"I've got an idea for a cigarette girl," Linda said.

Lou was still thinking it had to do with selling her body. He gave her a sideways glance, a look of incredulity.

"I know what you're thinking," she said to her future boss. "But I'm not looking to do any flesh peddling." She immediately remembered the joke her mother told her as a youth, about the prostitute who got on a bicycle and pedaled (peddled) herself all over town.

"Good," said Lou. "The last thing I need is trouble."

"In fact," she said, "having the position of cigarette girl would help you avoid trouble."

"How's that?"

"Well," she continued, laying out her thoughts on the subject, "the cigarette girl could be an additional set of eyes and ears for you, keeping an eye open for people scheming to hurt some customer or to commit some sort of crime. I could become another set of eyes to head off all sorts of nefarious activity.

"If you hire me as cigarette girl," she went on, "I'd sell cigarettes and sundries, sure, but as I wander around, I can keep an eye out for bad stuff about to happen. Also, my sense of hearing is excellent, and I could loiter near tables where you direct me, to monitor any suspicious activity."

Lou was fascinated not only by the concept of a set of roving eyes and ears, but by the ingenuity of the woman. It's got to take guts to come up with a position that's not in existence.

"How I am gonna properly pay you for all this work? Doesn't seem like you'd be able to earn a living by just selling cigarettes and doodads," he said. "I don't have much of a margin here at the bar, so I don't know if I could pay you."

"I'll tell you what we should do," she said. "I'm so convinced that the position will work out, and that you'll want to pay me something decent, that I'm willing to work for free for the first week. I know it's gutsy, but I think I can make it work."

Linda also added that she'd be willing to help out dispensing drink and food – with the wage negotiable.

Lou pondered the idea. He said he'd get back to Linda within a week with his decision.

Linda was so convinced Lou would say yes, she began to gather some of the items she'd need to create the position. Cigarettes. Odd and ends. The condoms.

Ultimately, Lou went for the idea and let Linda ply her trade. It didn't take long for Linda to prove her worth.

She did a fantastic job as cigarette girl, and gave the place a bit of class with the hawking of her wares. Older people were reminded of all the places in bigger cities that they'd been, places with cigarette girls. Younger people instantly knew what a cigarette girl was all about by remembering classic black and white movies like The Sweet Smell of Success with Tony Curtis and Burt Lancaster.

But it was on her first Friday night, late, that Linda's concept of being Lou's "eyes and ears" came in handy and proved her worth.

Near 11 p.m. that Friday, she had grown tired of standing all night, and took a load off those lovely gams in the back of the club.

It was there she overheard two seedy-looking white guys hunkered down at a table, whispering to each other. The two began arguing, and their whispers became barely audible.

"I'm not sure about this, Lennie," one lowlife said to the other.

"Don't worry, I got it all figured out," the other said. "You create a big disturbance in the back here, maybe pick a fight with someone, and I'll go to the cash register and quietly demand the money. Then I'll leave, you finish the fight and join me. No one will be the wiser. We're not known around here, and I don't see any cameras. We can do it in a flash."

Linda knew what to do.

She calmly got up, strolled first to another end of the rear of the club, then moved to the bar. She told the bartender to get the manager.

Lou came out from the back almost immediately. Linda crooked her finger and signaled Lou over to where she was standing. Lou came up to Linda, curious as all get out.

"What's up, Linda?" he asked.

"Lou, there are a couple of creeps in the back who are planning to rob you. Don't look in that direction, you'll give yourself away."

Lou's attention was riveted on Linda. He stared straight at her, not looking to the back. But then, without moving his head, he pivoted his eyes to the back. He saw the two seedy individuals she was talking about. He didn't recognize them, and that itself was enough to confirm what Linda was telling him.

"I'll take care of it," he told her.

Linda walked away. Lou reached under the bar, grabbed his .38, and sauntered over to the table where the two men were situated. He stood right next to the table, in a menacing stance.

"OK, guys," Lou said. "Time to hit the road."

The two simultaneously looked up at him, stunned and

embarrassed.

“But we didn’t do nothing,” one of them said. “We’re just sittin’ here minding our own business.”

Lou moved his kitchen apron to the side, revealing the weapon.

“Hit the bricks,” were his last words as the two men stood up and marched towards the backdoor.

Lou took a deep breath. He both loathed and loved confrontations. It made life exciting and nerve-racking.

Later, he thanked Linda, and told her that he would hire her.

“Minimum wage to begin with,” he said. “Then we’ll see where you take the job. You can keep your profits from sales, and any tips. But if you’re gonna start doing anything beyond that, keep me informed. I don’t want to hear from anyone else that you’re doing something beyond our agreement. If you do, you’re fired.”

“Lou,” the cigarette girl, newly hired, said, “I’ll always be straight with you.”

“Shove off, you brainless ninny!”

The shout rose from the back of the club, where a group of several men had gathered. They’d been drinking all night, ordering plenty of hard liquor and no food.

“I’ve got every right to be here,” cried out another man, sunk to the depths of his depravity. It was as if every man there was talking to himself, keeping company with himself, and with no care for any of the others clustered about the table.

The table was strewn with the detritus of a night of high spirits. Spilt drinks, baubles and castoffs from the men covered the table. There had been some argument as to who had the better watch and the reasons why, so each man who wore a wristwatch had it lying on the table. In a bygone era, there would be at least one cigarette ashtray filled with butts; but with modern society’s disdain for smoking indoors, there was no such accoutrement.

Cigarette smoking was limited to outside the club, on the sidewalk. Some bars and taverns in Portland built exterior smoking facilities, "butt huts," as it were, after the ban on indoor smoking took place in 2009. Those who had to smoke, suffering from nicotine addiction, were relegated to the outdoors year around.

"Everybody be quiet!" a drunken man at the table shouted. "I have something to say!"

Dipsomania engulfed the man in a stupor so thoroughly, as he stood to get the attention of his fellow rabble, he became the poster child for Alcoholics Anonymous. He was neither good looking or bad, but held sway over the other men as he swayed back and forth.

"I have something important to say!" he repeated.

"Go ahead, whip it on us!" one of his drinking mates reported.

The booze-soaked man stood for a second in silence, composing his thoughts. His declaration was as clear as his thinking.

"I forgot what I was gonna say," he said, sheepishly. The crowd around the table erupted in laughter and backslapping. It was the funniest thing they'd ever heard.

The man once standing quickly sank back into his chair, ashamed that he couldn't remember the most important thing he wanted to share with his mates.

"Oh, don't take it so bad," one man said to him. "Have another drink!"

If there had been someone there with an ounce of sense, he would have advised the man to slow down on the drink. It's the same all over with these sauce hounds. Shoulda. Woulda. Coulda. Always some mitigating factor.

If only someone had given him some good advice. Instead, he kept drinking, and would later be found dead on the streets, with his head caved in by some blunt instrument. Not a musical instrument. Probably a crowbar or baseball bat. He might have pissed off the wrong person, but no matter the cause of his demise, the result was the same.

So his last night on earth was spent rabblerousing and careening about town in a haze of alcohol. Not a very inspiring way to go, but it was his way of doing things.

CHAPTER 7

There was a rancid smell that permeated the entire apartment. So rank that upon entering, the fetid stench was so offensive, there was an instant gag reflex. You felt like vomiting. To keep from retching, you had to hold your breath. Either that or breathe through your mouth. Become a mouth breather of sorts.

"What did you expect?" she asked herself. Any place that's above a drinking establishment isn't exactly considered a penthouse.

The music wafted gently through the floor and from the baseboard heating units. "Glenn Miller, it must be, maybe Tommy Dorsey," Linda thought to herself. Some big band sound that has passed into history.

Lou told her that she could use the premises any time it was necessary, and she'd come upstairs for a look-see. She'd have to be pretty desperate to have to consider this an alternative to using her legs and hoofing it home.

At the time she gets off work, around 3 a.m., the least savory characters can be seen wandering the streets. Some have that disturbing habit of talking to themselves. Very creepy stuff, even to a tough broad like Linda. So finding a place she could crash for a few hours seemed like good preparation.

She'd aged to being called a "tough broad," but there was a classic beauty in this cigarette girl. For one thing, she always stood tall and proud, no matter the circumstance.

What Linda had learned over the years could in itself make a book.

She remembered her mother telling her to "consider the source" when it came to someone stating what they called a "fact." Linda's perceptions became intuitive after 30 or 40 years.

She remembered that acquaintances would ask, "Did you know…?" and would proceed to tell her some supposed matter of fact. After the acquaintance was finished, she'd say, "You know, you said, 'Did you know?' and even after you told me what you believe, I can't say I really know the fact." She insulted many a know-it-all person, many a clever man, with that line.

Her stepfather was also instilling common sense as she grew up. He'd trick her by catching her off guard with off-color jokes and bromides he'd picked up working at the mill. What Linda came away with after a childhood of lessons from parents, friends and the public school system was a street-savvy approach to everything. She became wise.

But for all that she learned as a child and adolescent at home and at school, there were thousands of little lessons Linda learned on her own.

Although work got in the way, she developed two maxims that kept her happy and healthy: Eat when hungry, and sleep when tired.

She'd always been able to maintain her slim and trim appearance through proper diet, and that did include eating food items when she desired. Starving herself was a sure way to build up a big hunger, and then all hell would break loose.

As for staying well rested, well, that was a no-brainer. She eschewed coffee. Coffee made her jittery and wired. No reason for that. She figured if she got the proper rest, everything else would follow, and it always did. Well rested, she was able to think clearly and act accordingly. Without the proper rest, there was no way to make the brain work properly.

Another lesson she learned was never to assume. She learned that the hard way.

Back in her younger days, when she first lived away from her parents in a tiny apartment in Southwest Portland, she dated a man named Gruber. When Gruber stopped calling her, she assumed he no longer had any interest in her. It was only months later, after talking to Gruber, she found out he wasn't avoiding her: His telephone number had changed, and he had lost her number.

By making an assumption, she'd missed out on an opportunity to date a man she really enjoyed talking with about a range of subjects. Gruber was not a good-looking man, but he made up for it in intellectual prowess. Linda didn't mind being with someone she considered smarter than herself; in fact, she made no bones about being interested in having men about her that stimulated her mind as well as her body.

Gruber was in fact proud of his capacity for mental gymnastics. He used to regale Linda with tales from his youth, including the audacity to claim having a subscription to a magazine called Intellectual Digest when he was in high school. Linda took that claim and others like it with a grain of salt.

"Yeah," he had told her, "I used to hang out with guys two, three, four years older than I was in high school. I had no problem keeping up with those guys intellectually. That was my métier."

"Your what?" Linda asked Gruber. She'd never heard the word, "métier" before, and thought at first he said "meatier." Linda's eyes narrowed as she stared at Gruber.

"'Métier' is a French word for an occupation or profession, that's all," said her friend.

"That burns me up," Linda said. She gave Gruber a look that would have turned anyone to stone. Her eyes were afire and her face was all puckered up, as if she'd sucked a lemon.

"What? What burns you up?" Gruber asked.

"People using foreign words that nobody knows," she said. "Latin and French are the most common, and it's so condescending to use those words or phrases to make themselves feel superior."

"Maybe it's you," Gruber said. "Maybe you have some sort of inferiority complex."

"There you go again," she said, "trying to sound all highfalutin and above the masses. It's so irritating to me the way you make yourself out as some sort of high-minded smart ass. And don't give me any 'inferiority complex' bullshit. You're no smarter than I am, I know that. Just because you've read more books than I have doesn't make you any wiser than I am. Fuck you."

"Alright, alright," Gruber said, exasperated by being chewed out by his female companion. He was thinking all the time listening to her that he really didn't have to take this kind of shit from anyone. He especially found it aggravating that he was taking shit from a woman with whom he wasn't having sex.

But Linda wasn't finished with Gruber. She had another bone to pick with him and all the other smart-ass men she'd run into over the course of her life.

"Oh, I'm not done yet," Linda said.

"I don't like people, and most of them are men, who use 75 cent words," she said, referring to multi-syllable words like "assuage" and "apocryphal," for example. "People who use big words are trying to show that somehow they're smarter than everyone else, but it shows their ignorance.

"The guys who use those two dollar words are showing their inadequacy of the English language; they're usually the ones who didn't go to college, and want to show the world that they're as smart as the college guy. Or they did go to college, but they dropped out, and are now trying to make up for that lack of sheepskin with fancy words."

Her friend Gruber looked at Linda in astonishment.

"It's a ruse," Linda continued. "It's their way of feeling secure in the midst of their insecurity."

"You're beginning to sound like Freud," said Gruber.

"No, I don't know anything about Freud," Linda replied, "except for popular cultural references. But that's not saying anything. Anybody can spout off shit they've heard other sources say, it's no big deal. Those are the same people who think in the same manner as bumper stickers. People who know slogans, but don't know anything deeper than that. It's like they're a huge, inch-deep lake: They cover lots of territory, but there's no depth."

"Wow, are you ever angry!" said Gruber.

"You betcha," she said back. "I'm angry because people who use big words are actually dumber than other folks with more common sense. They're trying to cloud the issue, to make people think they know what they're talking about. A person doesn't have to use big words to get a point across. That's something I learned a long time ago. It's not the words, it's how you combine them. A truly wise person combines words in interesting and unusual ways, to create a new thought. It's like painting.

"Painters don't necessarily use a paint that no one else is using," Linda continued. "It's not a different kind of paint, it's a different way of using it, of expressing yourself. Same for words. There is no magic in being able to use big words. That's subterfuge; those people are hiding their lack of imagination and their lack of the command of the English language."

"It sounds like you have quite a command of the English language," Linda's male friend said.

"No," Linda replied. "I'm no smarter than the next person. I'm still learning and growing and changing. I don't have the answers. But at least I don't pretend that I do, that's disingenuous."

"Now there's a 75 cent word," Gruber said, self-satisfied that he'd caught her contradicting herself by using a complex-sounding word such as "disingenuous."

"I'm sorry," Linda said, "I didn't mean to throw that out there. Just slipped out."

At her age, another woman would wear her hair shorter and her skirts lower. But Linda had that classic Nordic skin: pale, soft and clean looking. The kind of woman who doesn't need to wear much if any makeup. She wore lightly-applied lipstick, but kept her blond hair basic. Sometimes she let it flow, easy and beautiful; other times, done up tightly with bobby pins. No matter, because she was Beauty, the men Beasts.

Her clothes were simple, too, not plain, but easy on the eyes, like her face. Easy on the eyes. She was the kind of a good lookin' dame you'd be proud to call your wife. She was innocent looking; yeah, well, that's one in her favor.

Because men trusted her, because she acted with such guileless innocence, she became confessor to numbers of men with no one else to turn to. The cigarette girl.

"Hey, babe!" Gunnar Swernbernin shouted as he snuck up behind Linda at the Club Festival.

"Eowww!" she shrieked as Gunnar grabbed her around the midsection.

Linda turned quickly around and slapped her molester. The sound reverberated throughout the club.

"Ouch!" Gunnar yelled. "You didn't have to do that!"

"Buster," she yelled back, "the next time you touch me, prepare to die!"

"Back off, sister!" Gunnar responded.

He knew that he'd met his match.

Linda later would review the entire incident, going over in her mind the details of each move leading up to Gunnar grabbing her. She wondered if she'd asked for his unwanted attention by the way she acted.

She mulled it over in her mind, time and time again that night. That was her personal technique both to live a fuller life and to set to memory what she'd experience of importance that day. She'd learned from a fellow who went to college, one of her good customers, that the way to learn was not only to attend classes and read the assignments, but to go over notes taken in class, to set the information firmly in the mind.

She'd only seen the man Gunnar Swernbernin once, when he'd stopped by to introduce himself to Lou as the new liquor distributor for the new Idaho vodka distiller; his particular brand was made from potatoes. Sounds weird, but the liquor was good, it was inexpensive and it was definitely tasty. Came in a variety of flavors.

She knew Gunnar, nicknamed "Tail Gunner," as a tall, handsome drink of water, but nothing special. He was another man, nothing more.

She couldn't quite remember if she'd said anything to him or not. Who knows? With some men, it doesn't matter what a woman does or doesn't do; if he has his sights on the woman, she's a target for his wily ways.

The next day, the day after the incident with Gunnar, and after a brief mental review of the situation, she casually approached Lou to see if he could give her any insight.

It was slow at the Club Festival, one of those weekday afternoons where the only customers are truck drivers, businessmen and salesmen. Most of the time, in the middle of the day, no one was into any serious drinking. That sort of thing happened mostly at night. Mostly. There are the rare occasions where a bunch of guys or gals would come in to celebrate a promotion or someone quitting a seriously bad position.

Emily Lou Resnick was tending bar; Lou was checking out the inventory. Emily Lou's job varied between barkeep and waitress, depending on the circumstances. That was the agreement with Lou, to add some variety and flexibility to the job of serving customers. Emily Lou and Randi Obvitz shared responsibilities, along with Lou, for keeping an eye on the bar; the two women also served as waitresses. They liked it, Lou liked it. There was also some flexibility for the cigarette girl, Linda Avery; depending on who was on shift that night, Linda would step in and work as a waitress, filling drink orders and getting food to tables. Linda enjoyed the flexibility for two reasons. One, it gave her something to do other than peddle her wares. Two, it was taxing walking around all night with her tray, so it gave her back a break.

"Lou, can I talk to you for a minute?" Linda asked him, hesitantly. Lou was always a busy man, always taking care of business, "TCB" as he'd say. Lou took his job seriously, although he had a sense of humor about him.

"Sure, honey, what can I do you out of?" he asked in his usual oddball way.

"I'm still kind of shaken up over what happened yesterday with that new liquor salesman, the guy named Gunnar."

"Oh, you mean 'Tail Gunner,'" he answered.

"Tail Gunner?" she in turn replied.

"Yeah, that's the name I heard from some of the other booze pushers," Lou said. "Seems the guy's got quite the reputation as a ladies' man. In fact, he uses that as his calling card. He says to folks that he's not a ladies' man, he's one lady's man. Get it? He's only dedicated to one lady. Turns out that really means he dedicates himself to one woman at a time."

"Nice guy," Linda said. "He sounds like a real heel."

"Oh, he's harmless enough," Lou continued. "He's just a womanizer, a guy looking for a gal to hook up with."

Linda thought carefully about how to phrase her question. Guys tend to defend their own kind, and she knew Lou was loyal to people, and that he didn't like to gossip or backbite.

"Lou, I want to know more about the guy. He grabbed me yesterday, and it kind of scared me. I don't like strangers grabbing me. Who would?"

"Nobody would," Lou said, being empathetic. He kept an eye out for the women in the club, knowing the atmosphere. He also knew that men who'd had too much to drink tend to get out of control. A man full of liquor is likely to do anything, to act out in strange and bizarre ways. But he felt Tail Gunner was being frisky, that's all. He said as much to Linda.

"Oh, he's checking you out," Lou told Linda. "He's testing you to see if you are friendly or cold. What exactly happened between you two?"

Linda explained the incident, and how Gunnar has snuck up and grabbed her from behind.

"Oh, I wouldn't worry about it," Lou said. "It was probably a good thing you set a boundary, so he wouldn't take advantage of you. With some men, you've got to be assertive, just this side of aggressive, because that's all they understand. Gunnar is obviously one of those thick-skinned chowderheads who need to be told what's expected of them."

Linda hung her head in shame. She'd overreacted, and probably sent a signal that she was a cold fish, no fun, not in on the joke.

She left the bar with nearly as many questions as she had before. Talking with Lou was good, it was a relief to vent, but to be honest, she wasn't any better off.

She was determined to ask someone else their take on the whole affair. It seemed like a logical step to ask another woman.

"I'm not sure what to do next," she said to her friend Marcia Calibri.

"Do next about what, sweetie?" Marcia responded.

"That guy. You know, Tail Gunner, I told you about him," Linda said, sighing heavily. Linda then explained what happened between them.

"What can you do about guys?" Marcia said. "I've been in a few relationships, and guys are so hard to predict. Trying to figure out guys is like trying to herd cats. Guys are all over the place, mentally, emotionally."

The two women had met on Linda's day off from the Club Festival, for lunch and a movie afterwards. They were sitting in the bar, drinking coffee after eating.

"I mean, it's not that important, maybe," Linda continued, "but I'm still worried about my reaction to this guy grabbing me. Maybe I should lighten up."

"No, sweetie," Marcia said. "You have every right not to be pestered by a guy, especially not to be manhandled. No guy has a right to touch you like that, especially a virtual stranger."

"Virtual?" Linda asked.

"Yeah," Marcia said. Then she understood Linda's question. "No, I don't mean an artificial stranger, like a hologram. Virtual as in, 'in essence but not in fact.' I mean, you knew the guy was a salesman. But you don't know him personally."

"I don't want to know him personally," Linda said. "He's just a good-lookin' hunk of meat to me."

CHAPTER 8

"What do I have to lose?" Lou asked Linda.

"Your call," is all she had to say.

So Lou, manager and owner of the Club Festival, stepped out into the nighttime street and confronted the three drunken men in front of his bar.

"What the fuck do you want, pops?" the shortest one quipped.

"You guys need to move along, it's getting late," Lou came back, not with a bark, but with some bite.

"I don't think that's gonna happen," said another one of the drunks.

"Well, I guess it's time to ratchet it up a notch," Lou said under his breath, a bit wryly.

At that moment Lou drew from his back pocket a .38 caliber snub nose revolver. He pointed it at the shortest man, and everybody froze.

There's nothing like the sight of a nasty looking weapon to put the kibosh on a festive moment. The three drunks visibly sagged, and began to slink away, mumbling apologies and regrets.

Linda and Lou were left in the quiet of the night. Somewhere, Frank Sinatra played from a hi-fidelity stereo, out of an apartment room, filling the night air with an embraceable feeling. It was the city. It was good.

Club Festival's Lou Brodsky knew the difference between right and wrong. He'd been in the service, the U.S. Army, and saw a lot of both right and wrong actions while stationed in the U.S. and overseas.

Linda Avery, cigarette girl at the Club Festival, also knew the difference between right and wrong, good and evil. She'd grown up near the big city, raised by parents with enough common sense to allow their daughter to explore the world, and come back with lessons.

It was a Monday night at the club, things were slow, and the two were chatting near the coat room.

"Lou," she asked, "did you see a lot of insanity while you were in the military?"

"Depends on what you mean," he replied, lazily.

"I mean," she said, "I mean, like, weren't the rules and regulations tough to follow, for an independent spirit like you?"

Lou puzzled for a moment over her question, scratching his chin.

"There were moments when I questioned what the hell I was doing there. I mean, it was the tail end of the Vietnam War, and the troops were coming home, slowly." He remembered but didn't necessarily enjoy talking about the fact that he was in the U.S. military during a war that the U.S. didn't win. He was a bit embarrassed by the fact, but at the same time, he'd protested the war while in high school, a couple years before joining the Army.

Lou was stationed in Taiwan, officially known as the "theater of conflict," on April 30, 1975, the day the North Vietnamese rolled into Saigon, ending the years-long war. His tour of duty was cut short and he was sent back to the U.S.

It's not a point of pride that he was in the military on the losing side. What he does feel good about is that he learned much while in the military, many skills that he was able to transfer to civilian life. He'd learned much.

"The whole concept of the military is insane," he finally commented. "The fact that we were always preparing for war, to kill someone, to kill whole groups of people, that was always kind of crazy.

"But if you mean," he continued, "the idea of being in the military as insane, or the way the military worked as insane, I guess it was, but I was too busy chasing skirts and getting drunk to worry about it too much."

Linda's thirst for knowledge was not abated.

"But I used to hear about all sorts of crazy stuff," she went on, probing. "It seemed like a big conspiracy, with all sorts of secrets and stuff hidden from the public. Wasn't there like some sort of evil mindset with the military?"

"Nah," he said, "it was never like that. Think of the military as a bunch of guys and gals hanging around, doing what needed to be done. Most of the time there wasn't any grand conspiracy, as far as I could tell. It was all pretty much out in the open. Admittedly, some of it was crazy, but no crazier than out on the streets in America.

"I never saw a grand conspiracy," he continued, "and I never saw anything approaching dark secrets. It was just people, like you and me, ordinary people doing their job." Or jobs, as he remembered being overseas during the Vietnam War, although a thousand miles away on the island of Taiwan. Though he'd not served in Vietnam, or in nearby Thailand or Laos, he was officially a member of the armed forces serving in the theater of conflict. As that was the case, he found out that during times of war, there wasn't any 9-5 job. In fact, since he had cross-trained into another U.S. Army occupation, he was "volunteered" to work two jobs. He'd work one job in the morning and afternoon, then in the mid afternoon he went to another military job, where he'd work from mid afternoon until late in the evening. It made for some long days.

"Never break the law while you're breaking the law," Lou told Linda one day, advice that came out of nowhere.

"You see," he continued pontificating, "when you are breaking the law, the last thing you need to do is come up on the cops' radar. For example, if you are transporting drugs in the trunk of your car, don't speed or make any illegal lane changes or turns. It makes sense not to attract attention to yourself in the middle of a scheme."

Linda thought about it for a second, then realized that Lou was right. It was the foolish person who flouted the law while breaking the law.

Linda was like a beautiful flower growing out of a crack in the concrete near the freeway. She was an oasis of goodness in a sea of badness.

"Lou," she began to ask, "have you ever broken the law?"

Lou thought about her question for a moment, and although he knew the answer instantly, he was hesitant to expose himself.

"Yeah," he answered, with a tone of resignation, "I've broken the law. But petty stuff, nothing violent."

"Come on, tell me about what you've done," she said, in an anxious tone.

"Well, it was stuff I did when I was young and stupid," he admitted. "Stuff that I'm not all that proud of, but it wasn't all that serious.

"You ever heard of the term, 'B & E'?" he asked her.

Linda hesitated. She'd seen enough crime movies and TV shows; it took her a matter of two seconds to answer.

"Breaking and entering, right?" she said.

"Yeah, that's it. I guess for me, those were times I used a skill I'd learned in the Army," he said. "When I was working at one job," he continued, "I showed up to work and the manager, who had the keys to the place, wasn't there. Then another enlisted man who also worked there showed up; he was necessary to be able to help with the work. The jobsite manager, he was about as worthless as…" Lou trailed off, about to say, "tits on a boar," but realized he was talking to a woman, and let the statement trail off.

"Anyway," he continued, "this buddy and I were standing around, waiting for the manager, when we realized it was getting mighty close to time to get busy with work. We realized that if we didn't somehow get into the building, nothing would start on time, which was a no-no.

"So my buddy, he pulled out his wallet, and out of his wallet he pulled out his driver's license. It was one of those plastic laminated types. He took the driver's license, stuck it in the door jamb alongside the doorknob, jiggled the damned thing, and voila, he opened the door."

"You consider that 'breaking and entering'?" Linda asked Lou.

"Patience, dear," Lou said to Linda. "I'm warming up. That was one of the many lessons I learned in the Army, lessons they don't teach you in basic training.

"Well, later on," he continued, "after I got out of the service, I was living in this old house, renovated into apartments. I'd met a guy who lived next door, across the hall, and we'd smoked dope. He was kind of a dope himself.

"One day, when I knew he wasn't home, I used that driver's license trick to jimmy his door open. Once I'd opened his door, well, I knew what I was gonna do.

"First of all, since I lived next door to the dude, I knew I couldn't rip him off for any of his possessions, because if he saw any of his stuff, he'd pound me. The only thing I figured I could do is take some of his stash, you know, some of his dope, his pot. Since I'd been there before, smoking with him, I knew where he kept his stash, and I pilfered a couple of joint's worth, you know, something, but not enough to make him suspicious."

"Lou," Linda said, "you are a bad boy."

"I know, I know," he said, "but, like I said, I was young and wild. Let me tell you another story, and this one's kind of funny, really."

"Is it about ripping someone off? How is that going to be funny?"

"Listen and you'll find out," he said.

Lou stood straight up and rotated his shoulders, to shake off some stiffness.

"Again, while I was young, I was living in another apartment complex," he said, "one with balconies in the back. The balconies had railings on them, and this was a new building. The only thing that separated the balconies between apartments was a wall.

"So," he casually continued his story, "I decided to try a little cat burglar routine one night. I knew my neighbors weren't home, and I'd been smoking pot and drinking a little, and I got the bright idea that I could step to the outside of the balcony railing, swing around the adjacent wall, and over the railing next door to get onto the neighbor's balcony.

"I tried it," he said, "and by God I pulled it off. If I had fallen, it was two stories down to the asphalt parking lot below, and I would have been injured, but I pulled it off. I went into the apartment next door, looked around, and the only thing I found that I wanted were some record albums. So I thumbed through them, picked about a half dozen I really wanted, and reversed myself so I was back at my place, via the balcony railing trick."

"Lou," she said, "that's not nice, ripping off your neighbors."

"Well, you're right," he confessed. "In fact, since I had been smoking pot, immediately after stealing the record albums, I sat there in my apartment and started getting all paranoid. I realized that since I was the only one with a simple opportunity to do the stealing, I was instantly prime A No. 1 suspect.

"So, like an idiot, I took the record albums, and repeated the exact same process of going over my balcony railing, around the dividing wall, back over their balcony railing, and returned the albums."

"Pretty stupid stuff, Lou," Linda said.

"I told you it wasn't anything too intense."

"So tell me," she questioned the big man, "what other bad boy stuff have you been up to?"

"Another time," he said. "I've got to get some work done. We'll chat more."

Linda went back to working the crowd at the club. Standing alone near the coat checkroom, she began to think. Think about men. Think about relationships. She was lonely, and knew in her heart of hearts she could use some company.

Linda knew better than to get involved with one of the customers at the Club Festival. She knew that getting involved with a man, creating a relationship, was the last thing she needed. The most basic problem would be what to do if the relationship went bad. How could she face a man at the workplace whom she knows carnally?

But sometimes people take chances. Linda had been taking chances all her life, and although she was still alive, she had emotional scars from past romances.

Squint Eye seemed different. He was kind and courteous, no matter how much he'd had to drink. But that was another issue: It was pretty obvious that Squint was an alcoholic, since he seemed always to be drinking, no matter what. Hell, she noticed he'd come into the bar with liquor on his breath.

Watching him with his head down, passed out at a table, was not an encouraging sight. There wasn't much poetry in a man so drunk he'd have to pass out in a bar. No matter how handsome or charming the man, no potential partner is appealing in that way. Unless that's the way you want a man or woman, drunk to the point of being wiped out.

Nevertheless, one day Linda, out of either desperation or sheer boredom, began to strike up a conversation with the man known only as Squint Eye.

"Hey, partner," she said, nudging him on the shoulder. She had sat down next to him, near closing time at the bar. The Club Festival was nearly empty, the music played Chet Baker's soft, West Coast jazz trumpet in the background, sweet and low.

"Hmmm…" was all Linda was able to get out of Squint at first.

"Squinty," she crooned, "time to rise and shine."

Slowly, methodically, Squint began to move. He shook his rear end on the chair seat, to begin the process. Then he took a deep breath. He raised his head and opened his eyes.

"What time is it?" he asked Linda in a groggy voice.

"Nearly closing time," she answered, sweetly.

"Time to go home, I guess," he said, mouth dry from the typical drinker's dehydration. "I need a stiff drink and a big glass of water, with ice."

"Right away, sir," Linda said, and scampered away to retrieve the necessary liquids. She knew what kind of "stiff drink" Squint preferred: Scotch, neat, no ice, no water. The glass of water she poured directly from the tap was none other than America's cleanest, freshest tap water, fresh from the Bull Run Watershed a few miles up the road and into the mountains outside of Portland. Fresh and clear as spring water.

Linda was the Club Festival cigarette girl, but over time she'd become a waitress, bouncer and all around helpful person at the club. Her relationship with Lou and the other waitresses was so solid, she felt part of the business.

By the time she got back to the table, Squint was sitting up straight. He'd pushed his hair back in alignment, straightened out his shirt and made himself look semi-presentable.

Linda brought the man his required drink and water. She stood by his side as Squint downed the Scotch in one shot, and then began sucking back the water. He practically chugalugged the clear liquid, he was so dehydrated and thirsty.

"More water," he asked, not demanded. "Please," he added.

"Sure, buddy," she said, and went back to get the thirsty man what he needed. Squint wasn't suffering from a headache, the usual physical result of the possible hangover, but he knew that he was damned close to getting one. A professional drinker knows the signs the body gives, and the signs were unmistakable. Dry mouth. Cobwebs in the head. An overall body feeling of the sickness of life.

"Here you go," she said, placing another glass of that good Bull Run water down for Squint. With great aplomb, he lifted the glass.

"And here's to you, my good friend," Squint said, as he downed the second glass of water.

He shook his head, and took another deep breath.

"Man," he said, as Linda took a seat next to him. "How long have I been passed out?"

"Not long," she said, "maybe an hour, hour and a half. No biggie. How you feeling?"

"Kind of rough around the edges," he said, "but the Scotch and then two glasses of water are getting me back into the pink."

He slowly got to his feet, and prepared to leave. He reached over and grabbed his coat, too cheap to use the coat check at the door. Anything to save money, that was Squint's motto.

Linda thought to herself that maybe Squint would make a fine date. Or maybe not. In her mind, although she had considered getting together with the club regular, she opted out for the moment. Maybe another time.

"See you," Squint said, not using Linda's name because he really didn't know her first name. All he knew was that she was the cigarette girl.

"See you," she said, and watched as Squint headed for the front door.

CHAPTER 9

Tail Gunner.

Funny.

His full name is Dieter Gunnar Swernbernin. Originally from Germany, moved to the United States when he was a kid.

Went by Gunnar. Then in college, when he proved to be the consummate ladies' man, the fraternity brothers started calling him "Tail Gunner."

He was called Tail Gunner because he knew how to score tail. "Scoring" being the word for obtaining sexual favors, and "tail" being the word for that part of the female anatomy some men find quite irresistible. He could connect with a member of the opposite sex in an efficient and lucrative manner. There was no stopping his ability to line up women with which to have sex.

His technique was powerful and subtle. To most folk, he was being humble, but his smooth, subtle ways cut through the coldest ice queen.

Women could not resist him, but, then again, he never turned down opportunities, and that in itself secured his future of guile, subterfuge and seduction.

The man had no morals.

"It's sweet poontang," he'd like to say. He was now an American, no longer a citizen of Germany. He was so ensconced in the deep pile carpet of life in these United States, he reeked of the Yankee way of living.

Tail Gunner.

Blond, tall and lean, built like a male model. The kind of man who is so obviously handsome that he knows it. The cock, so to speak, of the walk.

Linda knew she was going to dislike the fellow the minute she heard the scuttlebutt about the new liquor distributor.

Calling Linda picky about her men is like calling a Mob boss picky about whom he trusts in his Mafia organization.

She'd had pretty good luck with men, mostly because she'd been smart enough to stay away from the worst of them. Men were bad news, pretty much always.

But, right away, ol' Tail Gunner started to put the make on Linda.

With his charming smile, witty banter and sparkling eyes, Tail Gunner was what the ladies called a dreamboat, a lothario by any other name. With his smooth talk and slick manner, he could charm the pants off of any woman. A man like that is dangerous to every woman.

"She's every inch a woman and every bit a man," Tail Gunner once told a friend about a woman he was dating.

Sincerity and honesty weren't his high points. Conniving, cunning creature he was, for all intents and purposes, he stalked women like a big game hunter. He was always looking for the next big catch, the next great trophy.

He had many notches on his belt, for the women he'd conquered. Find 'em, feed 'em, fuck 'em and forget 'em, the four Fs, that was his mantra.

He loved talking about "getting poontang," as he called the triumph of the sexual act.

"Women," he'd say, sarcastically, "can't live with 'em, can't kill 'em." Tail Gunner was, in his mean spirited way, paraphrasing the more appropriate, "Women: Can't live with 'em, can't live without 'em."

To any woman with an ounce of self-esteem, being with such a man would be an embarrassment. Yet, women flocked to him. Well, not every woman.

"I haven't met a woman I couldn't satisfy," the cocksure Tail Gunner would announce. "They all fall for me, sooner or later, and it's usually sooner."

As a liquor distributor and lounge lizard, he knew all too well the power of alcohol to ply a woman.

Tail Gunner was sitting in his liquor delivery truck, reminiscing about a woman he'd put the make on several years ago. He'd recently received a call from her, and enjoyed some game playing with her over the phone. He teased her about how he missed her, and how much he enjoyed having sex with her.

Ultimately, though, he had no intention of ever having sex with her again. He wasn't interested in working that hard. So he ignored her, not returning her telephone calls and messages.

When he finally talked to her, one sleepy night, he was curt and dismissive of her. He called her a whiner.

"I could tear your eyes out," she told him. There's nothing like a woman scorned. "You made it bad, you really hurt me," she told him in no uncertain terms.

He was cold.

"I like it when you hate me," he said, "it makes me feel good."

She was shocked.

"What do you want with me?" she asked, plaintively, with a voice both sour and submissive.

"I want to tell you how much it means to me when you tell me you hate me," Tail Gunner said. "I love it when women hate me."

"You are one sick puppy," she told the abusive man.

"Oh, yeah, I know."

Then, without warning, she hung up the phone.

Silence.

Tail Gunner was nonplussed. He went over to the refrigerator and got a cold drink, sat back down in his large recliner and continued watching the detective movie on TV.

Tail Gunner's attitude towards women didn't improve after he was involved in a solid grift. He got mesmerized by a woman he was convinced not only could he bed, but get the best of in a shady transaction.

He'd met a woman at a tony bar who had something to offer. Not sex, not right away. But something that glittered and shined, something valuable.

Or at least that's what she seemed to have.

Making a stop at one of the local watering holes, a few blocks from the Club Festival, Tail Gunner was servicing a client with his particular brand of hooch. After dealing with the bar manager at the Chaise Lounge, he was having an imported beer at the bar when a woman sidled next to him.

"Hey, good looking," she said, demurely. "Watcha got cooking?"

Tail Gunner wasn't used to women approaching him in such a friendly manner, but found her low-cut blouse and raspy voice enticing. Dressed to the nines, the young shapely blond looked like a successful businesswoman.

"Nothing, baby, what's up with you?" he said, checking out the woman's measurements, dazzling smile and haute couture outfit.

"Oh, passing the time before my next appointment," she said. "I just had a sales meeting with a client around the corner."

"Sales, huh?" he said. "Funny, that's my line of work, too. I'm with a liquor distributing company, and this is one of my customers. My name's Gunnar, what's yours?"

"Andrea," she said. "Andrea Carnegie."

The two eyed each other like hungry animals. Tail Gunner thought this might be an easy score. His new woman friend was thinking the same thing, but not in a sexual way.

"I deal in high-end men's accessories," she purred. "It's a great business, and I get to meet clients who know high-end merchandise when they see it."

As she finished the sentence, she subtly moved the black leather briefcase she had with her closer to Tail Gunner.

"In fact," she said, "I was showing my new clients some of my latest samples."

Tail Gunner's curiosity got the better of him.

"Let's see what you got," he requested.

With great panache, the fashionable woman pulled the briefcase up to the bar, and expertly opened the case.

Inside, set in a red velvet backdrop, were some beautiful looking items. A set of David Yurman Black Diamond cufflinks, a matching Yurman Black Diamond ring, a Gucci bracelet watch and a Stephen Webster sapphire dagger necklace.

"Sweet looking stuff," he said, first looking at the merchandise, then at the woman. "Must be expensive."

"Thousands of dollars worth," she said, "and they're not knockoffs. This is the real deal. Take a look."

Tail Gunner removed the bracelet watch, pretending to know what he was looking at. It sure looked real.

"I've got a problem, though," she said. "I've got to get rid of this stuff before I get back to the office, because my boss always wants me to hand out expensive samples. I know it sounds silly, but that's how it works in our business. It's baiting the potential client, and it works surprisingly well. But this potential new client didn't want to touch it, he was so cheap. The bastard."

Tail Gunner was flush with cash, from a day's worth of collecting invoices. Bars like to pay in cash; getting rid of cash in the register was a good way to make sure cash wasn't around if a robbery occurred.

"I know good stuff when I see it," Tail Gunner said, trying to impress the woman with his knowledge of expensive jewelry. "How much would it cost for me to take this stuff off your hands?"

"This stuff didn't cost me anything," she said, "but I'm not going to give it away. $500 and it's yours."

Tail Gunner hesitated. The deal seemed good, and her story made some amount of sense.

"You think about it while I use the little girl's room," she said. As she stood up to head to the ladies' room, she picked up the briefcase.

"Don't you trust me?" Tail Gunner groused, with a hurt look in his eyes.

"With this stuff, I'm not taking any chances. See you in a minute."

As she walked away, Tail Gunner watched her behind wiggle seductively.

While she was in the restroom, Tail Gunner thought about the transaction. "Portland's a small town," he thought to himself, and if there was any problem, he felt confident he could find her if he tried. He figured buying the men's accessories was a good way to show the woman he prided himself in looking sharp, and that is an excellent way to get a woman into bed.

He knew he'd be taking a chance. The money he had wasn't his, but he could juggle the account temporarily, and quickly make up for it somehow.

He also realized she could be in the bathroom taking the goods out of the briefcase. But she went in with only the briefcase and a wallet, and the outfit she was wearing was so form fitting it didn't allow for any hiding places.

What the hell, he thought. He decided to go for it.

When the woman returned, briefcase in hand, he let her take the lead.

"Well, what do you say?" as she stood next to Tail Gunner. She handed him an embossed business card. "Andrea Carnegie, Sales Executive, Neiman Marcus," the card said.

"Let's do it," Tail Gunner said. He reached into his pocket, got out his special collection wallet, and counted out $500 in 20s and 50s.

"Good deal, Gunnar," she rasped. "Let's get together later this week and have a drink."

"Sounds good," he said. "I've got your card, I'll give you a call."

The woman handed over the briefcase, and headed to the front door. She moved slowly and deliberately, turning around at the door to give Tail Gunner a wink.

Tail Gunner sat at the bar for several minutes, daydreaming about how he was going to make his next move with his new woman friend.

He picked up the briefcase, placed it on the counter and opened it. Empty.

"That slut screwed me," he thought, as he stared at the empty briefcase. He got up from the bar, walked as fast as allowable to the front door without attracting attention and went outside. The woman was long gone.

It was later he realized that not only did he get ripped off for the jewelry, the briefcase was faux leather.

He didn't comprehend it until later that the woman had set the whole thing up, and had the replacement briefcase waiting in the bathroom. All she had to do was drop the real briefcase out the window and retrieve it after she left.

Tail Gunner's experiences with women, mostly bad, began as a child.

His mother was domineering, and his sisters nagging and berating. That, combined with poor experiences in school and on the playground, left him a perfect candidate to become a womanizer.

Tail Gunner was the sum of a thousand small nuances, ten thousand different turns. He was not traumatized early in life by girls or women, but nonetheless, by the time he was a full-fledged adult, he was ready to "teach the women some lessons," as he put it to some college buddies.

He'd come to the United States on an athletic scholarship. His English skills were actually superb, and by the time he'd graduated from college, there was little or no German accent left in his speech.

In college he groomed his ability to manipulate women. He'd learned from the hundreds of different media perspectives that women existed to be manipulated. It was a subtle indoctrination.

Again, though, why blame society? It was up to each individual to carve out their own moral or immoral, ethical or unethical existence, at least past a certain point.

With Tail Gunner, all it took was a push from parents and teachers to make him feel as if he was the king of the world.

"There's no stopping me now!" Tail Gunner said to himself as he lay on his comfortable yet firm bed, arms back, hands behind his head, fingers interlocked. "I'm a genius!"

There's nothing more pitiful than the sight of a man caught up in his own delusion, a self delusion.

But his self delusion added fuel to his self confidence, so to him he was in the right, he was fulfilling the American Dream of becoming top dog. He enjoyed coming out on top, that's for sure, and anyone or anything that got in his way was merely shoved aside. He had his eyes on the prize; the prize was the next piece of ass, another notch on the belt.

Back to society's blame for creating Tail Gunner's attitude.

Since the main avenue in modern society to gaining knowledge of the world is the mass media, each branch of the media has a role to play.

Not much of a book reader, Tail Gunner was reliant on newspapers and magazines, radio and television, movies and stage plays for his development, past what parents and teachers bestowed upon him.

All that mass media, in every case, in modern society is supported by advertising and marketing. What America advertised was the good life, with sporty cars, luxurious abodes and the good looking woman on your arm.

Anything less, you were a loser.

Tail Gunner did not want to be a loser.

He was convinced the world was his oyster, and that he'd be a winner if he portrayed himself as a winner. He was convinced.

He tried slick pickup lines.

"Hey, babe," he said to the semi-good looking woman at the bar.

"Hey, handsome," she replied.

He placed the index finger of his right hand on the woman's left thigh.

"If this is Thanksgiving," he said to her, in a smarmy voice, moving his finger to the right thigh, "and if this is Christmas," he continued, alternating his gaze between her legs and her eyes, "then I sure would like to spend some time with you between the holidays."

The woman, or better put, his next intended victim, looked puzzled for a moment, trying to understand what the hell he was talking about. Then she got it.

"Asshole!" she spit out, and slapped him across the face. She got up and walked away.

"Bitch," he said, under his breath, embarrassed and trying to hide the incident from any onlookers. Another poor attempt by a man at communicating with the opposite sex. He'd learn quickly enough that pick-up lines were meant for other men. He found out there was no reason to get so aggressive, and take unnecessary chances.

But his disrespect and disdain for women's rights and freedoms weren't diminished.

One of the best sources of how to act like a man, and, conversely, how to treat women, came from the pages of men's magazines. Playboy, Hustler, Penthouse were staples to him as a young man. He liked photographs of the naked women, sure, but what he most enjoyed was the wit and wisdom to be found between the pages of the nearest girly magazine.

Those magazines were simply founts of information when it came to women. From the photographs, articles and advertisements, signposts and guides on how to be a man were tossed out like fishing lines, luring men into their net. The net? Buying products like cars, after shave lotion, clothes. It didn't matter how you did it, but sales had to be made.

Could Tail Gunner have turned out differently? Could he have turned out to be a compassionate, caring man who appreciated womanhood on a more wholesome level? Sure. Why not? But, again, the circumstances of his life directed him in a certain way, and that wasn't going to be good for women.

Never a man to turn down a challenge, the sporting nature within him saw conquering women as the greatest sport, the greatest challenge. It wasn't that he hated women; he didn't have any respect for them. They were, as the ads so brilliantly showed him, there for the dominating, there for the winner to take all.

CHAPTER 10

When she finally found his weak spot, Linda knew she could bring Tail Gunner down a notch. She knew she could bring him down a notch or three. Linda knew that his weak spot was really his weakest spot. A man like Dieter Gunnar Swernbernin had many weak spots. Women, booze, money, to name a few.

But when Linda found out Tail Gunner had a soft spot in his soft brain for rough sex, she saw a way to give the stud muffin a bit of his own medicine. She'd get hold of one of her prostitute friends, promise her the guy's not a psycho, and then let nature take its course.

"What do you want me to do?" asked Gloria, Linda's friend and a steady working gal at another club in town. Working gal as in the world's oldest profession, prostitution.

"Here's the deal," Linda said. "This guy, Tail Gunner, Gunnar, he's in need of a lesson. He's been abusing women all his life, now's our chance to get a little payback, for us and for all the other women he's abused."

"But I've never met him," Gloria said in a plaintive voice. "So he's never abused me."

"Come on, honey," Linda said, "trust me. I'm gonna make this worth your while, don't worry."

"Did he do anything to you?

"He tried to," she said, "but I stopped him before he could get away with anything. A guy like that would take advantage of a woman in a minute if he knew he could get away with it. That's the thing: He's got a bad attitude, and I'm making it my mission to improve his attitude. But I've got to have some help."

"Alright, I'm game," she said, not entirely convinced of the whole shebang.

"OK," Linda continued, "so this clown's big thrill in life is getting and giving rough sex with women, when he can find it. I'll tell him you love to get roughed up, and will give him a rough time if he wants it."

"So you're gonna introduce me to him? Where?"

"At the Club Festival," Linda said. "I'll have you show up 'accidentally' at one of the times he's sure to be there. He stops in regularly to service the client. He's a liquor distributor, besides being an asshole to women."

"OK, I get it. So what do you want me to do?"

"You can fool around for a while," she went on, "but at one point, I want you to strongly suggest you restrain him with these handcuffs," which Linda brought out of her purse. "These aren't the toy variety, they're the real deal. So handcuff him to the bed frame, nice and secure."

"Where are we gonna try to pull this stunt off?" Gloria asked.

"Where do you generally take your johns?"

"The Fleece Motel, in North Portland."

"Perfect. The Fleece it is."

"What next?"

"I'll be hiding in the closet," Linda said, "and when he's secure, come to the closet and open the door. I'll come out."

"What are you gonna do then?" Gloria asked, a little concerned over the sound of the scheme.

"Leave that up to me," Linda said.

"Wait a minute," Gloria said. "I'm supposed to handcuff him to the bed, right? I've seen the beds in the Fleece, and they don't have much of a headboard. In fact," she said, whining, "I don't think they have a headboard."

Linda's eyes darting up and to the right, making a face to suggest that Gloria wasn't being very smart or very cooperative.

"I already thought of that," Linda said. "Handcuff him to the railing under the corner of the bed. You'll have to convince him to lie on his stomach, and that you're gonna give him a severe spanking. After you've locked the handcuffs, both of them, come get me out of the closet and I'll do my thing."

Linda really had no idea what she was going to do to Tail Gunner once he was completely vulnerable. Threaten to cut off his balls. Threaten to cut off his penis. She was thinking about bringing a big, scary-looking Bowie-style knife, for effect. With him lying on his stomach, she might get away with not being identified.

Whatever was going to happen to Tail Gunner, Linda would be the judge, jury and executioner. She was ready to wreak some havoc on the man who thought he was the top dog, the best in the business, the man about town.

Whatever it took, Linda was determined to teach Tail Gunner a lesson.

The cigarette girl's caper would go as planned. Linda had made certain that Gloria happened to meet Tail Gunner at the Club Festival on the day he usually stopped in, which was every other Tuesday around 2 p.m. Gloria was there waiting for him, like the spider waiting for the fly.

When Tail Gunner showed up at the club, Gloria instinctively knew it was him. When Linda gave her the nod towards their intended victim, Gloria was positive.

All Gloria needed to do was walk up to the bar and grab a seat next to Tail Gunner. His nature as a prowler took over from there. The two chatted, and arranged to meet that coming Saturday night at the Fleece Motel in North Portland.

Once in the motel, all the preplanning paid off in spades. Within

15 minutes Tail Gunner was handcuffed to the bed.

One problem.

During the exercise, the prostitute brought a couple of scented candles with her, to add some romance to an otherwise tawdry scene. With the lights out, and only candles burning, Gloria felt more comfortable with Linda hiding in the closet. But after a few minutes of foreplay, one of the candles caught a curtain on fire. One wall in the room became engulfed in flames.

In the middle of the brouhaha, Gunnar Swernbernin nearly died. If it weren't for the speedy work of the cigarette girl.

She set him up for some form of torture, and then came to his rescue when the chips fell in a different direction.

Hiding in the closet, she came charging in when she heard the screams of her prostitute acquaintance. Tail Gunner was handcuffed securely to the metal bed frame. Flames were running from the curtains up the wall. Quickly.

In the terror of seeing flames everywhere, Linda couldn't remember where she put the keys to the handcuffs. In a snap, she remembered a scene from the TV show Cops, where one of the officers undid handcuffs with a ballpoint pen. Linda grabbed a pen from the nightstand, undid the cuffs, and the prostitute and the cigarette girl dragged Tail Gunner from the burning motel room. The prostitute, still dressed in her bra and underpants, grabbed a blanket to put around the naked Tail Gunner.

The fire alarm had been set off, warning nearby guests and the motel manager. The fire department was called, by who knows who, and firefighters arrived within a couple of minutes. As Linda, Gloria and Tail Gunner were coming out of the motel room, firefighters went in. Although the room was about to be consumed in flames, the quick action by the men and women put out the burgeoning inferno within seconds.

Sitting on the curb together, down from the motel room, a firefighter approached the trio.

“OK,” said the burly fireman, “who’s gonna tell me what happened here?”

Linda and Gloria looked at each other, unsure as how to explain why they were there. Not knowing why Linda was there didn’t seem to bother Tail Gunner; all he wanted was to leave, and not to get in trouble for hooking up with a hooker. He figured he could quiz the ladies later as to what the hell was going on.

The trio made an interesting spectacle. Linda was fully dressed, but Tail Gunner had only a blanket draped over him, and Gloria was still in her Victoria’s Secret underwear.

“Oh, we were having some fun,” Tail Gunner said, innocently. “Nothing was going on. I guess the candle my girlfriend brought caught the curtain on fire.”

“Which one is your girlfriend?”

“She is,” Tail Gunner responded, nodding towards Gloria.

“So what was the other lady doing there?”

Tail Gunner was flummoxed. He didn’t have an answer for that one. He didn’t know what the hell Linda was doing there, so he couldn’t answer. Linda spoke up.

“Oh, I’m their friend. I stopped by to say hi.”

“Right,” the firefighter said, his voice indicating he wasn’t entirely convinced of the whole story, as dicey as it was. The fact that Tail Gunner was nude under the blanket, and the prostitute in her underwear, with Linda fully dressed, made him suspicious.

Just then two officers with the Portland Police Bureau walked up to the firefighter talking to the three people. Officers Joe Blankenship and Mel Roswell were seasoned veterans with Portland’s finest.

“So what’s the story here?” Officer Blankenship asked the three sitting on the curb.

"No story, officer," Tail Gunner said, sounding simultaneously guilty and innocent. "We were explaining to the fireman what happened."

"Why don't you tell us what was going on?" Officer Roswell asked.

"Well," Tail Gunner began, stammering, "me and the girlfriend were having a bit of fun, you know, and somehow the candles started a fire. That's it. That's the whole story."

The two police officers looked at each other. Blankenship tilted his head slightly to the side, showing his lack of belief.

"So that's the story you all agree on?" Blankenship asked.

The two women looked at each other, then looked at the officers and nodded agreement.

"So are you saying a candle or more than one candle started the fire?" Roswell said. "I find that hard to believe. I don't think motels like this are in the habit of supplying candles to the guests."

"Oh, no, officer, I brought the candles with me," Gloria explained. "They were my candles. I was trying to set a mood."

Then one of the firefighters delivered to the police officers the handcuffs that they found in the room.

"And these handcuffs," said Blankenship, holding them up in the air for all to see. "They were part of 'setting the mood,' as you call it?"

Linda grimaced, Gloria hung her head in shame and Tail Gunner's face turned red. The firefighter and the police officers smiled.

"Yes, officer," Gloria mumbled.

The police officers thanked the firefighter for bringing the handcuffs to their attention. The two police officers then spoke quietly between themselves for about 30 seconds. The three sitting on the curb were numb from the excitement and letdown, and sat there silently.

"OK," said Blankenship, "we're pretty much satisfied with your explanation. Pretty much. There's only one problem."

The three guilty parties all tensed up, waiting for the next bomb to drop.

"My partner there recognizes the one in the underwear as a hooker," Blankenship said. "So let's drop this 'girlfriend' crap and be honest with each other. As for the fully dressed lady," he continued, "I don't know who you are and I don't care. But, sir, you need to come clean. Did you hire this woman for sex?"

Tail Gunner's face turned from bright red to pale white in a flash. Busted. "This is the last thing I need," he thought to himself. He may have been born in Germany, but he was brought up in America, and knew about his rights. He also knew that he could either get a lawyer before speaking further or simply deny everything.

"In fact," said Blankenship, taking the lead role, "I'm going to have to advise you of your rights. This is for all three of you. You all have the right to remain silent, and anything that you say can be used against you in a court of law. You also have the right to consult an attorney, and to have an attorney present during questioning. If you cannot afford an attorney, an attorney will be provided at no cost to you. Do you all understand your rights?"

All three ashamed human beings sitting on the curb nodded their assent.

"I need to hear you say it," he said.

"Yes, officer," Linda said.

"Yes, sir," Tail Gunner added.

"Yes, I do," said Gloria.

"OK, now, who's going to tell me the truth?" Blankenship said, sternly and directly.

A fire truck siren wailed in the distance. It was late. The lights from the motel and the streetlights gave a grave image to the whole craven scene. The firefighters were still mopping up, inspecting the damage to the motel. The curious looky-loos had drifted away. One fire truck and one police cruiser sat in the parking lot.

With the trio temporarily stunned, the two officers took each one aside separately and grilled them to see if their stories jibed.

As the stories began to fall apart, the chance that Linda would end up in jail for conspiracy to commit a crime increased dramatically. There was also a good chance the other two would end up arrested for soliciting prostitution services and accepting the services of a prostitute.

But thankfully, each one, in their own way, had enough criminal sense to keep from tripping each other up.

Tail Gunner became that stellar example of American manhood by admitting his weakness for sex, but saying that he actually knew the girl for more than five minutes. He had no idea what Linda was doing there, although he admitted he knew her from the Club Festival, where she was the cigarette girl.

"I don't know anything more than that," Tail Gunner said.

Gloria kept insisting she already knew Tail Gunner from a previous engagement. She said that Linda was hiding in the closet to make sure Gloria wasn't in danger during the rough sex. She and Linda had their stories straight on that one.

Linda knew better than to admit anything. She said she was there at the behest of Gloria, to protect her from being harmed during the rough sex. She knew if she said anything more than that, she'd be getting in way over her head. So she basically kept her mouth shut.

The two cops traded off investigating the three suspects.

"OK you three, just sit tight," said Roswell.

Linda, Gloria and Tail Gunner stood on the sidewalk in front of the motel room, not saying anything. They were each so completely drained from the experience that there wasn't an ounce of energy left in any of them.

After a few anxious minutes, officers Blankenship and Roswell approached the three suspects.

"We're convinced the fire was an accident," Blankenship said to the trio. "That's pretty clear. What's also clear is that there was some hanky panky going on between the man and Gloria. But since there doesn't seem to be much evidence of actual solicitation, we're gonna have to let all of you go."

Not totally satisfied with everything that had gone on, but without further evidence or some nefarious motive, the police officers had to let Linda, Gloria and Tail Gunner go.

"We don't really know what was going on in that motel room," Roswell said, "but whatever was going on, we don't want to see any of you again anywhere near this motel or any other motel trying to pull this kind of a stunt again. Besides," he continued, "you boneheads were mighty careless with the open flame. You folks need to grow up and get lives. Do you hear me?"

"But I want to say this much," Blankenship added. "We've written down your names and addresses, and if we ever see any of you out on the streets of North Portland trying to pull off any more mischief, you'll pay the price. Now get the hell out of here!"

Before the three could go, there was a small matter of a burned-out motel room. The manager was waiting around the edges of the investigation, wanting to know what happened. He'd have to file a report to the City of Portland Bureau of Business Licenses and his insurance company to cover the cost of repairs.

He needed to get some official story from someone, so at first he asked one of the firefighters. The firefighter he talked with told him to talk to one of the police officers. The police officer he cornered told him to go to the police station downtown the next day, which actually meant later that day, to get a copy of the official report.

With the firefighters finished mopping up and inspecting the damage, and able fairly quickly to assess the cause of the fire, the firefighting crew and their truck left before the cops were done interrogating the three involved.

The cops got back into their patrol car.

"Joe," Roswell asked his partner, "what the hell do you think was really going on there?"

"I don't know, Mel," Blankenship replied. "I don't know. But whatever it was, it wasn't anything we need to worry about. Those three clowns looked pretty shook up, first by the fire, then by our putting them on the spot."

"What's amazing to me," Roswell said, "is how mature adults can get themselves into so much trouble."

"Yeah, I know what you mean. Let's get out of here."

The police cruiser pulled out of the parking lot and into traffic.

"Say, how did you get here?" Tail Gunner asked Linda.

"Don't worry about me. I'm going home. Later, guys."

Tail Gunner was perplexed as to why Linda was hiding in the closet, but was too tired to continue putting questions to her. He knew he'd see her again, probably at the Club Festival, so he could ask her then.

Gloria started to walk away when Tail Gunner stopped her.

"Where you going, sweetheart," he said to Gloria. "The evening's young!"

"You've got to be kidding me," Gloria said, with more than a hint of exhaustion in her voice. "The evening may be young, but I'm not getting any younger. I'm taking off."

"So that's it, nothing more?"

"Nothing more, sailor. Stick a fork in me, I'm done. We'll talk another time."

Tail Gunner was disappointed. The whole evening had been a waste to him, and getting hassled by the cops was certainly no picnic.

Then he realized how much he'd been through that night, and began to feel his level of energy at first slip away, then spark.

"Maybe I should head over to the Dew Drop Inn," he said to himself as he got into his automobile, thinking of one of his favorite watering holes. "The guys would love to hear this story."

CHAPTER 11

A siren screamed down the street from the Club Festival; within a few minutes an ambulance was passing by at high speed.

It was a wet night in the city, and the whole swollen patch of humanity surrounding the highlife nightclub pulsated and throbbed. Rain was coming down in a drizzle. A soaking kind of drizzle that you'd think would give you a break. No.

"The rain doesn't seem to slow them down," Linda lamented to Lou, as they stood in the doorway of the club.

"No, sweetheart, nothin' slows 'em down," Lou replied, in a tired voice.

Although actually the same height as the woman, Lou was a mass of muscle, from his days as a boxer. He never lost that bulldog look, even after a decade of work behind the bar.

Linda was remembering last week, when she saved that rotten Dieter Gunnar Swernbernin's life. Tail Gunner. She swore she was gonna do him some harm, but in the end, she saved him from an inferno.

Retribution it was supposed to be. Revenge for all the nasty things other men had done to her and to other women over the years. But when the rubber met the road, she couldn't do it. She couldn't sink to their level.

She began to get philosophical.

Retribution and revenge, she thought to herself, are highly overrated. How are you any better than the next person if you commit the same heinous act that they do? Where's the justice there?

What was supposed to be a life-changing experience for Tail Gunner turned out to be a life-changing experience for Linda.

She was going to teach him a lesson, but she learned a different lesson herself. Instead of harming him and "getting payback," she saved his life. As she mulled the whole affair over in her mind, time and time again, she realized how compassion is a stellar replacement for revenge.

"Revenge isn't always sweeter," she thought to herself, paraphrasing the cliché.

She began to realize the effect the incident was having on her.

She realized that if she had mutilated Tail Gunner by cutting off some part of his manhood, she'd be wracked with guilt for the rest of her life.

Instead, she felt like a hero, after saving his life.

What a difference between the two feelings.

"I'm goin' back into the club," Linda said to Lou. "It's drier inside."

"See you back inside, babe," Lou replied.

The rain was still coming down in a drizzle.

Linda was a cigarette girl who'd seen quite a lot of mischief over the years.

Now, aging fast, she knew her good looks were changing. But as the looks changed, the stash of knowledge concerning the wild, wacky, who-done-it world was blossoming. It was all coming together for her, after all the years of paying attention.

One of her problems was that as she became smarter, with regard to the street, to men, to the hustle of marketing and advertising, she had witnessed a marked decline in her friends. Not the number of friends, but the quality of their lives.

Some became mental cripples who lost their way because of too many drugs, too much alcohol, too much and too soon of the cornucopia that America had become.

Linda had experimented slightly with drugs and alcohol, but never to the point of having negative physical or mental issues. She'd done every drug under the sun, except heroin, and lived to tell about it. She'd consumed beer, wine and spirits in massive quantities, sure, but never for very long.

Her tale was one of not merely survival, but of success. With barely a high school education, she'd learned many things over the years, lessons not taught in books and magazines or in movies and TV. Lessons sometimes hard earned, but earned nonetheless.

She also knew she was living on borrowed time. There were the physical challenges of growing old, but more than that, how to adjust mentally to a world seemingly gone insane.

It seemed that although she felt good about saving her abuser Tail Gunner, she was still not totally satisfied he actually had learned a lesson and had changed. She wondered seriously if he'd ever change. She realized there was only so much a person can do to help another human being. She realized that maybe the most important change was within her.

Yet, Tail Gunner was grateful to Linda for saving his life.

"Thanks, babe," he said, as he sat on the curb outside the motel. "Thanks for saving my life."

"No problem," Linda said. "It was an automatic response."

"What the hell were you doing there at the motel? That was pretty weird when all of a sudden you were getting me out of the handcuffs. What the hell was going on?"

Now her story would begin to unravel unless she could think quickly. She needed to come up with a reason for her being there, and it was apparent Tail Gunner was perplexed by the whole sordid affair. If Linda didn't come up with a good story, she might find out how truly abusive he was.

In the nick of time, they were interrupted by the firefighter seeking answers. Then the two police officers came onto the scene, with a few questions of their own.

Tail Gunner would never figure out the real truth of the matter, no matter how much time you gave him. He brought the subject up more than once with Linda when he chanced to run into her at the Club Festival, but she always avoided a direct answer. He finally forgot about the incident. He was a good looking dumb guy, more of a reincarnation of a dog than anything else.

One of the few books Linda had ever read was Demian by Hermann Hesse. She couldn't say what the book was about, but she remembered the introduction to the book, and how it talked about how some people aren't actually completely evolved, describing someone as a human being above the waist, dog or fish below.

Well, Tail Gunner was like that. He was a still-evolving human being.

But maybe the same thing could be said of anyone, including our heroine Linda. She was evolving, too, from baser instincts to a high morality and ethic.

You see, she'd already evolved by taking a higher road, by not letting Tail Gunner die in the fire, the supreme revenge.

The next day, back at the club, she'd put the whole incident with Tail Gunner behind her for the moment. She'd let the whole thing percolate in her mind, reviewing each detail carefully. She felt good about what she'd done.

She was plying her trade during a dark, rainy evening when she noticed the man known as Squint Eye motioning for her to come over to his table.

"What can I do you for you, sir?" she asked the club regular, with a tone of respect.

"I'm in the mood for a pack of cigarettes," he quietly explained.

"I didn't know you smoked," she said.

"I don't, usually," he said to her, "but tonight I'm making an exception. I enjoy a good smoke on the walk home, and it's been quite a while since I've indulged myself."

"Not a regular habit?" she asked.

"No, just a random feeling."

Her case of goodies hung from a strap slung over her shoulders and around her neck. Her wares were there for all to see.

"Have you got any extra light cigarettes?" he asked. "I'm a lightweight."

"Sure, partner, right here," she replied.

She picked a pack of extra light smokes, handing them to her customer with finesse.

"That'll be $7," she said.

"Kind of high, don't you think?" he asked.

"Well," she said, sighing heavily, "I've got to make a living."

"Fine," he said, reaching into his pocket. He handed her a ten dollar bill. "Keep the change, good looking."

The two parted company, with Squint getting back to some serious drinking before last call and closing time, and Linda heading to the bar for a drink of water.

Linda thought about Squint, and felt good about all that had transpired with him over the past few days and weeks. He was a customer who treated her with respect and dignity, a rare thing in the world of the cigarette girl. She remembered one such negative exchange that happened earlier in the day.

She had started her shift at the Club Festival, when two customers, young white trash, signaled for her to come hither.

"Hey, blondie, what'd ya got in the case?" one of them asked of her cigarette girl tray. "Got any firecrackers?"

"You're kidding, right?" she replied, giving the young man a severe stare down.

"No, baby, I'm not," he said back, giving her a mean look.

"No, young man," she said, haughtily, "I've got no firecrackers. Aren't you a little old to be playing games?"

The two young men, looking barely over the legal age to drink in the state of Oregon, gave her sideway glances. They were going to play a game of verbal fencing with the cigarette girl. Or at least they thought they were.

"Oh, aren't you the wiseass," said the other. "Don't you know that the customer is always right?"

"Sonny," she said to the other youngster, "I'm about to go get the manager to card you to see if you're old enough to be in this place. How would you like them apples?"

"Hey, lady," the other one replied, "we're not looking for trouble."

"Well, trouble is what you got, big guy," she said. "So is there anything I can do for you two?"

"No," the first one said. "Buzz off. We're tired of playing games with you."

Without responding, Linda turned around abruptly and headed back to the bar.

To get her mind off the oafish twins she'd encountered, she started to think about Squint again. She remembered that at one point, a few days ago, she was beginning to think about hooking up with Squint, but changed her mind. Now, compared to the two she dealt with, Squint began to look like a prince.

"What you thinkin' about so heavily, honey?" Emily Lou Resnick asked her. The question broke Linda's daydreaming, and she looked right at the waitress.

"I'm thinking about dating one of the customers," Linda said to Emily Lou.

"I don't think that's such a good idea," Emily Lou returned.

"Why?"

"Well," Emily Lou continued, "besides the fact that you'd have to face the guy again if things didn't work out, there are a million reasons not to date men you meet on the job. With customers, they're already in a bar. Isn't that enough reason right there?"

"Maybe you're right," Linda said.

Emily Lou wandered off to attend to some chore, and left Linda alone to ponder the infinite possibilities of life.

As she examined her nails, Linda wondered with what her day would be filled.

She actually enjoyed being a cigarette girl, it gave her the income she needed without too much strain, and it provided an interesting milieu of people with which to interact.

"I hope I see the Bosleys," she thought to herself, remembering how genuine and kind the couple had been to her. Nothing smarmy or greasy. Regular folks out to have a good time. Might have kids at home. Nice couple.

She noticed Lou was staring at her.

Linda, like some women, hated her father, in this case her stepfather, growing up, but missed that brutal presence so much she kept hanging around men who were like her father. She hated her stepfather, deep inside, for the violence, the yelling. At the same time, it molded her forever.

She was a product of her childhood.

Always trying to please a man, to give him what he wants, when, of course, no man ever really knows what he wants. They're all faking it. Linda remembered the really smart kid in high school, the athlete and straight A student who had it all, his father was one of the executives down at the mill. The kid hung himself by a rope until he died, by his own hand. Why? Why would a person with so much going for him end it all so young?

She remembered her stepfather would brag that one day Linda

would write a memoir of all his witty sayings.

"Girl, do you know what a pheletus is?" he'd ask her. "No, dad," she'd innocently reply. His response: "It's a turd floating around the heart." Or the one where he told her some fake name of a disease, and told her it was "a turd caught in sideways."

Frightening, really, fecal matter caught up in the system. Thankfully, that never happened to her. Happened to a friend of hers, when he was young, got all caught up inside, had to put a balloon up his ass. He walked funny for years, finally straightened up from riding bike and walking all over town as an adolescent.

Dad repeated all sorts of outrageous things. The strange and sad part is, in a way Linda honored his request by remembering all the insane and often inane witticisms; with no warning they'd pop up in her mind, floating to the top of her consciousness randomly and without reason. In this way she created a transient memorial to the old man.

"Teach me how to be a tough guy," Linda pleaded with Lou, bartending at the moment. "Teach me what it takes to not be afraid when you go out into the street so late at night."

"Lady, I don't know if you got what it takes," he said to her, his head tilted in an odd manner, giving him a buffoonish look, one that he was trying for.

"You're giving me a hard time," she barked at him. "Tell me something useful for once, you worthless lump of flesh."

"All right, all right, don't get your panties in a wad."

He thought about what he should tell her. It didn't take a lot of thinking.

"You've got to be prepared," he explained, "and be one step ahead of the bad guys." He thought for another moment. "You don't have to turn into a bad guy, you have to think like they do by thinking bad thoughts. Think sneaky, lowlife thoughts."

Linda gave him a look of disbelief.

"What the hell are you talking about?" she asked him.

"Well, first of all, don't go walking down the street whistling like the guy from The Happy Wanderer," he said. "You've got to project something that makes you not appear to be a victim."

He thought again.

"But you don't have to be a tough guy," he insisted. "Sometimes all it takes is acting like the weird guy, the unpredictable street person, or the not-to-be-relied-on mental case. If you act like you are out of your mind, and have nothing to lose in a street brawl, the common mugger will avoid you. Your potential attacker looks at some potential victim as too much trouble, too much chance of them getting hurt. The person who displays the nature of the wild beast is to be avoided."

Linda nodded.

"Who wants the drama, who wants the pain?" he continued. "Criminals and bad guys look for the weak in the pack, like the cheetah or lion hunting the weakest wildebeest. You look for the easiest target."

Linda was beginning to catch the clue, to get the point. Her eyes narrowed, her glance suddenly had a knowing look. Lou continued.

"You don't have to be the toughest monkey," he said. "Instead, you can be the nuttiest monkey, or the quickest one with the punch. I advise catching your opponent off guard with some quick movement to the face, neck or groin. Works every time.

"Getting the upper hand in the confrontation is key," he added.

Linda took a deep breath. Time to absorb. Time to absorb some good alcohol. To relax. To rest. To forget the rest of the world. The world can go fuck itself. Linda asked for and received a nice, stiff drink from Lou.

"Thanks," she said to Lou as he set down a double Scotch on the rocks, some of the good stuff, Glenlivet to be exact.

"No problem, Linda," he said, as the two sat in silence at the bar.

Lou thought about some of the advice he'd given Linda, and hoped it would help her in the future. His own experience with the world included nothing all that violent, and he went back to work.

He remembered being in the right, and taking the high road. He thought about the phrase, "the high road," and recalled a couple of instances in the military when he nearly got busted for breaking the law. He felt lucky.

Lou had more than his share of drug experiences in the military.

One time, while hanging out with some of his soldier buddies, he ended up in a barracks room smoking pot with a bunch of the guys. There was a little experimentation with "poppers," amyl nitrate, heady stuff. But a quick whiff, nothing too intense.

The men had purchased some high-powered Jamaican weed; it smelled slightly moldy, but was fairly potent. There were a couple of ounces of the stuff, and it had been cleaned of stems and seeds and placed in a thick LP record album cover, similar to the All Things Must Pass album by George Harrison.

All of a sudden, a fellow burst in through the door.

"The MPs are here!" he said. "They've got dogs and are searching for drugs." MPs, or military police, constantly patrolled the barracks for suspected crime, including the use of illicit drugs.

Before Lou's eyes, he watched everyone either dive out the first floor window or exit the barracks room. On the way out, one of the fellows handed him the LP with the drugs in it.

He was left holding the bag.

Lou stood there for a second, not knowing what to do. He decided he'd act casual. He calmly walked out of the barracks room, down a hall and out of the barracks. Lou didn't see any MPs, and so he casually walked back to his own barracks room across the post.

You'd think he'd kept the pot, but he didn't. He gave it back to his buddies.

Another time, he was smoking hash in a pipe on the post, near the running track, at around 8 or 9 at night. He was with another soldier, a woman, and the two were smoking and laughing and enjoying the night.

All of a sudden, lights were in their eyes. A military police jeep had pulled up 50-60 feet from them. Lou quickly tossed the hash pipe in the grass.

The MPs approached the two scofflaws. Questioned by the MPs, they denied they were doing anything. One of the MPs crouched down, picked up the pipe and presented it to Lou.

"Oops," Lou said. "Sorry" was all he could say.

For whatever reason, the MP stuffed the pipe in his pocket and told the two to vamoose. The luck. Always the luck.

CHAPTER 12

Linda Avery's childhood was perfect. Perfectly uneventful. In her small Oregon town, on weekends there was only a movie theater for entertainment, which meant if you already saw the featured movie on Saturday, played once in the afternoon and once in the evening, there wasn't anything to do on Sundays.

For lack of anything better to do on Sundays, Linda and her brother Joe would walk over to Peterson's School of Dance and watch the young ladies practice their tap dance, ballet and whatever else they may be rehearsing. It was at the very least something to do. Not much of something, but something.

Peterson's School of Dance was located a block down the street from the theater, one of many storefronts that lined the main street of the ancient downtown. Along the same side of the street in the same block as the school of dance there was a greasy spoon restaurant, the Greyhound Bus station and some boarded up former retail stores. It was a moldering remnant of the glory days of the post-World War II era, barely viable and clinging to a fast-changing world. Suburbia and television were replacing community gatherings and front porch conversations as quickly as the latest women's fashions.

The exterior of the dance school was pure 1940s, alive in the 1960s, with an air of shabby dignity in the old downtown core. Inside, the smell of mildewed wood and of a basketball court, that is, of human perspiration, permeated the space from end to end. It was unheated in the winter, not cooled in the summer, and generally gave to visitors the air of austerity and meagerness.

Guests were welcome to come into the studios of Peterson's School of Dance, where visitors could watch the children, mostly small girls, practice their ballet or tap dancing routines. Unaccompanied children were welcome only if they behaved; the town was small enough that everyone knew everyone, and children weren't as well known by their first names as by their parent's names; you weren't Johnny or Jill, you were "Bud's child" or "Maxine's daughter." The identity also gave testament to how a misbehaving child was disciplined by adults other than their parents; there wasn't any need to directly scold a child, for all an adult needed to do was call the parent directly. Discipline was meted out at home, where the heart, and the belt, lived.

At Peterson's School of Dance the actual dance studio practice area and the viewing area were located in long rooms perpendicular to the store front. There was a combination hallway and viewing area, with a row of metal folding chairs lined opposite to a huge wall-sized window, stretching from floor to ceiling, from one end of the practice room to the other.

Within the dance studio practice space, a piano was placed in the viewing area. It created a living tableau carried on for the masses, akin to a store window display. The difference from a store window display was that the viewing area was located inside, not outside from the street, and there were chairs for seating.

Along with dancing, which ranged from beginner to expert, there was the frequent emotional breakdown of a child. Some little girl would make an error, or two, and break down and begin to openly sob.

"I never wanted to do this, mommy made me!" could be heard from the emoting child. Then mommy would come into the practice area, grab the little girl by the arm and march her out.

It was human drama played out in real time. It could be considered the best entertainment in town for Linda and her brother

Joe, but it was simultaneously the only entertainment in a small town in Oregon during the 1960s. Watching the students at Peterson's School of Dance was occasionally interesting, sometimes funny and oftentimes just plain touching.

Life in the big city offered a different form of living montage, sometimes entertaining, but more often bizarre or dangerous. Linda did not necessarily seek out the human drama alive on the streets of Portland. The one time she did seek out drama, it turned out to be a bit much for her to stomach.

When traveling through downtown Portland on a TriMet bus one Sunday morning in the late '90s, planning to show early to work, she noticed a couple of Portland Police Bureau cruisers pulled up alongside a building. Curious, and with some time on her hands before having to be at work, she signaled to get off at the next stop. Once off the bus, she walked to near where the hubbub was occurring.

She got more than she bargained for, because several police officers surrounded what was apparently a homeless man covered in blood from head to toe. The scene was upsetting and stomach-churning to Linda, who, although had seen much blood and guts on TV and in the movies, wasn't prepared to see such a visceral display in real life. She made a mental note never to be so curious again, unless of course there was something she could do to help.

But there are times when the action comes to you, when there's no stopping fate from bringing life on the street right to your front door.

As Linda relaxed at home on one of her days off, she enjoyed a couple of beers while she watched TV in her apartment. It was late afternoon on a sunny, fairly warm day in the late spring.

As she sat on the couch, her eyes wandered to the street. There she saw something she'd never forget. Down below, in the gutter, a large rat, black and slimy, crawled along slowly. Its rear legs were crippled, and it was using its front legs to drag itself forward.

A city of rats.

She'd seen rats scurrying around at night, along buildings, down alleyways. Rats. They're everywhere. Because of the labyrinth of sewer and storm drains under the city, those in the know say that city dwellers are only a few feet away from a rat at any one moment.

The handicapped rat, fighting to survive, skittered down a storm drain grating and out of sight. Linda continued watching the TV.

Rats were part and parcel of the city. Some months prior, she'd had an up close and personal introduction to the city's rat population.

It was late at night in her apartment. She heard some strange scratching in her bathroom. Going in to investigate, at first she saw nothing. She continued to hear the noise. Recognizing that the noise was coming from the toilet, she lifted the lid and seat. Inside the toilet bowl was not the Tidy Bowl Man but rather a rat. Startled, she threw the toilet lid and seat back down, and flushed the toilet. She heard the gurgling and clawing from the rat as it tried to get out of the toilet. But toilets being what they are, there's not much to grab. Down the toilet drain went the rodent. After the commode was finished recycling, there was silence.

Cautiously, Linda lifted the lid again. The rat was gone.

For whatever reason, all she could think of was a phrase from her stepfather, from her childhood. "Crazier than a shithouse rat," dad used to say about certain people. The 1960s comical phrase, "We don't swim in your toilet, so don't pee in our pool," also came to her mind.

The late afternoon sun was beginning to set. Bored, with nothing better to do, she thought she'd saunter outside her tiny apartment to smoke a cigarette and see what was happening on the street. When she got outside, the bright sunlight blinded her, and she felt a bit unsteady on her feet. She knew then she'd forgotten to eat anything for breakfast or lunch, and the minor amount of alcohol she'd consumed made her feel a little bit dizzy.

She casually looked down the block, then up the block as she stood on the sidewalk in front of her apartment. Looking up the block was an accurate description of the situation, because the street in front of her apartment was not level.

She looked up the block and saw a form, some lump, on a bicycle. For whatever reason, she thought to herself, "Trouble." She saw trouble coming. She lit her cigarette. The human being was several blocks away, but somehow she knew that trouble was coming her way. It seemed natural, since the person on the bicycle was uphill from her, and it would be nature and gravity that would send trouble wheeling her way. Trouble, it seemed, was riding a bicycle.

Then trouble arrived.

A stocky black man with fire-red eyes slowly came to a stop on the street, directly in front of her. It was obvious to anyone that he was seething with anger, teeth gritted, fully in the depths of an alcohol- and drug-fueled fit of pique.

Seeing that Linda was smoking a good American tobacco cigarette, the crazed black man firmly requested that she provide him one. Linda, of course, being the streetwise diplomat, humbly yet quickly obliged. Nothing in her experience would have led her to any other course of action. Whereupon the man deftly slipped the cigarette behind his left ear.

The two immediately created a bond. It helped that Linda had been tippling; the two were on an equal footing, so to speak. He sat atop his two-wheeled machine and proceeded to relate some major drama regarding an argument with a girlfriend; a short description of the domestic squabble morphed into a lament that he "had nothing in the world."

Linda immediately became the devil's advocate, disagreeing, telling her new, wild-eyed black friend what she thought of his statement.

"That's not true," she said to the stranger. "You have at least two things in this world: A bicycle, and a cigarette."

Assuaged, and for some reason doubly thankful for the donation of the cigarette, he nodded good day and cycled on down the road.

As was said, Linda's looks were changing. At first, when describing her, someone thought of using the word, "fading," instead of "changing," but it was clear to anyone that this woman, like many women, was maturing in a way hard to define, hard to delineate.

Like men growing older, a woman can grow older and still retain the grace and charm possessed as a younger person. It's all in how one carries oneself. It's true. There's no denying it.

Of course, grace and charm are qualities that can't be purchased at the local supermarket, can't be bought online and can't be earned through study. Either one has grace and charm, or one does not.

Linda Avery had grace and charm in spades.

The way she walked, self assured and with a bit of swagger, portrayed a woman totally engaged in the waking world. There's nothing like it. Of course, the first benefit to someone like Linda was that she was not messed with on the street; she was the last person who filled a "victim profile." Her carriage and demeanor was such that she exuded confidence and strength. Men or women who looked to take advantage of "helpless" women avoided a confrontation with someone as full of life and verve as Linda. That's approaching the issue from a negative view.

From a more positive perspective, her grace and charm were used to their best influence on men. Especially men who considered themselves a "cock of the walk." Linda attracted men, but she ironically repelled men who came onto her with masculine bravado and machismo. It wouldn't matter if he were a Latin Lover, a Stud Muffin or a Sex Machine. All men bowed to Linda.

"You really think you're something, don't you?" her ex-friend

Gruber once told her.

Linda didn't have to think about that statement very long.

"Yeah," she said, in a haughty tone. "I'm something. But you got the wrong idea if you think I think I'm above everybody else. I want respect, not admiration."

"You think you're the queen of all you survey, don't you?"

"What is wrong with you?" she snapped back. "You really are starting to get on my nerves. Back off, and give me a break, will you?"

"Oh, I'll give you a break, baby. I'll break you of being an egg sucking, man-eating bitch!"

"That snaps it, fella! I'm outta here, and I'm not taking any of your shit."

"I wouldn't give you any shit, baby," Gruber snapped back, "because you're my favorite turd!"

Linda had enough class, enough grace to know when she'd had enough, when to cut her losses and get out of a relationship that was turning bad. With Gruber, she'd had enough of his verbal abuse. She also knew from other women that a man like that only got more abusive, more demanding, until the pressure either cracked him or cracked her. She wasn't waiting around to find out what more he had in store for her. She had it up to her chin with a man like that. She knew there must be a better man out there, somewhere.

She also knew she had retained enough of her good looks to attract another man.

Beauty, desire, physical attractiveness, all these features can be found in men and women who carry themselves with dignity and pride. The bloom of youth, faded, is replaced by a quiet and calm air of self respect and self esteem. It takes years to achieve this sort of aura, but those who stick with it can accomplish any goal.

The flame of youth burns brightly within the aging woman or man who retains common sense, a sense of humor and horse sense.

There's no replacing those qualities within a person. It's something that Linda learned at home, at school and on her own.

These days, everyone complains about bad parents and the poor public school system. To Linda, that's a bunch of bunk.

"Parents are universally condemned," she told her friend Bev. "That's the way it is. So is school. When you are young, everything seems to be against you, but as you grow older, you see the wisdom in most things."

Although only a high school graduate, Linda had continued to mature and grow by reading, attending seminars and watching educational television. She knew what all intelligent people know: Attending college is no stamp of brilliance or achievement. What really counts in life is what you do with your life each and every day, not for a few days. Becoming wise isn't merely collecting facts and figures; it's what you do with your mind on a daily basis that guarantees success.

"You make me proud," Bev said. "You make me proud to call you a friend of mine. I don't know too many other women who have as much confidence as you do."

"Thanks, darling, I appreciate that." Linda had a big smile on her face, and raised her chin up high.

"I'm not sure why you think that about me," Linda said, "but whatever your reasons, I'm glad you have the guts to tell me what you really think of me. You'd tell me if I was way off on something, wouldn't you?"

"What do you mean?"

"I mean, if I had something completely backwards, like some opinion I had on a subject, or if I was being too judgmental about someone."

"You'd be the first to know," Bev said in a sarcastic tone, "right after me."

"You're not blowing smoke up my ass, are you?"

"Linda, don't worry, we're friends, and I wouldn't just tell you what you want to hear."

"That's what I don't want in a friend," Linda said. "I don't want someone to automatically agree with me, to tell me what I want to hear. I want a friend who'll be honest with me, who'll lay it on the line. I value honesty in a friend, complete honesty. You know that."

"I know."

"Like with Tail Gunner. I did do the right thing by saving him from the fire, didn't I?"

Bev gave her friend a look of disbelief. Bev's face scrunched, the corners of her mouth went up and her eyebrows came down.

"Come on, girlfriend," Bev said. "You did what had to be done. You wouldn't have been able to live with yourself if you let that piece of shit die. He was a piece of shit. Hell, he still is a piece of shit. But letting another human being die in a fire? That would have been inhuman. And you are a good human being."

"Thanks. I appreciate that. I still don't know what I was thinking when I went to teach that son of a bitch a lesson. I was so tired of being used and abused by men."

"You were gonna do it for all of us, babe. You were on a mission. I understand that. But I think you learned a lesson."

"You're right," Linda said, taking a deep breath. "I learned that I couldn't do the same thing that he was doing to all those women, and to me. I couldn't stoop to his level. I learned that I'm better than that, and I didn't know it. I guess it took an extreme circumstance to bring out what I'm really all about. It took saving his life."

"Like I said, you didn't have any other choice."

"Oh, I had a choice, we all have a choice. I chose the right way. I chose life over death. It still amazes me that I did what I did. I didn't think I had it in me. I thought I could teach him a lesson. Instead I learned a lesson."

"What was that?"

"That revenge isn't sweeter, that we humans can evolve, that we can become better people."

"Like I said," Bev repeated, "you're a great friend. I'm proud of you, I'm proud of me knowing you, I'm proud of everything you did that time for Tail Gunner. He's still a son of a bitch, but at least you didn't sink to his level. You're better than that."

CHAPTER 13

Not everything that Beverley Beech did was kosher bananas. She'd been known to get into more than a little trouble.

Bev and her boyfriend at the time had been drinking cheap liquor and smoking expensive marijuana, hour after hour. While her boyfriend sat in the kitchen continuing the excess, she decided, for some ungodly reason, to strip off all of her clothing and run outside naked.

Before she could get to the front door of her apartment, the boyfriend caught her, grabbed her by the waist and threw her on the couch. She bounced up and immediately made another run for the front door. Again, the boyfriend thwarted her plan.

Her boyfriend would let her drunkenly recline on the couch while he returned to the kitchen to continue his own guzzling and imbibing. He positioned his chair so as to keep an eye on the front door. After another couple of attempts by the inebriated Bev to run naked through the streets, the boyfriend devised a plan.

He hooked a wire coat hanger on the front doorknob, with other wire hangers dangling from it. That way, before Bev could maneuver the two front door locks to make her attempted escape, there would be noise from the hangers. He also piled some boxes in front of the door, and placed a chair there.

Bev, drunk as the proverbial skunk, tried to quietly pick her way through the obstacles, but she was no deft thief; the noise invariably aroused the boyfriend, who made a successful grab at her.

One time, though, she was able to make it to the outside of the front door; the boyfriend grabbed Bev by the hair and pulled her back inside the apartment.

Finally, after an hour and a half of that madness, Bev passed out on the couch. Her boyfriend, thinking it a fine opportunity to reap a little reward for all his efforts, stripped his clothes off and proceeded to rest alongside her, exhausted.

Bev was not perfect, by a long shot. Because one is a nurse doesn't make one immune to all the poorest leanings and proclivities of society.

For instance, she had a weak spot for TV infomercials. Easily influenced by others, the barkers and shills on TV sold her everything from knife sets to pasta makers to massive cooking devices. One cooking implement could cook two chickens, a mess of shrimp and several beef steaks, all at the same time.

She piled up a wealth of such extraneous items, until she ran out of money and had to file bankruptcy. Bev picked herself up, dusted off the detritus of bad decisions and straightened out her life.

Well, with the help of a 10-week inpatient drug and alcohol treatment program.

That in itself was a nightmare for everyone involved, including Linda. As Bev's friend, Linda had to watch Bev spiral down, as with the flushing of a toilet, watching the swirling water go around and around, and there's Bev, about to head down the drain.

Bev's penchant and thirst for hard liquor became insatiable. Linda had seen it, and remembered partying with Bev for a short time. It was a full decade prior to Linda finding work as the cigarette girl at the Club Festival. At that time, Linda could keep up with other professionals in the field of drinking or doing drugs, but she was never a non-stop professional; she knew when to call a halt to the snorting of the Bolivian marching powder or to the lure of the wasty wonderland that is drink. To do it on an ongoing basis for more than a few months was not Linda's way of enjoying what life had to offer.

But Bev was heavily into the drink.

Linda would come over to Bev's on a night they both had off from work, and for a few months the two would go through at least one if not two fifths of hard liquor together. There were many nights where Linda was too drunk to try to get home, by taxi or by bus. Passing out on Bev's couch was Linda's last remembrance of a debauched evening.

The two would have drinking contests, listen to loud rock 'n' roll and generally have a hell of a good time. Then Linda would go home and not drink for days or weeks, until she saw Bev again. This went on for several months.

What Linda came to realize, slowly, was that Bev continued to drink during the nights she had off from the hospital. The drinking became a serious habit, then a problematic addiction.

"What are you going to do about your drinking?" Linda asked Bev one night while the two were downing straight shots of inexpensive Scotch whisky.

"What do you mean?"

"I saw your storage pantry."

"What?"

"The storage pantry, where you keep your recycling," Linda said. "I've never seen so many empty bottles of Scotch. I know we've been getting into some heavy drinking when I show up, but there must be 100 empty bottles back there. And a couple of months ago, I know for sure there weren't any."

Bev hung her head in shame.

"Don't worry, honey, it's OK," Linda said to her friend. "Do you think you need help?"

Bev hesitated.

"Yes," Bev said, "I'll admit it's gotten a bit out of control. I don't know what happened. It sort of crept up on me. One day I'm drinking a little, the next day more, the next day more, the next day more…"

"I get it."

"I got it. I got the habit. I don't know why or how, but there it is. Now I don't know what to do. What do you think I ought to do?"

Linda paused for a second.

"I don't know either," Linda said. "But I could take a stab at it. Do you want me to candy coat it so you can swallow it better, or do you want me to give it to you straight?"

"I want you to be honest with me, no matter how much it hurts. I'm at wit's end."

"Let me ask you this," Linda began. "Can you stop drinking today?"

"I don't think so. I don't want to. I like it too much."

"You got a problem, girl."

"I know, I know I know. I'll have to think about what to do."

"Don't think about it too long, girlfriend," Linda said. "You need to do something about it, before alcohol starts eating at your liver and your brain."

"Do you think it's that bad?"

"Unless you've got a bevy of friends coming over for drinks," Linda said, "you've obviously been drinking enough cheap whisky to float a ship. Let me ask you this: Do you drink every day?"

"Yes," Bev admitted. "Some days I'm so hung over I'd like to give it a break, and sometimes I have to bite the bullet and show up to work with a hangover, looking like and feeling like shit. It's none too pleasant."

Linda closed her eyes and shook her head.

"You've got it bad girl."

"Yeah, I got it bad. I guess I need to get some help. In the meantime, pass me the bottle."

A twinge of guilt passed through Linda's psyche as she lifted the bottle of Scotch and passed it to her friend.

"I'm enabling you by drinking with you, aren't I?"

"Let's not worry about it now. Let's enjoy the moment."

All the words of wisdom and care flew out the window as the two women let loose. The drinks flowed freely between them and Scotch was downed by the shot glass. The two were also smoking pot, which Linda knew was not a good idea. As she loaded the pipe, took a hit and then passed it to Bev, Linda spoke up.

"Is this also part of the problem?"

Bev grabbed the pipe without hesitation, applied flame to the bowl and filled her lungs. She took more than she was able, and began coughing and hacking with tremendous force.

"God, are you gonna be alright?"

Bev stopped coughing after a minute.

"Yeah," Bev said, her voice raspy from the coughing jag. "I'll be fine."

"So is the pot part of the problem?"

Bev took another hit from the pipe before passing it to Linda. Bev blew out the smoke with pride.

"Probably," Bev said. "I don't care at the moment. I want to party. You're not gonna start lecturing me on partying, are you?"

"No, I'm not. I'm not your conscience. But I don't know if I should continue doing this with you."

"More for me," Bev said, as she poured another shot of whisky. She downed it in a hurry, filled her shot glass, then filled Linda's.

"Jesus, girl, I don't know which one of us is more wicked: You for being such a fiend with the drugs and alcohol, or me for helping you do it."

"We're both wicked," Bev said. "But don't feel guilty for enjoying yourself. If I've got a problem, then it's my problem."

The two continued to abuse the whisky and marijuana for the rest of the evening.

Near midnight, the two were soaked in whisky. Bev started ranting about the state of nursing, then grew silent.

At one point, Bev excused herself and left her apartment.

"I'll be back in a minute," Bev said. "Enjoy."

Linda sat in Bev's apartment for a half hour waiting for her friend to return. Linda wondered where Bev could be going at that hour.

When she returned, Bev had two houseplants in her possession, both in rather nice pots.

"Where the hell did you get those?" Linda asked. "It's kind of late to go shopping. I don't think there are any stores open at this hour. So where'd you get the plants?"

"You don't want to know."

"If I didn't want to know, I wouldn't ask."

"I picked these up from a neighbor."

"A neighbor?"

"Yeah, from outside of an apartment down the street. They looked ripe for the plucking. So I took them."

"You mean you stole them?"

"Well, I didn't knock on the door and ask the people if I could buy them, if that's what you mean."

"I mean, did you steal them?"

"Yes, I stole them."

"Christ! Are you kidding? What's wrong with you?"

Bev sat down and poured herself another drink. She threw back the shot of whisky and gave a rebel yell.

"Yahoo! Yippee tie one on!"

Linda's eyes grew big. She was watching the birth of a monster, a person who had no other desire than to get drunk and stoned and raise hell.

Too tired to argue with her friend, Linda lay on the couch and simply passed out.

In the morning, both women were suffering from hangovers.

As they gathered themselves and sat at Bev's kitchen table, they lamented the prior evening's affairs.

"We shouldn't have drank so much," Bev said.

"Yeah, you're right," Linda said, nursing a powerful headache.

"We should have drank some water before going to bed," Bev said. "That's a good way to prevent a hangover."

Linda rolled her eyes, yet nodded her head in approval.

It was the last time the two drank so much together. It was the last time Linda would drink with her friend Bev.

At the end of it, there was the rehab.

Ten weeks of drug and alcohol in-patient rehabilitation.

Linda remembered one particular incident, in the middle of the rehab, at about the fifth or sixth week. Bev called Linda from the rehab center.

"Linda?"

"Yes."

"It's Beverley."

"Beverley, where are you?"

"I'm at the rehabilitation center. I've only got a minute. I want you to do me a big favor."

Linda hadn't heard from Bev for weeks, and was immediately suspicious.

"I'll do my best. What do you want me to do?"

"I want you to go to my apartment. There's a key hidden above the door. When you get inside, I want you to go to the closet in my bedroom. In the closet, on the shelf above where the clothes are hanging, there's a small wooden box. Inside the box you'll find a marijuana pipe and some marijuana."

Linda knew from watching television dramas what was coming

next.

"I want you to take the pipe and the pot and bring them to me here at the rehab center. All you have to do is sneak it in by hiding it in your shoe. They'll want to inspect your purse, but they won't do a complete search of your body, so you can get it into the center."

"Oh, Bev," Linda said. "That's the craziest thing I've ever heard."

"Do it for me, please? If you do this for me, I'll owe you one."

"I'll try."

"Thanks. I gotta go."

Linda got the pipe and the pot, alright, but she didn't do "the wrong thing" by taking the paraphernalia and the substance to the woman in the rehabilitation treatment center. Linda did the much wiser but more self-centered thing: She sat in Bev's apartment and smoked the weed herself, while kicking back watching bad movies on TV. It seemed like the only logical thing to do at the moment, to Linda at least. Bev was none too pleased, but while she was in treatment, there wasn't much she could do to Linda anyway.

By the time Bev got out of the rehab center, getting back on the pipe or the bottle was the last thing on her mind. As Linda recalled, Bev in fact stayed in rehab for probably more like 11 or 12 weeks, to make certain the cure took.

Bev Beech wasn't the only woman in Portland with a back story to tell.

Randi Obvitz remembered with fondness and some amusement living with Concertina Fluke and her daughters at The House of the Scorched Egg in New Jersey.

With the guns and the drugs and the craziness at the house, it wouldn't seem like a place to feel safe, but Randi did feel safe. She was on their side; Lord pity the person who wasn't, or who tried to break into the house when the occupants were home.

Randi also enjoyed the Wild West atmosphere at the house, and with the young women coming and going as they pleased, it was easy for Randi to do the same. Getting dressed up and going out at midnight was no big deal to Concertina and her daughters. Randi came and went as she pleased, and felt what few possessions she owned were safe at the house.

Randi had hooked up with a good looking man of Norwegian descent from New York City, who enjoyed cross country-skiing at Mohonk Preserve in New York state's Ulster County and at Wawayanda State Park in New Jersey's Passaic County.

Cross-country or Nordic skiing was different than downhill or alpine skiing. It all had to do with the ski boot bindings. In cross-country, the heel is not fixed to the skis; in downhill, the binding is fixed heel.

When she first started to learn to cross-country ski, Nicolette Fox, a friend of the Fluke family staying at The House of the Scorched Egg gave Randi one important tip when it came to skiing.

"No matter what's happening," Nicolette explained to Randi, with a devilish look in her eyes, "don't worry about going downhill out of control."

Randi's eyes narrowed, and she gave Nicolette a sideways glance.

"You know that most of the time cross-country skiers use tracks in the snow already made by other skiers, right?" Nicolette asked Randi. Randi had been out once already, and knew what Nicolette was talking about; cross-country skiers left a virtual highway of grooved tracks in their wake.

"Yeah, so?" Randi replied.

"How are you at stopping yourself?" Nicolette asked.

"Well," Randi admitted, "that's been a problem. Once I get going down the hill, I find it hard to stop. It's kind of dicey, because there always seem to be people in the way, so I dive off to the side, to keep from hitting someone in the tracks."

"I've got the answer to your problem," said Nicolette.

"Oh, yeah?"

"Sure," Nicolette continued. "Whenever you're totally out of control and can't stop, start yelling at the top of your lungs, 'Get the hell out of the way!' People will hear you and'll get out of the way."

"Sure," Randi said. "Sounds good."

Randi took the advice and kept it to herself. She really didn't believe Nicolette, and felt that somehow Nicolette was pulling her leg. She didn't tell her cross-country skiing partner about the advice. No reason to be considered a kook.

Oddly enough, the next winter, when she was out skiing with her partner, Randi found herself heading down the hillside at high speed. She could see ahead there were several skiers in her collision path. Randi didn't feel like diving off to the side, and for whatever reason remembered what Nicolette had said.

Randi started to yell.

"Get the hell out of the way! Get the hell out of the way now!"

To her surprise and amazement, it was almost cinematic how the various skiers further down the hill began themselves diving out of the way to avoid being hit.

CHAPTER 14

Squint Eye could be found at the Club Festival usually on a daily basis. He was the only regular that could be counted on to be drowning his sorrows in Scotch, which he lovingly described as "the delicious brown liquid."

He was the kind of heavy drinker who was never out of alcohol at his home. You might see him at the local Oregon Liquor Control Commission-sanctioned liquor store early in the morning, making purchases. State law cut off liquor sales at 2:30 a.m., but at 7 a.m. retail outlets could, theoretically, begin selling the stuff.

Because as anyone who drinks alcohol professionally knows, you don't want to run out of liquor. There's no reason to run out anyway, since the stuff is available in its many forms at grocery stores and convenience markets; except for hard liquor, which in a state like Oregon is only available at the OLCC outlets.

An early morning run assured that the hard stuff was available by noon. Squint Eye was enough of a gentleman at least to wait until noon to start drinking. Of course, that might mean that he'd be passed out by 3 p.m. Then, after a good rest, he'd be back at the stuff by dinner time.

Squint Eye was a former media maven, a man who'd been involved in the mass media nearly all his life. Starting in his sophomore year in high school with the school literary magazine, then the school newspaper his senior year. He took a photography class his junior year.

After high school, he joined the U.S. Air Force, where he worked on several base newspapers; while in the military, he also worked as a radio station disk jockey, and a TV producer and broadcaster. After serving his country, he became a writer and editor for magazines and newspapers.

Growing up in the '60s, he looked forward to a lucrative career in the media industry.

He'd grouse later that the women's liberation movement had changed the playing field, so that by the time he began looking for work in public relations in the '70s, the landscape had changed so that women dominated the field. Women also seeped into the rest of the media industry, from print to radio to TV. Like much of the world of work, women, rightly, had found a place to succeed in mass media.

But for Squint, there was only some sort of conspiracy, some sort of rigged game with marked cards and loaded dice. Struggle as he might, he never found success in his dream career of public relations, so he stuck to what he knew. He stuck with the craft of writing. He was a consummate writer, and as he found out, that led to many writing and editing gigs.

After he became a newspaper editor, he'd developed a rule: All editors need to be good writers, but not all writers make good editors.

Here's how his logic worked:

An editor needs thoroughly to understand the craft of writing, the hard work and mental toughness it takes to create out of thin air a coherent sentence, a well-turned phrase and ultimately a thoughtful article. Grammar, syntax and an innate understanding of the language are requisites for the writer.

But not all writers can be editors. Not all writers want to be editors. Some writers, those who have crossed swords with strict editors, dislike the role the editor plays. Some writers go so far as to contend that no matter how well a piece is written, an editor will change something in the article. It was like a dog marking a fire hydrant by urinating on it, marking its territory. Not that the concept is true, but there is some merit in the statement. Some writers also feel that to justify their paid occupation, an editor must do something to the article, to prove that the editor is paying attention.

Writing as a craft is hard work, but admittedly not in the sense of working in a factory or being a lumberjack; that is most certainly hard, physical work, along with the stress of having to stay alert at all times to what you are doing. Squint's father was lead man when his dad worked at the mill, so Squint knew that being a "Mill Willy" wasn't necessarily brainless work.

But one thing aspiring writers find out right away: It's easy to churn out one or two articles, that's fun, but to have to write interesting copy day in and day out, week after week, month after month, that takes dedication and discipline.

It really doesn't matter if you work on a daily newspaper or on a monthly magazine, each article is a challenge, each subject a mountain to climb. It's also a challenge to make some subjects interesting, but as the wise editor once said, there are no dull subjects, just dull writers.

Squint Eye had a long and fairly illustrious writing and editing career. He'd enjoyed the game, and got to meet hundreds of interesting people. His life was richer for the experience, both professionally and personally. He felt lucky to have been able to do what he loved to do, and to be paid for it. The personal benefit meant that what he learned "on the job" was how other people viewed life, how others lived and worked. He'd learned much over the years.

One aspect of the craft that Squint particularly enjoyed was the fact that to write an article, the writer absorbs anywhere from twice as much to ten times as much information as will ultimately go into the article. It's a matter of space, be it time in a broadcast or inches in a magazine and newspaper. There's only so much time or space available. The most stimulating aspect of that equation is that the writer often times gets to know the whole story, and sometimes gets to know facts that the subject doesn't want the public to know; and you have to respect your subject, Squint found out, if you want to be able ever to speak to that subject again. So there's a bit of a gentleman's agreement about the whole thing. There really is such a thing as "off the record."

Sometimes, though, what people feel should be off the record is made public record, and oft times, in Squint's experience, it had more to do with "running off at the mouth" as opposed to the writer digging up some secreted fact. More than once in his writing career, a subject called after an article had been printed, and exclaimed, "I never said that!" when, in fact, the subject did say that, but was associating so freely that he or she didn't remember. Then it's a case of the subject's word against the author's word, but the argument usually doesn't go far. In the best case, there's a recording of the conversation; at the least, though, there's the concept that the writer wouldn't have said it if he or she didn't first hear it somewhere.

So Squint Eye would be found pretty much on a daily basis at his favorite watering hole, living his life through memory. But as the philosopher once said, the life lived in memory can be as fulfilling as a life lived in the here and now; memories cannot be taken away, only forgotten, and they can be relived time and time again.

Squint Eye raised his left hand, extending his index finger.

"One more round," he croaked, and the waitress knew what to get.

Squint was sharing his table with another former journalist; unfortunately, although an excellent reporter, Squint had a mental block when it came to names. He couldn't remember the fellow's name sitting across from him, but that didn't matter.

Out of the blue, Squint's buddy began pontificating.

"A punch in the eye is worth two in the jaw," he slurred, ostensibly to Squint Eye, although the general audience included anyone within ear shot. The din at the Club Festival was audibly like a concrete block of noise. The aggregate racket included glass breaking, men screaming, women moaning and the beat of some form of music from the bar's audio system.

"Get to them first, I always say," his buddy continued, but by this time Squint had his mind on other action in the club. Twenty feet away a woman with jet black hair caught Squint's attention. Squint's friend put his head down on the table to rest.

Squint was a good judge of character, a skill he'd acquired as a journalist, trying to determine if a source was reliable or not. There were many ways to tell if a person is telling the truth or lying. It's in their look, in the structure of their words, in any number of body language expressions that give away a poker face.

With decades in the writing craft, he knew he possessed not only the ability to come up with the right word at the right moment, with the ability to instantly express any desire, want or need, but he also possessed the ability to tell exactly what a person is feeling, not thinking, from the look in their eyes and face, including the angle of the head on the shoulders.

"The eyes give it away," Squint Eye told the drunk friend at the table at the Club Festival. "It has to do with the integrity of the eyes. The eyes don't lie, Chico."

The last reference was to the movie Scarface with Al Pacino, with Pacino's character, Tony Montana, mapping out his personal philosophy.

"But it's the whole face," he continued, with no particular attention from his buddy, "the look around the eyes, above and below, and around the mouth. The tilt of the head, that's important, too. It's been a lifetime of looking at photographs of men and women, in mug shots, pornography, newspapers, magazines, books, movies and TV. It's been a lifetime of observing, Chico."

The weary man finally raised his head.

"Don't call me Chico," he said. "My name is Ted."

"Sorry, partner," Squint Eye said truly apologetically.

He noticed the woman with the jet black hair immediately, but couldn't place her. He recognized the hair, and the approximate height and weight, but there were several items out of place. For instance, the girl he knew didn't wear glasses, and wasn't in high heels, and the makeup was all wrong.

Then, after going over her visage gently, he hit on something that was unmistakable. She was wearing the same damned hoop earrings! Of course! She tried to change everything else about herself, but those signature hoops caught his attention, and he immediately recognized them from a prior engagement.

The power of observation can be uncanny, if let loose from the restraints of day-to-day living.

Squint thought to himself, "I am a professional!" He'd seen and participated in many an editorial battle, usually writer versus editor, and of course you know the editor's got the edge on you.

Squint had known what it is to be a professional at anything you do – from driving a fork lift to editing a book – and he especially enjoyed the word "executive" added to his title.

Squint sat starring at his drink, contemplating his life and the world of mass media.

He'd seen and done it all over the course of 40 years as a writer. He'd not just been a scribe and on-the-air talent in radio and TV broadcasting, he'd worked in radio and newspaper advertising sales. He chuckled to himself that shock radio talk show host Howard Stern considered himself to be the "King of All Media."

"If anyone is king of all media," Squint thought to himself, "that's me." Squint saw Howard Stern as merely talent, a radio station voice with little actual experience in the mass media. Squint, on the other hand, had been writing for all manner of newspapers, magazines and Web sites for years, and had generated millions of original, hard-thinking words.

He'd seen the world of the mass media from the inside, and had plenty of stories to tell.

He also knew that his experiences shaped him as a person, outside of the work place. As he reflected, he looked at the whole of his life from a sociological perspective.

He remembered that one sociological view said men in the 20th century were identified by their work. To sociologists, men defined themselves by how they earned money, be it logger, factory worker or white collar worker.

That same logic, again in the 20th century, defined women by what they typically did, which was run the house and raise the kids. "Housewife" was the phrase that was used for many years. The role of women began to change significantly during World War II, as women went into the industrialized workplace to accomplish work formerly only done by men. With that introduction to the "real world of work," women were on the brink of a revolution.

The 1960s and 1970s solidified that change in roles with women's liberation. Women were no longer tied to the home, and began doing work previously dominated by men. Think of the military, fire fighting and law enforcement, to begin with, and then branch out into mill work and construction, all manner of dangerous work and top-flight executives in major corporations.

So as the 21st century dawned, women worked alongside men in virtually every occupation.

So it could be said that by the 21st century, men and women would begin to identify themselves by their occupations.

Squint saw it all clearly. Through his squinty eyes.

He saw that a nurse, whether female or male, saw the world

through a nurse's eyes, whether on the job or off the job. A nurse's background influenced the way that person functioned in the non-work world.

"It's something I've seen in myself," he thought to himself. That is, being a journalist has colored his non-work life with its own attitude. Same might be said of a cop or a private detective, that after work, before work, when work is not being accomplished, that cop or private eye would use some of the same work skills for everyday living.

In his experience, Squint witnessed nurses treat anyone they encountered as if they were medical cases to be observed and managed, while cops viewed strangers with eyes wide open, as if at any moment a person could turn from stranger to suspect.

From his personal and professional point of view, Squint thought of himself as a person who held back judgment on all people he ran into, because he found out through years of reporting that the truth of the matter was always concealed, never obvious and often times transient.

"The truth is a slippery thing," he'd tell his friends, the few he had. Facts, they might be abundant, but to get to the truth of the matter, that was another question entirely.

Squint knew that the average citizen relied on the mass media to expose the truth about the world, and those truths ranged from the actions of politicians to the safety of consumer goods. It was a constant battle to try to figure out where the truth was, and which news organization was the most straightforward about telling the truth.

He rejected the alternative media notion of corporate media not telling the whole story, while alternative media had some sort of magic formula for discerning the truth. It wasn't that simple, he thought.

For Squint, he'd also found out something odd.

For years he thought of President John F. Kennedy as a saint, and thought of someone like Frank Sinatra as immoral and corrupt.

Strangely enough, through the years, the more he found out about Jack Kennedy, the less impressed he was with the man. He'd been part of a rich family that practically bought the presidency for him.

Conversely, the more he read about Frank Sinatra, the more impressed he was with how unbigoted and free-minded the man was, supporting black performers and fighting for equal rights for all men. Squint had to remind himself that the phrase "all men" was telling, because as far as he could tell, Frank Sinatra possessed the old fashion male chauvinism that dominated America up until the late 20th century.

Squint had a lot on his mind. Always.

One of the customers in the Club Festival was waving his hand at Emily Lou Resnick.

"What now?" she thought as she ambled over to the table.

She had been serving the man and his buddy straight shots of tequila for the past hour, and they were both good and drunk.

"Hey there," the customer slurred, still waving his hand. "I got a question for you."

Emily Lou tried to keep from rolling her eyes, but she couldn't help it.

"Sorry to bother you, sister," he said, with a disgusted tone.

"I'm sorry," she said. "I didn't mean any disrespect. It's been a long night, that's all."

The two drunken men looked at each other and laughed. They didn't really care what the waitress had to say. They were fully tanked and filled with none-too-bright ideas.

"Anyway," the customer continued, "I need to know something."

"Shoot," Emily Lou said.

"Why is there a worm in a bottle of tequila?"

She tried not to smirk, and this time succeeded in hiding her disdain. It wasn't a bad question, she thought to herself. But she didn't have the answer.

"I don't know," she said. "I'll go ask the manager."

She did an about face and headed to the back of the club.

The two drunken men returned to a previous conversation and quickly forgot the about the waitress.

Emily Lou knew that their query was strange, but now her interest was piqued.

"Why is there a worm in that stuff?" she asked herself on the way to Lou's office. Now she wanted to know.

She walked down a corridor to the back room where Lou's office was located, all the while mulling the question over in her mind. She had no idea why the worm was there, yet she'd heard about it since she was old enough to drink.

She stood in front of Lou's office; the door was closed; she could hear some sort of noise or music inside, and hesitated to knock on the door. She didn't want to interrupt Lou if he was occupied with someone else or otherwise busy. She liked Lou well enough, and he was a decent boss, but he could get cranky.

She knocked on the door.

"Come in," he said, almost immediately. He was sitting at his cluttered desk in the cramped office, with the lone television set in the club broadcasting some program. Emily Lou paused for a second or two, still working over the question in her mind.

"Do you hear them?" Lou said as he turned to her. "Do you hear them?"

All Emily Lou could hear was some rhythmic noise coming from the TV. She had no idea what he was talking about.

"Hear what, Lou?" she said.

"It's the choppers," he said in a serious tone. "They're comin' in!"

Emily Lou had a puzzled look on her face.

"Choppers?" she asked.

"They're coming in for a landing!" Lou exclaimed.

Emily Lou looked around the room, still not really comprehending what Lou was talking about. Then she looked over at the TV and saw a motion picture of old style Army helicopters on the screen.

"Lou, are you OK?"

"Yeah, yeah," he said, and started to laugh.

He was watching the Public Broadcasting Service's rebroadcast of Vietnam: A Television History, which began each episode with the sound and film of helicopters landing.

She got the joke, if there was much of one, and shrugged her shoulders.

"Lou, you are so weird sometimes," she said.

Lou took a deep breath, realizing that watching old films of the Vietnam War was interesting only to him. Lou Brodsky was still fighting the war in his mind. He'd known buddies in the Army and Marines who had died fighting that long, losing war. He also had buddies that were forever scarred by their service in, as he called it, "The Nam."

"Sorry," he said, "I get worked up a bit watching this program. What can I do for you?"

Emily Lou had forgotten why she came to see Lou. She thought back, then remembered.

"Lou, some customer wants to know why there's a worm in a bottle of tequila."

Lou grimaced. He looked to the side and gathered his thoughts.

"That's a good question," he responded. "From what I understand, the whole tequila worm thing is a myth, and if there is a worm, it's not in tequila, but in similar hard liquor from Mexico called mescal. Who's asking, anyway?"

"Some bonehead out in the bar who's been doing straight shots of tequila for the past hour."

"Well," Lou said, "tell your bonehead customer that the whole thing is a joke, that it was probably started as some sort of marketing scheme. Tell him the worm's not in tequila, it's in another drink, a similar drink. Is this really important?"

"No," she said, realizing she was wasting her boss's time. "But you know customers, when they get a burr up their ass, they get twitchy. I'll do my best."

"That's all you can do," Lou said. "I understand. The customer's always right. I appreciate what you're tryin' to do."

"Thanks, Lou," she said, turning around. "I'll get out of your hair."

By the time she returned to the barroom, the men had paid their bill and vamoosed. Emily Lou was relieved that she didn't have to deal with the situation.

CHAPTER 15

Linda and Bev were enjoying some time off from work, Linda from the Club Festival, Bev from her hospital job. They were spending some time shopping at the Clackamas Town Center mall south of Portland.

Linda's experience with Tail Gunner had changed her mind about the sweetness of revenge, yet she couldn't help remembering the evil things men had done to her and to other women. Linda was privy to the tale of one man's life, that of her brother Joe. For reasons she couldn't understand, he'd become a punisher of women.

"I want to tell you about my brother," Linda said quietly to her close friend. "Please keep this between you and me. I want you to know this information." The two were having some lunch at the shopping center's food court. Chinese food.

"I'll keep it to myself, honey," Bev replied to Linda. She continued to eat her spicy chicken dish.

"My brother Joe had been through several relationships," Linda began. "He was a gentle soul as a young person, with no history of abuse to any living thing. He'd been particularly gentle with pets. The one time he'd shot a bird with his bb gun, he'd felt such remorse that he destroyed the gun."

"I like that," Bev said.

"Wait. There's more. When he got married, all hell broke loose."

Bev shifted uncomfortably in her seat.

"At first, everything was nicey nice with the new wife. But the minute she began with the backtalk, he began with the slapping."

Bev put down her fork. She stared at Linda.

"I guess that's what he was taught growing up in American society. When your wife gives you any backtalk, you give her the backhand."

"So he hit his wife?"

"Yeah," Linda said. "I guess that was his way of expressing his anger. He liked slapping his wife around. She reacted well to it, meaning she reacted poorly, breaking down, crying, whimpering. He liked that. His wife divorced him."

"So that taught him a lesson?"

"No," Linda said. "Things only got worse."

By this time Bev had stopped eating and was paying rapt attention to Linda.

"He learned to hand out the punishment not in dribs and drabs, but in a withering display of human firepower. The next woman he'd push around," Linda continued, "was a girl he'd met after the divorce. Here's the strange part: I guess she had been involved in sex with multiple partners at the same time, what the boys call a 'gang bang.' Well, she became known by the guys in her high-rise apartment as a slut."

"Man," Bev said, "that's sad."

"It gets sadder for her. Her solution to her shame was attempting suicide."

"I'm not surprised."

"My brother Joe tried to help. He started to pick up the pieces of her life. He wanted to help her get over her suicide attempt and the depression that followed. He really did want to help her."

"I know a bit about psychology," Bev said. "I studied it in school to get my bachelor's degree in nursing. Depression, huh?"

"Yeah," Linda said, "but he also was not so helpful. He'd tell his friends, 'Did you see the set of knockers on that Amazon queen?' Joe told me he considered her like the woman in the Brick House song by Lionel Richie and the Commodores."

By this time Bev had lost her appetite. Listening to Joe's treatment of more than one woman had given Bev a sickening feeling in her stomach.

"He told me one thing he hated was her platform shoes. He called the highest stacked platforms, with at least three inches of thick soles, 'Cripplers' and the lower stacked platforms, with only one or two inches of stacked soles, 'Crippler Juniors.' He was very descriptive about those shoes."

"Why did he call them 'Cripplers'?" Bev asked.

"He called them 'Cripplers' because invariably she'd be walking down the street or down stairs, catch them on something uneven on a surface and come tumbling down.

"In fact," she continued, "he knew so well the physics of her shoes that one night at a party he noticed she was standing in a pool of water on slick linoleum. He gave her quick push to the shoulder. The ripple effect started at the shoulders, ran down the length of the body, and ended up causing her to lose her balance and, as I said before, come tumbling down."

"Your brother sounds like quite the jerk," Bev said.

"Yeah," Linda said, "he was a jerk. He's a lot better now. But back then, he was out of control. That's not the end of the story.

"He continued to punish that particular girlfriend, at one time pushing her down the stairs at their apartment building, following her down and threatening to kill her as he held her by the throat."

"Whoa."

"Next girlfriend," Linda said, "same thing. He remembers strangling her and threatening to kill her. That always went over big. His girlfriend became hysterical and just about went nuts when he threatened to kill her, she was so desperate to escape the grip he had on her neck. He liked to go for the throat, I guess."

"Tell me that he didn't kill some poor woman," Bev said, eyes wide open, jaw dropped.

"Finally," Linda said, "one of the exploited women asked that he see a therapist. Which he did. Then after the first group therapy sessions were finished, he slapped and kicked his latest woman friend in front of witnesses, which got the cops called, which got the fellow straightened out for sure. Before the court ordered he get back into therapy, he was enrolled.

"Therapy was good for the man," Linda said, "and he straightened out, for over two decades."

Bev's eyes narrowed.

"You mean up until recently?"

"Yeah," Linda said. "He met a woman, got engaged to her, though she understood his past problem with anger and violence. In his defense," she said, "she took it upon herself to tease, taunt and torment him until he lashed out at her. But there is never an excuse for any form of violence."

Linda knew there is no excuse for roughing up a woman. She knew at the root of the problem must be an understanding of the psychological and sociological reasons for domestic abuse. She'd heard the statistics of how many women in the U.S. are battered by their significant others.

She also knew that even if you did take the time to look at the stats, the numbers might create a disconnected image, and might not really hit home emotionally. It's much like when people hear of a war. They have a hard time relating to a mass of unknown combatants fighting and dying, on both sides, but it's hard to ignore the story of one person. One person makes it personal and more relatable. One person can be related to intimately.

The issue of domestic violence is probably one of the most serious yet seriously underappreciated aspects of our American society. Linda felt that unless there is a revolution in the thinking process, this country cannot address the issue with enough gravity.

An avid TV watcher, Linda had seen hard evidence, irrefutable evidence, of the epidemic of domestic violence in America. She found it in the TV show Cops.

In many of the 30-minute programs, there were at least three sub-episodes of police encounters. Many of the encounters, possibly one out of three, involved domestic abuse. A pattern within that pattern is to see how, sadly, even after being abused, the women insisted they loved their men. In the filmed follow-up narration to the incident, viewers find out from police officers it wasn't the first time the women had been abused. Viewers also discover how men are liars, rarely admitting their crimes.

Linda knew there were safe houses for battered women and their children. She knew that the media does report the instances of domestic abuse, especially when they involve some Hollywood movie star or New York musician. But as an overall theme, domestic violence is swept under the table, like the issue of how America is hooked on drugs, or of how Americans are becoming brainwashed with the concept of entitlement to social services.

Domestic violence is woven into the thread of American culture. Movies and TV shows depicting the psychological and physical abuse of women and men abound. So much that it becomes numbing after it's portrayed enough.

From a feminist perspective, the culture of dominating and abusing women is part and parcel of the patriarchal society in which we live. In other words, men have the final word, and when looking at it from a purely physical attitude, the last word is a slap on the face, a push into a wall. Portrayed in popular media for ages, all one has to do is play back some of the images, both visual and aural, created by artistic media.

Linda not so fondly remembered a song from the 1970s and 1980s that used to play on the Portland classic rock radio station.

Boom, Boom (Out Goes the Lights) by the Pat Travers Band was a popular tune, getting some amount of play on the classic rock radio station.

Its lyrics are chilling.

Roughly, the lyrics to Pat Travers Band's Boom, Boom (Out Go the Lights), written by song hit maker Stan Lewis, per the live version:

"No kiddin'/I'm ready to fight/I've been lookin' for my baby all night/If I get her in my sight/Boom, boom, right here, out go the lights!

"No kiddin'/I'm ready to go/When I find her boy don't you know/If I get her in my sight/Boom, boom, what is it? Out go the lights!

"I thought I treated my baby fair/I just found out she don't want me here/If I get her in my sight/Boom, boom, come on, out go the lights!

"I never felt this mad before/When I just found out she don't want me no more/If I get her in my sight/Boom, boom, come on, out go the lights!

"No kiddin'/I'm ready to fight/I've been lookin' for my baby all night/If I get her in my sight/Boom, boom, one more, out go the lights!"

The radio stations don't play the song any more, but the image of spousal abuse is of no doubt.

Linda felt as if it would take a radical change, a sea change, in attitude before the abuse of women is finally eliminated.

"But let's not fool ourselves," Linda said to Bev. "There is also abuse of men by women."

Linda related a case she personally knew about, where a wife got so out of control that she bit her husband's hand, and then threatened to burn down the house with the kids in it. The husband had to call the police, who had enough evidence, with the bite on the hand, to take her away in handcuffs and charge her with domestic abuse.

"It's as if there will have to be a complete change of attitude with regard to the treatment of both men and women before there can be any change," Linda said. "The same can be said of the issue of the crazy-stupid number of guns in America, and the American proclivity to ingest massive amounts of drugs. It's part of our culture."

"I sure hope those things do improve," Bev said. "I hope they aren't part of our culture forever."

"Me, too."

"I've got a novel idea," Bev said. "Why don't we consider domestic abuse a disease and treat it like cancer or addictive behavior? We could treat it like the disease it is, maybe with counseling, maybe with medication."

"I don't care what happens," Linda said. "Something has got to be done."

What Linda had seen regarding domestic violence had been shocking and saddening. She received a startling education in how destructive it can be from one man, her brother; luckily she was not one in a series of women having a relationship with someone like him. Her knowledge, although not first hand, was not from a detached source such as an article or news broadcast. She knew the truth, the sad and difficult truth of a scourge that plagues society.

It was shocking what men do to women as a result of either repressed or overt anger issues. Linda had known more than one woman who put up with all manner of abuse, including being called disgusting names like "stupid cunt" or "fat whore." Those were actual names that men had used to call their significant others. Linda had heard it, not second hand, but first hand as a witness, out of the mouths of men. Not only had Linda heard such abusive language, she'd seen the results of the physical abuse perpetrated by men on women.

To add to her own personal witness, she'd also seen photographs and videos of abuse. She knew the situation was bad. She couldn't say whether the situation was getting any better. Certainly the awareness of such violence had increased in the last part of the 20th century, but by the first part of the 21st century she really hadn't seen much improvement in the statistics.

For her own sake, she'd educated herself. She knew there were many forms of abuse.

Some of those forms included men controlling the actions of their spouses, one of the forms of psychological abuse. There was the taunting of a spouse by calling her fat or lazy, a form of abuse not actually involving physical contact. These were forms of abuse, not physical, but hurtful and real nonetheless.

Stepping up the intensity of the forms of psychological abuse, there's what can only be called "yelling at the top of your lungs" at your spouse, which is demeaning.

The next step is actual physical abuse. There again, there are many layers. It might start with a simple shove. Maybe throwing an object at the spouse. Pushing her into the wall.

Linda had known one fellow to throw an entire milkshake into the face of a woman with whom he was having an argument. She related that incident to her nurse friend Bev.

"What would have happened if that were a cup of coffee?" she asked Bev.

"That'd be horrible!" Bev said. "Why are men such maniacs?" Bev had seen her share of trauma working in the hospital, with multiple cases of partners beating up on each other.

The next step after pushing and shoving is actually slapping, kicking, punching, hitting.

The final step is killing. By knife. By gun. By baseball bat.

Again, Linda personally knew of at least one instance of a woman having anger problems leading to getting physical with her husband. But that instance of domestic abuse is in the statistical minority. Most instances come from men and are aimed at their dates, their girlfriends and their wives.

Linda researched some of the different organizations that promote the prevention of domestic violence, and although all those organizations are necessary and needed, they only strike at the symptoms, not at the disease itself. Bev knew what Linda was talking about.

"It's like trying to stop the problem of heroin or methamphetamine addiction," Bev told Linda, "by closing down the places where people deal and take the drugs. Drug houses. That doesn't stop the problem, it only slows it down, for a bit.

"Sure," Bev continued, "closing down a drug house probably makes it safer for the neighbors, but the problem doesn't end there, it moves to another part of town. To solve the issue of drug addiction, or the addiction to domestic violence, we need to get to the root of the problem."

Bev and Linda agreed the work domestic violence partnerships are doing is vital in helping to keep women safe from abusive men. No issue there. But both also agreed on the fact that there's a deep-seated culture of relationship abuse that is ingrained into the psyche of the American male.

"Do you think it would help if all men turned into feminists?" Linda asked Bev.

"I don't know," Bev admitted. "All I know is that things are not working now, and we're only sticking our finger in the dike in trying to stop the eventual flood, always about to overflow and drown us."

"If they can send a man to the moon," Linda asked, "why can't they send them all?"

Bev gave Linda a stern look, then laughed out loud.

"I haven't heard that one in a long time," Bev said. "Pretty funny."

The women were comfortable with each other, and so sat quietly without saying anything for several minutes.

"So what is the answer?" Linda again put it to Bev. "What is our society going to do to put a stop to women getting beat up? How are we going to stop it?"

"That's a good question," Bev said. "I don't know what to say."

Bev paused for a moment and thought.

"I don't know," Bev said. "Men kill men in wars. Everyone in the United States seems to own a gun. Boxing matches are still taking place. We're a society and country steeped in violence. How are we supposed to stop men beating up women when we approve of kick boxing matches?"

"I don't know either," Linda responded. "Maybe we'll have to evolve out of the tendency to beat the shit out of each other. I mean, look at what we both do for a living."

"What do you mean?"

"I mean," Linda continued, "I work in a bar where there's a least one fight a week, if not more, and you work in a hospital, where you are constantly putting people back together after a fight."

"It's a crazy world," Bev said. "But I'm not giving up hope. I think the fact that you and I are talking about it and that the cops have domestic violence laws counts for something."

With nothing left of their appetites, the two women continued to sit at the tables in the mall's food court. Around them swirled young and old people, couples and singles and parents with small children. Bev spoke once again, with gravity.

"The struggle of good versus evil truly exists today, right now," she said. "It's not some concept that's found in old books describing chivalrous knights or gallant deeds accomplished by men in white hats on horses.

"It's a life and death struggle," she said, "and not something 'ripped from today's headlines' to create television dramas featuring cops, perps and victims."

"I know you've seen a lot of the results of domestic violence working in the hospital's emergency room," Linda said. "You've told me some pretty hair-raising stories of the lowlifes who abuse women."

"You know, though," Bev said, "that it's not only trailer trash that bung up their spouses. I've seen rich people, I've dealt with folks from the inner city and from out in the sticks. And from watching TV, you and I both know famous people who've gotten into trouble with the law for working out on a spouse."

"I guess we all personally know somebody who has been abused," Linda replied.

"I remember from basic psych class in college," Bev said, "Abraham Maslow said that a human being's most fundamental needs are first the needs of the body, including breathing, eating, water, sex and sleep. Let me think for a second."

Bev stirred her cold, congealed Chinese food with her fork. Her left eyebrow arched.

"Now I remember. Once those basic needs are met, we want to satisfy the need for safety." She paused for a second. "That includes the security of the body, employment, resources, morality, the family, health and property.

"Women who are abused live without the satisfaction of the safety and security of the body. Many live with a big unknown with regard to family, property, employment."

Linda nodded her head in approval.

"But what can be done," she said, "to change a man's attitude so that he doesn't threaten the physical safety of his spouse? I don't want to get bogged down with the gender issue, because in our society we see women abusing men, women abusing women, men abusing men.

When will it stop?"

"It's good versus evil," Bev said. "It's that simple."

Linda Avery and Beverley Beech both had witnessed the root of evil. Although not victims themselves of the abuse from a partner, they both had seen the effects. They both were struggling to understand the causes.

CHAPTER 16

Outside the Club Festival, people walked as if in a trance.

The city was a place where people moved about without caring about the details, where trash littered the street and people's lives meant nothing.

It was a city of heartache, heartbreak and heartlessness. That's the way it is with the big, big city. You're lucky if someone cuts you some slack and gives you the time of day.

But for Linda, the city had its gritty charms. Losers, winners, down-on-their-luck players, all types. But everyone needed a little something. Linda, the consummate cigarette girl, was always there, ready to provide that little something extra to make life tolerable.

Cigs, candy, a novelty.

Condoms, cover-ups and a little weed on the side.

It's all part of the scene.

The cigarettes, sweets and novelty gifts were all on the surface, in view of every customer whom she walked by. Lucky Strikes, Pall Malls, Kools. A little Hershey's chocolate, Lifesavers, Sen-Sen. A novelty magic trick, maybe a wind-up mechanical toy rabbit, something to amuse.

It was stuff below the surface, behind the counter, that some men yearned for.

It seemed to cover the whole gamut of activity, especially meant to add to sexual activity. If you examined it, it was a time of before, during and after sex. For the most part, it was meant for the world of men. For the most part. A novelty to amuse her. Condoms hopefully to keep her from getting pregnant and to avoid sexual diseases. Sen-Sen and other cover-ups to keep the world from knowing what the hell you've been up to.

Linda didn't mind working in a bar, but she didn't particularly enjoy dealing with a customer who was drunk. It was easy to tell when someone's had too much to drink. A drunken customer walks odd, talks odd and sometimes flies off the handle.

"What do you mean, I've had too much to drink?" one customer, a black man, told Linda. "It's a bar, goddammit, and I'm here to celebrate."

"Sorry, sir," Linda said back, "but you're hanging all over me, drooling and acting stupid."

"You can't talk to me like that," said the man, and he took a swing at Linda.

Since Linda was totally in control of her faculties, all she needed to do was move out of the way of the punch, and the momentum of the angry man's swing had him swerving and diving for the floor.

The commotion attracted Lou's attention. This was the part of running a bar that he didn't like. Handling drunks was not that difficult, but not entirely pleasurable.

Lou came over to help Linda with the messy situation, and clear out the rabble.

"OK, buddy," Lou said, as he picked the man off the floor by his left arm. "Time to leave."

"Hey, you fuckin' cracker, leave me the fuck alone," yelled the man. When Lou had the man on his feet, the drunken customer took a swing at Lou. Bad idea.

Lou, also not inebriated, was able to avoid the punch, and the man staggered forward. Lou grabbed him by the right arm, put the arm behind the man, and forcibly pushed him towards the backdoor.

At the backdoor, Lou shoved the man outside.

"Shove off, you nitwit," he yelled as the man staggered out into the parking lot, falling down on the asphalt and broken glass. "And don't come back."

Linda was straightening out her outfit and wares when Lou came back to the front of the Club Festival.

"You all right, sweetie?" Lou asked Linda.

"Sure, Lou," she replied. "Thanks for taking care of that guy."

"I've never seen him here before," Lou said to Linda. "Was he new?"

"Yeah," she said. "I'd never seen him before either. I hope never to see him again."

Lou started laughing.

"What's so funny?" Linda asked.

"I don't know," Lou said. "It's so much damned fun running a bar, you know what I mean?"

Linda couldn't help but start laughing herself, which made Lou laugh harder. Lou started laughing, coughing and hacking.

"Lou," she said to her boss. "If laughter's the best medicine, I think you're about to overdose."

Linda, Randi Obvitz and Lou all went back to their routine at the Club Festival, serving customers what they needed and what they wanted.

Linda kept a sharp eye out for more trouble, Randi served drinks and food, and Lou went behind the bar to make an inventory of what liquor needed to be ordered.

Like a well-oiled machine, the club chugged along nicely enough.

Still not convinced Squint Eye was the man for her, Linda was conflicted. She knew that it would be easy to get involved with a man like Squint, but not so easy to disentangle herself from a relationship with him. Dangers lurked all about in the murky waters of a relationship, if her past experiences were any indication.

It was another slow night during a weekday, a Thursday. Since Lou eschewed having any TV sets in the bar, if there was a football, basketball, baseball or soccer game on, a small percentage of customers headed to what's known as a "sports bar" or partied at home with friends.

After Randi had delivered some delicious fried food items to some customers, she hung out at the bar with Lou.

"Lou, you know we're missing a big basketball game on the boob tube," Randi said.

"I don't give a shit about sports," he said to Randi, who wished he'd a least get one TV set in the place; tonight was a good example of what she was talking about. Randi tried to think of an argument she could give Lou that would change his mind about getting a TV set into the bar.

"Lou, what happens if there's some sort of breaking news story?" she asked, wiping her hands on her apron. "Don't you want to be in the loop?" Randi tried to act casual about the whole thing.

"The loop?" he replied. "The loop? I don't care about any stinking loop! I've got a radio in the back, that's enough for me. I'd rather have jazz music playing in my club, that's a whole lot classier."

Lou had become slightly agitated defending himself. He put down his inventory list, only half done, and steamed for a bit. His face was red, and he sighed heavily. Randi knew she was in over her head; she decided to back down and leave the boss alone.

"OK, boss, you're the man," Randi whispered, trying to calm him down. The waitress then got the signal from a customer to bring her another drink.

On her way to serve the customer, Randi walked by Linda.

"Watch out," Randi said to Linda in a low voice. "The boss's in a bad mood. You can blame me."

"Thanks for the warning," Linda replied.

Linda wandered over to where Squint Eye was sitting, nursing his drink, lost in some thought.

"What's going on in that brain of yours?" she asked Squint.

Squint shook his head, the thought process broken.

"Thinking about dark films," he said.

"Dark films?" she asked him.

"Yeah," he said back, "a style of movie known as film noir, French for 'dark film.' I've been watching a bunch of them on video and on the Internet."

"What exactly is a 'dark film,' anyway?" she asked.

"That's a good question," he said. "Do you have a minute?"

Linda's head shifted down and to the left, her lips pursed and her left eyebrow rose, indicating she had to think about his question for a second or two. Squint immediately saw her quandary.

"Just a minute," he repeated. "I know you're working, so I won't waste your time. I think you'll find this interesting."

"Oh, what the hell," she said, "it's slow and I am curious. I'm Linda, by the way."

"Oh," he said, "I never knew your name. Everybody calls me Squint Eye."

"I know," she said, "Squint for short."

Linda took a seat, placing her tray on the chair next to her.

"Anyway," he said, "film noir is something the French named American films from the '40s and '50s that had a certain attitude toward life, a cynical attitude, left from soldiers returning from the devastation of World War II."

"OK," Linda said, "I'm following you."

"Those films showed the seedy side of life, with men getting caught up in a series of events that seemed beyond their control. Most of them that I've seen also have a woman in them giving men bad advice, and leading them down a bad road."

Linda was listening, and paying attention. She suddenly realized that the man she thought she knew she didn't know at all. He had depth, intelligence and feeling. He wasn't another drunk at the club.

"Can I go on?" he asked. Linda nodded in the affirmative, making a mental note that this man, as opposed to most other men, seemed to think of her welfare before his own. He was a special man, a caring man. Her heart began to soften. Maybe not all men are like Tail Gunner.

"Anyhow," Squint continued, "these films also have a look to them, with intense lighting and sometimes gritty shots of actual city streets at night. It's a whole thing, very interesting."

"Can you name a couple of these films?" Linda asked, finally realizing that she probably needed to get back to work.

"They say the first one was The Maltese Falcon with Humphrey Bogart," he said. "Let me see… there's also Out of the Past and Detour, those are excellent examples."

"Squint," she began to ask, "can we continue this conversation later? I've got to get back to work."

Slightly offended by being interrupted, Squint realized he was taking up the cigarette girl's valuable time.

"Sure," he tried to remember her name, but couldn't. "That's OK, I understand."

"Thanks," she said, gathering her tray and standing up. "But don't get me wrong, I love movies, and this stuff sounds cool. We'll talk again."

"Sure, sure," he said, trying to be as casual as possible.

"I'll be seeing you," Linda said, and began to turn away.

"Hey," he said as she was walking away.

"Yeah?" she said, turning around to address Squint directly.

"What was your name again?"

"Linda."

"Thanks, Linda," Squint said. "See you around."

Linda walked away and resumed hawking her goods.

"Film nwar," she thought to herself. "Sounds interesting."

After losing her mind smoking artificial marijuana, Marcia Calibri stayed in touch with her friend Linda, by telephone from another state. Another state and another state of mind.

After nearly living in the streets, Marcia finally manipulated the government system and found herself living in Section 8 housing, subsisting on government handouts of rent, food and money. It was best this way. Rather than becoming homeless or worse, she found refuge in the system. Without government help, she could have become a statistic of another nature, that of criminal or wastrel.

"I'm doing better," Marcia told Linda, a few weeks after Linda had last heard from her old friend. "I'm doing much better."

"I'm glad," Linda told her friend during the first over-the-telephone conversation. "I'm glad you're inside, not outside," Linda said, referring to the fact that Marcia was sheltered instead of homeless.

Homeless. In the old days, Linda thought to herself, before political correctness, people called the homeless, "bums."

Marcia may have found shelter and subsistence, but over the years she'd become a whiny complainer. Marcia complained about aches and pains, and about her sister's pestering. Turned out Marcia's sister was also living in Section 8 housing nearby. The two Calibri siblings were not good for each other, causing each other pain, enabling each other's penchant for illicit drugs, and generally making every encounter a reason for drama. Unnecessary drama.

Marcia's sister, in fact, lost her grip on reality quicker than Marcia. Fran Calibri had developed a methamphetamine habit.

She began using the stuff, infrequently at first. Methamphetamine. Speed. Crank. Meth. Before you knew it, Fran was out of control.

The first thing Marcia noticed is that her sister would stay up all night doing meaningless, repetitive chores. One time she was found at a computer, switching entire programs between the dual hard drives; it didn't take long to completely disable the poor computer.

Then there were the telltale signs of meth addiction. Her arms were covered with scabs from the constant obsessive picking. Fran picked at imagined sores, then picked at the scabs. It got so bad that she was forced to wear long-sleeved blouses at work to cover up the sores and scabs.

Then there was the workplace. The more meth she took, the more paranoid she became. Everyone was plotting against her. She also began indiscriminately pilfering goods from work. Something as simple as toilet paper. Or as cumbersome as a protective plastic mat for a rolling office chair.

Finally, after a scant few weeks of paranoid delusions and bizarre behavior at the workplace, she was fired.

Although Fran Calibri went through drug rehabilitation and was seemingly "cured" of the meth habit, it had left her mentally scarred and totally twitchy. Fran was convinced that people were using the crawlspace above and below the Section 8 housing to create havoc; she found holes in her ceiling, and was convinced she was being spied upon.

Marcia wasn't much better. She had experimented with a strange form of artificial marijuana that had damaged her psyche. Emotionally, she lived as if someone had peeled off all of her skin, leaving her hypersensitive to every slight breeze of change or alteration of routine.

Another case of drugs not doing someone any good. Linda was convinced that certain people should never take drugs. Never. Alternately, she was convinced that some drugs, heavy drugs like LSD, could be useful, in the right situation, with the right person.

But Marcia Calibri's experimentation with artificial marijuana had pretty much taken its toll. Linda was also convinced that it wasn't only the artificial pot. Linda was convinced the illicit drug combined with isolation and, believe it or not, poor nutrition, sent her friend Marcia over the edge.

It's always like that: There's never only one thing that tips a person over, sending them spiraling towards madness. It's a combination of the physical, that is, the chemical balance in the brain, along with environmental factors, like what kind of parents, what kind of schooling and what kinds of friends, all are influential.

Marcia continued to bitch and moan about all the problems in her life. Linda listened patiently, but knew in her heart that the problems that Marcia had were problems Marcia created. Maybe it had to be that way, because Marcia's life was so devoid of meaning she needed to create drama and madness for something to do.

Sometimes Linda was convinced she herself was the only sane person she knew. But that thought only lingered for a second, when she thought of her boss Lou, or the many successful and happy people in her social circle.

Her friend Marcia wasn't one of them, and she was glad Marcia was far, far away, and not so close as to make Linda's life a living hell. People can do that to you. They can make your life a living hell.

Randi was no stranger herself to inviting trouble. She'd been in trouble with the law for drug possession, marijuana specifically, and had learned how to avoid being busted for possession.

But she'd also caused trouble where there was no trouble before. Maybe you could call her a troublemaker.

While still in her early 20s, she was visiting friends in New York City at their spacious loft. A party was going on, music was playing loudly, the drinks were flowing and drugs were the option. Separated from the main loft space was an area cordoned off for the private use of drugs like cocaine and marijuana.

A small group was sitting cross-legged in the cordoned-off area snorting cocaine. Randi knew the two women because she'd come to the party with them. The other three were men, a couple of Hispanic gentlemen and some tall, pasty white guy wearing a T-shirt with the spray-painted Warriors logo from the Walter Hill film The Warriors.

The music was your typical rock 'n' roll: The Beatles, the Rolling Stones, The Who represented the British bands, along with music from American groups like the Jefferson Airplane, Jefferson Starship, Santana, MC5 and Bob Dylan.

The drinks? Hard liquor like Beefeater's Gin, Stoli Vodka and Jameson Irish Whiskey. The bar was well stocked with carbonated mixes and ice, along with a few select imported beers. Someone had done their homework.

The cocaine was straight from the streets of New York, heavily cut with mannitol.

Randi had done cocaine previously, and found it made her nervous and hyper-alert; she could have found the same effect in several cups of coffee. That and the expense of cocaine made her no fan of the drug.

She also felt disdain for those people who continued to champion the use of the drug. To her it was a big waste of time.

So when she was invited to join the inner circle of coke users, she was determined to do something nasty. She was brewing a plot in her mind, fueled by a combination of the liquor, the pot and the dislike for the drug cocaine.

"Hey, Randi, let's do some lines," said one of the ladies.

"Sounds like a winner," she said, and sat down on the floor in front of a coffee table with a large mirror in the center. One of the Hispanic gentlemen was methodically chopping up the white powder with a single-edge razor, lovingly preparing the coke for ingestion up the snout.

One of Randi's friends wanted to use a rolled up twenty dollar bill for ingestion, but the other Hispanic man reached under the table to magically produce a plain drinking straw. He got out a Swiss Army knife and cut the straw in half, making it only a few inches long.

Lines were prepared. Everybody leaned forward to inspect. Then Randi took in a deep breath and blew the several prepared lines into the air.

"What the fuck!" said one of Randi's friends. "Why the fuck did you do that? You fucking idiot!"

Randi laughed.

"The stuff's a waste of effort anyway," she said. "You'll thank me some day."

The two Hispanic gentlemen stopped being gentlemen and stood up. Both were agitated; it was their cocaine that Randi had squandered.

"Get her out of here," said one. "Get her the fuck away from our shit."

"OK, OK," Randi said. "No need to get physical. I'm leaving."

Randi returned to the general mill of the party, but as the evening went on, news of the incident circulated, and Randi was looked on as an interloper, no better than a narcotics agent. As she slinked about the loft, fewer and fewer people would talk to her.

CHAPTER 17

"Listen, bitch, I ain't afraid of you," said the Hispanic man in his early 20s. "I've got nothing to lose, so hand it over!"

The man was nervous, so he became loud. It was his first robbery on the street; all of his previous crimes were petty, only shoplifting and vandalism. He'd steeled himself for the illicit act by drinking copious beers and smoking robust marijuana with friends. He'd told them he was going to go out to rob someone, and although they didn't believe him, when he returned with the evidence, his friends were at once appalled and enthralled. Appalled that he had done such a heinous act; enthralled that at least one of them had some guts.

He had appeared as if out of nowhere, because he'd been waiting behind a metal fence near an empty storefront.

Linda had been doing her best to pay attention to the activity on the street, but if someone wants to remain hidden, it doesn't take much to accomplish that goal. To all animals, humans of course included, we notice movement easily, but if some other creature is preying upon us, staying perfectly still and being camouflaged is all that's necessary to be nearly invisible.

Standing at only 5-foot, 5-inches tall, the man was not a tower of power. But his demeanor was threatening enough to intimidate.

"Now!" he yelled. "I said hand it over!"

All Linda knew was that he was mighty serious sounding. She also decided the smart thing to do would be to lose the battle in order to win the war. The battle was her wallet and its meager contents, and the war was her life. No need to exchange one for the other, although this fellow didn't look armed.

It was then that he pulled out a nasty looking weapon, a Saturday night special.

"I said, 'Hand it over,' and I mean it!" he snapped at her.

His desperate attitude and the sight of the handgun made Linda move fast. When he pulled out the gun, all the words became engraved on her mind, echoing and bouncing around the inside of her skull. The handgun made the man look bigger, for some reason, but no matter what happened from this point on, Linda was not going to lose her life over a wallet.

She shoved her wallet into his eager hands, and looked away. She remembered something about preventing a robber from getting violent by showing that she won't be able to identify the assailant. She was reacting instantly, not really thinking; when and where she picked up the information about looking away, she couldn't have told you at the time. But that's what she did.

"Don't turn around, lady," he choked out the words as he took off, wallet in hand. He was off and running down the street, around the corner as Linda turned around to see the last of the thug.

She stood alone in the street. The noise of traffic from adjoining streets continued to fill the air, but there was nothing else going on. She was the center of attention. She had become a victim.

"Damn," she said to herself. "Royally ripped off!"

She wasn't far from home, and with rapid precision marched back to her apartment, partially in shock, partially in fear. When she got home, she immediately dialed 9-1-1 on her cell phone; why she didn't do so on the street we'll never know. The police told her they'd send an officer to take a report, but she declined, saying she'd come into the precinct the following day and make an official report.

"No reason to bother one of your fine officers," she told the police dispatcher. "I'm home safe now, that's the most important thing."

The next day, after a trip to the police station, Linda told the whole story to Lou at the Club Festival. He listened to her tale while he polished glasses at the bar.

"It happened so fast, Lou, it was all over in an instant," Linda told her boss, over a cold one at the club.

"Crime on the street," Lou said, "it's like that, over in a blink of the eye."

"Lucky for me there wasn't much money in the wallet," she rationalized.

"But did I do the right thing?" she asked her boss. "I handed over my entire wallet. Was there something else I should have done?"

"Like what?" he said.

"Oh, I don't know, kick him in the crotch or run?"

"In the face of a gun," he said, "I don't think so. With shit like that, it's not like in the movies, this is real, and you're no martial arts expert, so you really did the only thing you could do."

Linda looked at her boss. She thought about what he said. They continued nursing their beers. Lou's face then became pinched and anxious.

"Hey," he said, "you're gonna have to excuse me for a minute."

Before Linda could respond, Lou quickly got up from the chair and headed to the back. He headed to the men's restroom.

It seemed that the Mexican food he had earlier was not agreeing with him. Or it could be something in the water, like the deadly parasite Cryptosporidium, attacking his bowels. Whatever the reason, he barely got into the stall and his pants down when a severe case of diarrhea evacuated his bowels.

He stayed in the men's restroom for the next ten minutes. Linda might have been alarmed, but she had other topics on her mind, like surviving her recent encounter with the Hispanic mugger. She was also mulling over in her mind what she might have done differently.

She remembered that one time a media report suggested that in the event of a robbery, a tactic might be to take the money out of a wallet and throw it on the ground. Since money was all most robbers are looking for, then the robber would be instantly fixated on the cash on the ground, and the victim might be able to slip away quickly.

But Linda remembered the gun, and that made her pause as she reflected. No reason to take any chances.

When Lou returned, Linda asked what took him so long. She never noticed that he had rushed back to the men's room; for all she knew, he had gone to his office, or taken the rear door exit to take care of some task. She'd learned not to take anything for granted; at the same time, she could consider all of the possibilities without obsessing or assuming.

"Had to go to my office," Lou responded. He lied, of course, but it was out of embarrassment and modesty, not out of malice or subterfuge. In Lou's mind, there was only so much information that people need to know. He almost instantly felt better after relieving himself.

"Lou," she said as he sat back down, "I was thinking."

"That's a dangerous proposition," he said, smiling. Linda realized he was joking, and giving her a hard time.

"Listen," he said. "Don't make too much of a thing out of this incident. You did the best you could under the circumstances, and you are alive and well and uninjured. What more could you ask for?"

"How about my ID?" she asked. "I was thinking, maybe I could have taken the small amount of money out of my wallet and thrown it on the ground, and then headed the other direction."

"Yeah, right," he said. "Hindsight is golden. We can all second guess ourselves later."

"I'm sorry, Lou, for wasting your time."

"Stop," he said. "It's good to talk to someone after such a

harrowing experience. That's what friends are for, to help process and vent."

"You're deep," she said, in a sweet tone.

"Cut it out," he responded. "I've learned over the years to share and open up with people I can trust. It's good therapy. It's good for both parties."

The two sat sipping their beers. Lou's stomach felt normal and the bubbly brew felt good going down.

Linda and Lou were becoming good friends, and felt comfortable with each other.

Linda was especially grateful that she found a man who had a heart and a mind, and was not afraid to open up. She'd known so many bad men, to find a good one was like finding gold. She felt good about what was transpiring between them. It wasn't a romantic feeling, more like the feeling you'd get from relating to a brother. She also knew it wasn't the beer, since she'd only had two or three swallows from the glass.

She had a funny feeling in the pit of her stomach, a feeling she'd use to have as a child when a parent or good friend was helping her do some craft or project. It was a good feeling. It seemed to her to be the opposite of having an upset stomach.

"Yeah," Lou said. "Sorry about what happened to you. But what about replacing your ID?"

"Well, there's that," she admitted, sheepishly, holding her head down. He was right. She'd lost all her current ID. That wouldn't be easy to wrangle up again. But it would have to be done.

A few years ago, she'd misplaced her wallet with all her ID and found out what a hassle it can be to get all that together again. In particular, she thought getting a new Oregon state driver's license would be difficult.

Her issue with the driver's license was that she didn't have a matching birth certificate. Her mom had divorced Linda's real father, and when her mother remarried, to the person who would become Linda's stepfather, there wasn't a legal adoption. She was automatically absorbed into the stepfather's world, and since infancy all the normal avenues of ID were easily handled by the parents.

Linda had a birth certificate, necessary to get a new driver's license, without her current name on it. Oh, it had her birthday and birth place, but a completely different name: Norma Rae Sinclair.

She was worried she'd have to file for a whole new birth certificate, but a friend of hers advised she go to the Oregon Department of Motor Vehicles with the original birth certificate.

"Try it," said the friend, "and see what happens. What do you have to lose? And if the person you're dealing with at the counter doesn't go along with it, ask for a supervisor."

Brilliant idea. Linda had learned from becoming an expert shopper that if you don't get satisfaction from the person on the sales floor, ask for a supervisor. At that point either the person you're dealing with gives in to your request, or the supervisor comes out and usually makes sure "the customer is always right."

Linda went into the DMV with her original birth certificate, with the "wrong name" on it, and attempted getting a replacement driver's license. Amazingly, no one at the DMV blinked an eye. Sure, Linda had brought along other pieces of ID to verify her address and phone number, like her electric bill and phone bill. The people at the DMV seemed nonplussed over the circumstance, as if they were faced with that dilemma all the time.

But there was more to being robbed than the loss of money or possessions. For Linda, it went much deeper. Her guilt over being taken advantage of, especially after Lou had given her some savvy advice about defending herself, had become oppressive to her. It was good to talk afterwards to Lou, and what he said made sense. It was a random act that no one could have predicted, and without foreknowledge there was nothing anyone could have done to prevent the crime.

As with anything that bothers Linda and makes it difficult to process the information or event, she found it helpful to talk with friends. Her friend Bev had been especially helpful in the past, but Linda didn't want to rely on her exclusively.

"What to do, what to do?" she thought to herself. She had a tight-knit cadre of close friends for support, and a brother in town, so why was she so stymied? She had become obsessed with attempting to figure out where she went wrong during the robbery. As important to her was the existential question of why did it have to happen to her?

She worked it over in her mind again and again, with still no wisdom forthcoming.

Finally, she decided to talk with someone. Lou had been as supportive as he could be, but this issue was not going away. Linda wanted her life back. She wanted some answers.

She decided to take a chance and talk with Squint Eye. To her it was a crazy idea spilling her guts to a stranger, especially a customer, but she was at the end of her rope. He was available, as a club regular, and the two of them had become better acquainted over the past few weeks. Maybe instead of looking at Squint Eye as a possible romantic encounter, she could use another friend, another person to share the load of life.

Squint was absent the day Linda decided to speak with him, for whatever reason, but the following night he was back.

It was around 9 o'clock, and the action during the weeknight was middling, not too busy, not too dead. As cigarette girl, Linda could make her own hours and take breaks whenever she felt the need. It was a sweet deal.

She saw Squint and moseyed his way.

"Hey, stranger," she said to Squint as he sat at a table, alone, contemplating the world.

Squint was lost in thought, and Linda's salutation startled him.

"Hey. Good seein' you. Oh, I've been helped by one of the waitresses," he said, pointing to the shot glass and beer in front of him.

"That's OK, I'm stopping by to see if I could bother you with a question."

Both of Squint's eyebrows rose, and he nodded.

"Sit down, take a load off."

Linda placed her cigarette girl tray of goodies down on the chair between them.

"What's on your mind?" Squint asked.

"First of all," she said in a low voice, "would it be alright if anything we talk about during this conversation be kept confidential?"

Squint was honored that Linda would share confidential material with him. He had only recently learned her name, and was impressed she had the fortitude to come to him to talk.

"Yeah, I got no problem with that. Share."

Linda described the recent violation of her personal property. She told the story without flourishes or emotion. Although she was roiling inside with emotion over the incident, she kept her composure in front of Squint. It was all she could do from breaking down and crying, reliving the crime again. Having to explain it again was painful.

"So how much money did he get away with?"

"I wasn't exactly rolling in dough," she said, "so he only got a few bucks."

"What about losing your ID? Aren't you afraid of identity theft?"

"I took care of all that right away. I don't have any credit cards. All I had in the wallet was a driver's license, a library card and a debit card. No big deal."

"If it's no big deal, then why are we talking?"

Linda was surprised to hear Squint say something so callous.

"I mean, you seem to be taking this whole thing in stride. Is there something here I'm not getting? Did he physically attack you?"

"No, I wasn't attacked," Linda said, beginning to think that maybe it was a mistake having a conversation with a man she didn't really know that well.

"Listen," he said. "I'd like to help. Tell me what's really bothering you."

Linda sat in silence for a few seconds. She took a deep breath.

"I don't know what's really bothering me," she confessed. "I can't seem to get this rotten thing out of my mind. I keep wondering what I could have done differently. I keep wondering why it had to happen to me."

Squint was feeling good. A nice lady was asking him for advice. He was in heaven. He lifted the shot glass, downed the shot and followed it with a sip of beer. He looked Linda right in the eye.

"I'm sorry about what happened to you," he said. "That's first. Second, without knowing more about the incident, I'd have to say at first glance that there was probably nothing you could have done to prevent it, obviously, and furthermore there wasn't any choice other than handing over your wallet. Unless you were Superwoman or something like that, what other choice would you have had?"

Squint's advice was similar to Lou's. The advice was simultaneously confirming and yet somehow not all that helpful.

"Lastly," he said, trying to express himself in a way that was reassuring and calming, "to answer your question of 'Why me?' I've got to be honest: It's a question that doesn't have an answer."

Linda had to think about that one. She appeared puzzled.

"Do you remember me talking about those 'dark films' the other night?"

Linda did remember, but she couldn't pinpoint the name he used.

"Didn't they have some sort of French name?"

"Yeah, you're right. They're called film noir."

"What about 'em?"

"Well, I didn't really get a chance to get into some of the nuances of those films, but there's a thought process that links most of them."

"What's that?" Linda sat back in her chair and relaxed. It was the first time in a couple of days she had been able to forget about the robbery.

"The characters in those films get into some pretty rough jams. And in the middle of it all, they ask, 'Why is this happening to me?' And do you know what the answer is?"

"No," Linda said, following each word from Squint, paying attention and feeling good about the interaction.

"No reason. No reason at all."

Linda looked to the side and thought about what Squint had said.

"I don't know if that's helpful," he said. "But I've thought about life quite a bit, and sometimes there just isn't any rhyme or reason to certain things. Sure, you could blame God or Allah or the stars or the fates…"

"But maybe there's no answer," Linda said, trying to finish his sentence.

"Right. I mean, I'm not saying there's no God, but at the same time, who said there's any kind of rule book to life. Hell, I figured out a long time ago there is no instruction manual for life. So maybe you shouldn't worry so much about why you got robbed. Maybe you should feel lucky you weren't seriously injured. Did you say he pulled a gun on you?"

"Yeah."

"We should throw all the guns away," he said. "They're too much trouble. But that's another subject. Are you gonna be OK?"

Linda was feeling better. It was good to speak to a man who

seemed both sensitive and smart. Squint Eye was turning out to be something of a find.

"I do feel better," she said. "I appreciate you being honest with me, and not babying me or patronizing me. I appreciate the advice."

At that moment Linda reached for her tray and began to stand up.

"Let me buy you another drink," she said. "Kind of a partial payment."

"No," he said, "I'm good. You don't owe me a thing. It was my pleasure to try to help you out with this situation. Good luck."

"Thanks," she said, and wandered away.

CHAPTER 18

"Don't worry about me, I'm alright."

Or at least that's what the woman in the bathroom said to Linda. Linda had taken a break, near closing time, to freshen up in the ladies' restroom at the Club Festival.

Upon entering said restroom, Linda noticed the smell of cheap perfume and vomit. One of the three bathroom stalls was obviously occupied, the door closed and locked. She heard a woman's voice moaning and groaning inside.

The kind of clientele that came to the Club Festival ranged from the tony crowd of the suburbs to the lowlife types who roam the city streets. You get all kinds at the Club Festival.

At a different time Linda had come into the women's restroom and immediately saw blood on the floor. It turned out that one of the women hadn't made it to the facilities in time to purchase a tampon and take care of her monthly cycle.

"The wound that never heals," she remembered one rather crude man describe a woman's biological function. "Never trust any animal that bleeds but doesn't die," was another. Linda didn't make up these tasteless references, but they swirled around in her brain as cultural residue.

This time, though, the drunken woman in the bathroom stall had her own problems. Linda peeked under the stall door and notice that one of her high heels was off of her foot. Linda wondered if the woman was alone, or if there was some poor sap of a man outside in the club in basically the same condition.

"Are you OK in there?" Linda asked.

"I'm fine, I'm fine," was the response. No matter how serious an injury, the person with the injury will always answer the same: "I'm fine." Their leg could have been amputated and they're bleeding to death, but typical human beings in these United States would always say, "I'm fine."

"Come on, lady, tell me the truth. I work here. Are you OK?" Linda asked, her voice straining to show concern.

"Listen," was the terse response. "If I said I was OK, I'm OK. Now get lost."

"Hey, don't give me a hard time, I was trying to help. I work here at the club. So there's no reason for me to call 9-1-1 or anything?"

"I don't know you, I don't want to know you and I don't want any help. Can I make it any clearer to you?"

"OK, OK. I'm outta here."

Linda shrugged her shoulders and left the restroom. Nothing to do there. She returned to the barroom of the club.

"Hey," Linda thought to herself, "if the lady don't want any help, then she don't want any help." Linda made a mental note of the time; it was about 10 minutes after 2 a.m. Last call was in a few minutes, with all liquor sales positively halted by 2:30 a.m., and the bar closed at 3. So Linda might check in a half hour to make sure the person was no longer in the bathroom, whatever her problem. If it really was a "her." It could have been anyone these days, transsexual, transgender, you name it, it was a regular free-thinking paradise in Portland, with the crazy gender bending things going on.

Linda circulated among the revelers, hoping to make a last minute sale on cigarettes or condoms. You never knew with the crowd at the Club Festival.

"Hang it all," said a customer sitting at one of the tables. To Linda, he looked as old as dirt. "The doctor said it'd kill me, but he didn't say when!"

The old man began to laugh at his own joke, but then fell into a fit of coughing, the likes of which would have made anyone think he was dying. He was dying. But with his last days on earth upon him, the crusty gentleman decided to go out swinging. He was tired of drinking at home, and thought for a change he'd come to a local bar. The Club Festival was close to his retirement high rise.

He gulped down the rest of his drink, then caught the attention of waitress Emily Lou Resnick.

"More grog, wench!" he barked at the server. Emily Lou heard his coughing from a distance, and noticed his wretched behavior.

"Are you sure you should be drinking?" asked Emily Lou.

"No, I'm not sure, but I'm free, white and over 21, so serve me!"

Emily Lou was glad Randi Obvitz wasn't around that night, or there'd be trouble for sure. Randi didn't take kindly to racist statements, even if they were simply some remnant of a bygone era, an era that the old man represented. Randi was a black woman who took guff from no one.

The kind of racism prevalent in the Pacific Northwest is less obvious than in the Deep South, but still there. In Portland, integration was part of the society, but for the oldest white residents racism still simmered deep down inside. Racism is taught, and learned, not part of a gene or bloodstream. Thankfully men like our dying friend were few and far between; hopefully racism would die with them.

"If it's drink you want," Emily Lou said, "then it's one last drink ye get," giving her best imitation of a pirate. "What'll you have, mate?"

"Make it a double Johnny Walker Black," he said. "I like my Scotch like I like my women! Old and tasty!"

Emily Lou took the old man's order with panache, trying to get into the spirit of the thing. She felt bad for the man, dying the way he was, but he was old enough to know better, so if he wanted to commit suicide by alcohol, well, at least the bar will make a profit off him.

"If not our bar," Emily Lou thought to herself, "then some other bar."

She brought the wheezing buzzard his Johnny Walker, set it on the table and proceeded to leave. The old man's hand slithered towards her and grabbed her by the sleeve.

"Thank you so much," he said. "I appreciate you humoring an old man."

"No problem, sir. Glad to help."

Emily Lou enjoyed being able to work both behind the bar and out in the barroom. Both had their advantages and disadvantages, and together as a mix gave her enough variety to keep work interesting.

Behind the bar was interesting because there was always that customer who liked to converse with his or her bartender. Bartenders were privy to lurid stories, true confessions, brazen lies, you name it, bartenders hear it all. But after a while, it's nice to take a break and serve customers out in the barroom. The tips were better and there wasn't a great deal of patter.

Another customer banged his fist on the table trying to get Emily Lou's attention.

"That'll be one more for the road," the stranger croaked. "Make it a double." Too cheap to tip the coat check girl, he had his trench coat draped over the chair next to him.

Emily Lou Resnick was prepared.

"It's past the last call, buddy," she said.

"Come on, baby, cut me some slack," he continued, "there's hardly anyone in this joint, and I'm a paying customer."

Paying customer, right. There would be a large payment to the Oregon Liquor Control Commission if Emily Lou were caught serving this late. The guy was also obviously drunk, so allowing more booze to flow down his throat would be another chance for either a fine… or litigation when the family of people he killed while driving sued the bar, and her.

"That's it, buddy, no more alcohol," she said with finality. "It's past last call, and the OLCC is strict about enforcing the law. I'm sorry, that's it."

The man got up, indignant as hell.

"Ah, fuck you," he barked. "I'm out of this dump."

He didn't leave it at that. He had to add some vague threat.

"Maybe I'll see you later, honey," he crooned in a syrupy voice, full of passive-aggressive warning.

Emily Lou shrugged off the threatening tone of the man's voice; she'd heard lots of goofball men say a lot of goofball things, and this goofball man was no different.

As the man put on his trench coat, he accidently bumped into Linda walking through the fast-emptying barroom.

"Sorry, sir," Linda said, as contrite and sincere as possible.

"Watch where you're going, sister," the man commanded.

"Sorry, sir," Linda repeated, feeling threatened. She wasn't in the mood to get into an argument with a customer, especially this late in the evening. She could tell by his breath that he had consumed quite a bit of alcohol.

The man struggled as he finished putting on his trench coat. He walked slowly to the front door, making sure everyone saw that he was not being pushed around. He left the bar.

Once outside, he began singing out loud. His voice was not something to be proud of, but he didn't care. He was going to sing no matter what anyone said.

He wandered down the street and around the corner, where he broke into one of his favorite ditties.

"If the river was whiskey," he sang, out of tune and sounding jangled, "and I were a duck, I'd swim to the bottom, and never come up."

He weaved down the boulevard, heading to he knew not where. All he knew in his greasy little heart was that he needed more to drink.

"Look out, buddy," he said as he careened into a streetlight post. "Get out of my way!"

Swerving down the sidewalk, the drunken man didn't get far from the Club Festival when he happened upon some sailors sitting in the recessed doorway of a retail shop, sharing a bottle of Cutty Sark Scotch. They had heard him singing as he weaved down the concrete path, and were tipsy enough themselves to appreciate a little entertainment.

"Hey, old man," one sailor exclaimed. "Sing us a song and we'll give you a drink!"

The man in the trench coat stopped in his tracks. He hadn't been paying much attention to his surroundings, having concentrated all his mental energy into figuring out how he was going to get hold of more booze. He turned to face the sailors.

"What did you say?"

Another sailor took up the cause.

"We said to sing us a song and we'll share some of this fine Cutty Sark, matey!"

Not wanting to wait much longer for more hooch, the drunk responded almost instantly by breaking out into another ditty.

"I love to go swimmin' with bow-legged women," he tried to sing, without much rhythm or melody. "How's that boys? Hand that bottle over!"

"Oh, come on, you can do better than that!"

"I could," the drunk said, "but I need a little inspiration, and my vocal cords need some proper lubricant."

The sailors moaned, laughed and handed the bottle to the man.

He wiped off the opening with his sleeve, causing another round of moans and laughter from the sailors. He then tipped the bottle back and took the equivalent to two or three shots.

"Christ! Shit! Hey!" the sailors said, all at once and all together. "Go easy on that stuff, old man!"

"Well, you boys sure are greedy with the good stuff," the drunk said. "Now I'm ready to sing another song!"

"Oh, get the hell out of here," said one of the sailors. "We're tired of your act."

"That's a fine 'How do you do?' Hey, why are you guys are dressed up like sailors?"

The man's question caused an uproar of guffaws from the sailors.

"Old dude," said one of them, "we are sailors. Why else do you think we're dressed like this?"

Arguing with the young men had created a powerful thirst in the older man.

"Hey, are you sure I can't sing you another song for another drink? Help a dry man out here."

"You're really not getting the hint, are you?" said one of the young sailors.

"I guess I'll be leaving now."

"Oh, hang on," said the sailor who had current possession of the bottle. The young men had purchased two bottles of the same Scotch, so it wasn't as if they were low on alcohol. He handed the bottle to the older man, who proceeded to take a deep pull on the bottle, quenching his thirst and giving him the jolt he needed to keep the maintenance dosage of booze flowing through his bloodstream. He handed the bottle back.

"Thanks, boys, I'm good!"

Away the drunk man went, in search of more booze. He staggered down the street, full of himself and filled with alcohol. The stiff pull on the bottle from the sailors gave him the perfect amount of inspiration he needed to continue his journey.

He ran into another streetlamp, but instead of excusing himself, he leaned against the pole and took a bit of a rest. It had been a long night. It was now after 3 a.m. He was on the edge of being totally exhausted, but the alcohol somehow gave him strength. He rested for a minute or two, then began his travels afresh.

Within a few paces he noticed two figures coming his way. Unafraid, he forged ahead. The two figures were headed straight at him. To avoid a confrontation, he moved to his left. In response, the two figures moved to their right, again heading directly for him. Once more he shifted his direction, but the figures matched his change of motion.

As he got within a few feet, he grasped the situation and took defensive action.

"Out of my way!" he yelled. "I'm loaded for bear and not afraid of a fight!"

The two figures, women in their 20s, started to laugh. One was tall and slender, the other shorter and Rubenesque.

"You old fool," the taller one said. "What the hell is your problem?"

"You're my problem, madam," he replied, and took a swing at her. She leaned back, letting the punch miss her, and due to the force of this own momentum, he went tumbling down.

As he lay on the sidewalk, mumbling, the two women stood over him and laughed.

"Look at the idiot lying on the sidewalk!" the Rubenesque woman said. "You're quite the sight, old fart!"

"Give me a chance, and I'll teach you two a lesson!"

"I don't think you're gonna teach anybody a lesson today, fuckface," the taller one said, and spit on the man as he lay on the sidewalk.

Infuriated, the man first got to his knees in an attempt to stand. With a shove to his posterior from the shorter woman's foot, he returned to the prone position.

"You know, it's assholes like you that make the world a terrible place," said the taller woman. "Darling," she said to her partner, "let's teach him a lesson."

The two women proceeded to boot stomp the man on the spot. They kicked him several times in the stomach and the back, but gave up the punishment abruptly.

"Quick," the taller one said, "I see a cop car, let's get out of here!"

The two women hustled their bustles away from the scene, leaving the man in the fetal position on the sidewalk. As it turned out, there was no police officer coming in their direction; the car was the right make and model, a Ford Crown Victoria, but it wasn't a cop car, it was a civilian's private rig.

The man lay there groaning, feeling sick and dizzy. A minute or two passed, then his sailor friends came by, singing and laughing. When they found their former drinking buddy laid out on the sidewalk, they recognized him and took pity.

"Hey, isn't that the same guy we saw a few minutes ago?" one said.

"Yeah, that's him alright," said another. "Hey, buddy, you OK?"

Realizing he was no longer being pummeled by the two aggressive women, he uncurled from the fetal position, sat up and spoke.

"Help me up, fellas."

Once on his feet, the sailors tried to get him back into some semblance of sartorial shape by brushing his trench coat and straightening it out.

"God, it's good to see you boys again," he said. "You don't happen to have any of that good Scotch whisky with you, would you?"

"Sure, buddy," said one, and took out a half-empty bottle of Cutty

Sark. "Have a drink on us."

He drank deeply from the bottle. It had been his fortune to have intersected with the sailors again. They not only helped him to regain his composure, but continued to keep him well lubricated.

"We gotta take off, buddy," one of the sailors said to the man. "Are you gonna be OK?"

"Fine, fine, I'm fine," he said, in his slurred English. "Did you boys see a couple of broads running down the street?"

"Yeah," said one, "we saw a couple of chicks high-tailing it down the street. Do you know them?"

"Know them? I got to know them! Witches! Bitches! They were trying to kick the shit out of me! Thankfully a cop car came around the corner."

"We didn't see any cops," said one.

"It don't matter, they took off before they could hurt me." At that instant the old guy winced; he felt a jolt in his right side, and stiffened from the jabbing pain. He weaved and bobbed in place, mostly from the booze, partly from the pain in his side. The sailors were no longer interested in the drunk's story; they had enough of him and his problems, and didn't notice his expression of pain.

"Take it easy, fella," said one of the sailors, as they wandered down the street.

"Yeah, yeah," the drunk said. "You, too." He felt a bit dizzy, but otherwise was ready to continue on his way.

After a night of excitement, danger, drinking and a boot stomping, the man in the trench coat was full of piss and vinegar. It would be a pity if anyone else had to deal with him again that day.

CHAPTER 19

Leaving the Club Festival after closing, around 3:30 a.m., cigarette girl Linda Avery slung her purse over her shoulder and began the long walk home. Not well off enough to afford a car, she was too poor to afford a taxi, at least that night.

"That's the breaks," she said to herself, and began to apply a little leg action to the journey. Her stepfather used a different term growing up; when she asked him one time to drive her somewhere, he advised her to use "shanks mare," an old timey term for walking.

Instinctively, she noticed someone following her right away. The first thing she heard were footsteps. She listened carefully to the clip-clop on the sidewalk. She crossed the street in the middle of the block, which gave her the natural opportunity to check both ways while in the middle of the street. As she turned to the right, she saw him.

She could tell it was a man, lurching across the street in parallel with her. She kept her pace and began to think about who it might be as she traversed the street. Linda sees so many people at the club during her shift that she didn't immediately recognize the man. Then it struck her: It was the same man who had been argumentative with both her and Emily Lou near closing time. It was the man in the trench coat that Emily Lou refused to serve after last call, the same rude man who bumped into her at the club.

After Linda cut across the boulevard in the middle of the block and to the sidewalk on the other side of the street, the man was still following, but getting closer. At last he made a beeline toward her.

"You're the sweet thing that sells cigarettes," the man said, clearly drunk and clearly menacing. Filled with alcohol and wanting to return some of the wrath he received from two very aggressive women earlier, he was ready to dish out some punishment. It wouldn't matter who was on the receiving end, as long as someone got hurt other than himself.

"Sir, I'm going to have to advise you to back away," she replied. She knew she sounded like some sort of police officer, but she also realized it didn't matter what you said at this instant, it mattered how you said it.

The drunk, menacing man stumbled forward a few steps, then stopped.

"Lady, don't get threatening with me," he spit out.

The cigarette girl knew she had to do something. The street was deserted, and no one was around to help her. All she had to defend herself was her wits.

The man stood there, weaving in place, mumbling something to himself and rummaging through his pockets. It was this last movement that gave Linda the impetus to take action.

Like a football running back, she sprung forward, running at full speed toward the man. She collided with him at a full clip, leaning forward at the last minute and catching the man between the gut and the rib cage. He flew up, back and down into the gutter, stunned.

Linda, who was prepared for the sudden maneuver, continued running in the same direction, back toward the club. She knew Lou would still be there, closing down the joint and checking the day's take.

She ran through the dark streets, looking behind her as she turned the blocks. She was still in a panic as she reached the front door of the Club Festival. She banged on the front door with her right hand in a fist.

"Lou, let me in, let me in!" she hollered.

He'd heard the hammering on the front door, and at first thought it was some crazy from the street.

But then he heard a woman's voice, yelling, practically screaming. He ran to the door; he peered through the tiny window and immediately recognized Linda. He hurriedly unbolted the deadbolt and opened the door. Lou let Linda into the club as quickly as he could.

Linda practically fell into the club's entrance.

At the same time, the man who had been threatening Linda lay in the gutter, stunned. After a few minutes, he began to realize that he'd been made the victim, that the woman he thought he was going to terrorize wasn't going to take it sitting down. Or, in her case, standing up.

The numbing effects of the booze began to wear off him in a hurry. He got up on his knees at first, then to his feet.

"I'm lucky to have my head still screwed on," he thought to himself, "after that slamming."

He stumbled down the street, heading home. It'd been a long day. Hell, it'd been a long night, and he was exhausted.

"Luck of the Irish," he thought to himself, as he ran his tongue around the inside of his mouth to see if he'd lost any teeth. "Luck o' the Irish."

Linda was still catching her breath at the Club Festival. Lou let his cigarette girl calm down, got her a drink and put on some quiet music.

Linda, shaken from the experience of being seriously menaced by a stranger, needed some time to relax. She was drenched in sweat, her blond hair matted with perspiration. Her heart was still pounding, her breath quickened.

It all happened so fast.

It was then that she noticed she had lost her favorite blue beret. It must have fallen off during the altercation. The whole incident was dreamlike, almost a fantasy.

Then she started to laugh.

"Lou," she said, half laughing, "you shoulda seen that sucker go down."

Lou was glad to help his female friend when she needed it. His philosophy was that with family, you were stuck, but with friends, you pick and choose. Loyalty to friends was more important than loyalty to family, in Lou Brodsky's world.

"Baby, you know I'm always here for you," he said, giving her a wink and a smile.

"Thanks, Lou, it's nice to know you can depend on someone," she said as she threw back her hair.

It was then that she noticed she'd probably injured her neck in the impact with her potential assailant. "That'll be stiff in the morning," she said to herself.

But for now it was nice to sit in the quiet bar, sipping on a nice, stiff drink. Lou never cheaped out on the drinks. Maybe customers got the watered-down version, but not a friend. Friends don't give friends watered-down drinks.

"Lou, I gotta get goin'," she said, expelling the words with a sigh. It was late, the adrenaline had worn off, and tomorrow, as they say, is another day.

"OK, baby, shag your svelte ass on down the road. Do you want me to call a cab?"

"No thanks, Lou, I can hoof it," she mumbled dismissively. "Whoever it was that attacked me, he's long gone, and I hope for his sake he doesn't try bothering me again."

"You did good, girl," he said to her. "Did our discussion about protecting yourself on the street we had the other day help at all?"

"I dunno, Lou," she admitted. "I'm not sure if it did or didn't, but I appreciate the advice. I guess it helped. It couldn't have hurt."

"Well, at least you're OK," he said.

"I'm better than OK, Lou. I feel like I did the right thing at the right time, so I guess your talk on self defense must have helped me at least gain a little confidence."

"Well, I'm glad if I helped."

"Thanks again, Lou," she said as Lou unlocked the front door and let the cigarette girl out into the night.

The minute she was out on the concrete, she immediately saw the problem with her decision to try walking home again. What if the same man was waiting around the corner? For a few seconds she thought about turning around, knocking on the door of the club and asking Lou for help. But in a flash, she caught herself doubting her own abilities, shook off the doubt and began hoofing it home.

"Fuck the bastard," she said to herself. "If he tries anything again, he'll get another dose of that medicine."

She walked briskly yet confidently home, taking an alternate route.

As she rounded a corner near her apartment, she was startled by a stray cat running in front of her. She took a deep breath, composed herself again and finished her journey.

Once home, she was too anxious and wound-up to go right to sleep. She changed out of her clothes, and again remembered that she'd lost her favorite beret.

"Damn," she said aloud to herself, "that's the only beret I ever liked."

She got into a comfortable set of PJs and turned on the stereo. The music that came out at first was rock 'n' roll, so she changed the channel to the classical radio station in town. Some calming classical guitar music came on. She looked at the clock, and it was 4:15 in the morning. She was thankful to be home, to be alive and to be in one piece. Life in the city was tough, but she was tougher.

Linda contacted the Portland Police Bureau the next day to describe her attack and the attacker.

"So, you're saying you're OK?" the woman at the police bureau making a record of the incident asked Linda.

"Yeah," Linda said, "except for a sore shoulder where I ran into the guy."

"You know, you could have gotten really hurt doing that. He could have had a knife or a gun, or grabbed you as you flew into him. What I'm saying is you might want to consider other options the next time."

"Like what?" Linda's voice was strained and cracked; she was getting impatient with the woman at the other end of the phone. Linda didn't think the woman was taking the incident seriously enough.

"Like running away from the man, going to a place of business and knocking on a door, anything but confront the man."

"You're kidding, right?"

"No, ma'am, I'm not," said the police bureau representative. "I'm serious. Can you give me a description of the man."

"I sure can, and so can one of the waitresses at the club where I work."

"OK, shoot."

"Well ..." she said, hesitating. Linda began to realize that she did not get a good look at the man either inside the club or outside on the street.

"Don't tell me you can't describe him."

"Yeah, yeah, give me minute."

"I haven't got all day, ma'am."

"Hold on to your horses."

"Sorry, ma'am."

"The one thing I know is that he was wearing a tan trench coat, you know, one of those coats that you see in old fashioned detective movies."

"I know what a trench coat is, ma'am."

The woman taking down the information for the report was getting impatient with Linda, but knew that the information had to be recorded properly. It was her job to make sure the incident had all the important details, details which might come in handy in the future, in case of an arrest and ultimate prosecution.

"Other than the trench coat, I'm not positive what he looked like. I know he was a white male, older…"

"How old do you think he was?"

"Maybe late 40s, maybe 50 years old, I dunno."

After several minutes, the police bureau had a report on an attempted assault by an adult white male, possibly in his 40s or 50s, wearing a trench coat. There wasn't much to go on, so the police couldn't do much more than make a record of the incident. Linda forgot to give Emily Lou's name to the woman taking down the information, and the woman forgot to ask for it.

Linda wasn't as obsessed by the episode as she was with the robbery where she lost her money and her ID. All she lost this time was her beret.

Trouble seemed to follow Linda of late, but she'd escaped being physically harmed by using her smarts and her wits.

It was a frustrating conversation with the police, and Linda was not thoroughly satisfied with her interaction.

"Those people don't give a shit about me," she said to herself. "I'm a statistic to them."

Her frustration was enough to put her into a depressive state. She still had a few hours before heading to work, so she took what she liked to call a "lay down" and napped for an hour.

She dreamed a devilishly weird dream, unlike any other.

She dreamed that her brother Joe developed an inoperable cancer and had been told by the doctors he only had a few weeks to live. In the dream her brother decided that if he was going to die, he was going to take a few people with him. Her brother Joe had made up his mind to go on a violent killing rampage, and to "take out" any of the people in his past that had wronged him.

Before her brother could begin his killing rampage, Linda awoke from the dream in a cold sweat. She lay in bed contemplating the nature of her dream, trying to make some sense of it. She couldn't. She decided not to attach any significance to it, since there didn't seem to be any meaning to the dream.

But the dream about her brother did inspire her to call him. It being the middle of the afternoon, he'd be at work. She couldn't remember his work telephone number, so she looked it up in her address book. She decided she'd pull a trick on him; hell, he was her brother, if she can't pull his leg, whose leg could she pull?

She got out her cell phone and dialed his number. He answered after the second ring.

"Joe Avery."

With her voice disguised, Linda was ready to pounce.

"Mr. Avery?"

"Yes, this is Joe Avery."

"Mr. Avery, this is the American Red Cross. We're calling to see if you'd be willing to come down to our North Portland center and donate blood."

"I'd like to," Joe said, "but last year, when I tried to donate blood, you folks checked my blood and found out I was anemic. They said it's because I don't eat enough fruits and vegetables."

Linda was completely caught off guard by her brother's confession. She intended to pull a prank, but instead found out more than she wanted to find out about her brother's medical condition.

"Joe, this is Linda."

"Linda, what the hell are you doing? I know you aren't working for the Red Cross!"

"I called to pull a joke, but I guess it backfired. I'm really embarrassed. I'm sorry I'm bothering you."

"Sis, you really take the cake, you know it? Here I am at work, busy as hell, and you have nothing better to do than give me grief. What is wrong with you?"

"Jeez, Joe, lighten up, there's no harm done."

"Sis, you can really be a royal pain in the ass, you know it?"

"Sorry, Joe, I'll go away now. I don't know what got into me. Maybe it was what happened last night."

"Huh? What happened last night?"

"You don't want to know. I'd better go and stop bothering you."

"No, no, you brought it up. Tell all."

Linda gave a thumbnail sketch of the turmoil with the man in the trench coat.

"So you're OK?" Joe said. "Did the man get hurt when you ran into him?"

"I didn't stick around to find out. Why would I care if he was hurt? Why are you more concerned about him than about me?"

"Come on, sis, I was only curious. So you're OK?"

"Yeah, I'm fine. I'd better go now."

"Well, I'd like to say it was fun talking with you, but it wasn't."

"Fine, Joe, I'll talk to you later."

Linda hung up and sat in her apartment steaming over Joe's seeming lack of sensitivity. After a few seconds she remembered that it was she who called him, in an attempt to pull a practical joke.

"I guess I'm just another woman giving Joe a hard time," she said aloud to herself.

She thought back on all his trouble with the female sex. She thought she knew her brother, but his history of abusing women perplexed Linda. He had never picked on her as children. Where did he get his aggressive nature?

Linda lay back down on the bed to catch another few winks before hoofing it to the workplace. Her interactions with other humans hadn't been very positive today, and she hoped that she might find refuge at the Club Festival. She knew she would. Lou had been so supportive of her, so kind to offer a shoulder to cry on. But it was more than that. Lou had provided some good information on defending herself on the streets, and she appreciated that. There were many things to be thankful for, and one of them was Lou Brodsky.

Linda's cell phone rang.

"Hello?"

"Are you Linda Avery?"

"Yes."

"I've got your beret."

"What? Who are you? Where'd you find it?"

"My name is Seymour. I live in Southeast Portland, and I was riding my bicycle through downtown Portland early this morning when I saw this beret hanging on a parking meter. I usually wouldn't touch anything like that, but it somehow drew me to it. You've got your name and phone number written on the inside."

"Oh, yeah, that's right."

"How can I get this thing to you?"

"Gosh, it's nice of you to offer to help. I work at the Club Festival in downtown, and I'll be at work in a few hours. You could drop it off there with anybody." Linda gave the fellow the address of the club.

"OK, sounds good. I'll see if I can stop by tomorrow and drop it off."

"Hey, thanks a million."

"No problem." He hung up the phone. He did drop the beret by the next day, dirty but otherwise intact. Sometimes there's a bit of good news to accompany the bad.

CHAPTER 20

Linda Avery remembered, as an adolescent, experimenting with all manner of drugs, licit and illicit, and one of her favorite, yet wicked, memories was sampling her friend's mother's medicine cabinet, medicine by medicine.

In fact, Linda being a bit of an amateur sleuth and scientist, she began the experiment by approaching the container of drugs at the very top left of the cabinet, and began a process of working each row from left to right. First the top row.

She'd, of course, at least look at the label of the drugs, and there were dozens of plastic containers, some prescribed, others over the counter.

There were, of course a few real duds, like a container filled with fake fingernails.

The second from the top row. Left to right.

She'd take maybe one or two of anything that sounded like it might give her a buzz. Yes, and as she went, she found nothing of interest, that is, until nearly the end.

A bottle on the bottom row filled with black gelatin capsules, lovely things. She tried one or two, and they made her a bit "speedy."

Turns out, of course, that she'd stumbled onto her friend's mom's stash of diet pills, known in the drug abuse world as "black beauties." Amphetamine, basically.

She left the bottle in the medicine cabinet. She didn't want to arouse any suspicions at that point; in the final analysis, she ended up downing the whole bottle one or two pills at a time.

She shared the black beauties with a friend of hers at high school. What was especially fun for Linda and her friend were taking them during Physical Education class, and for once they enjoyed at least of couple of PE classes at the school.

PE classes for Linda were either deadly dull or a pit of verbal abuse from the class ahead of you. Especially if you were a little different or weird. The abuse. The abuse was psychological in nature, never physical, but she still did not enjoy being targeted and bullied by those girls. Taunting, name calling, it all became part of the experience of "PE." She enjoyed the physical activity, but the stress of being belittled and picked on made the whole experience subpar. It did teach her one thing about the "real world" and its inhabitants: There are a lot of nasty people out there. She also realized that there were a lot of good people out there, too, you had to separate them from the bad eggs and rotten apples.

No wonder she took drugs during PE.

But Linda knew from a personal perspective that it was possible to get something positive out of the drug experience. She knew that herself, and she knew from talking with Lou, her boss at the Club Festival. Linda and Lou were rare examples of how the drug experience can be helpful. Again, though, only rare examples.

Lou'd done his share of drugs, starting young. Not too young, mind you; the way Lou looked at it, he was lucky to have been delayed in the drug taking experience until he was midway through his high school education. Back in the day, he watched very young kids taking drugs and becoming wrapped up in the drug culture. It was sad to him, because it seemed those kids would miss the regular, normal stuff that everyone goes through, and instead have the world colored and tainted by the mystification that was the drug experience.

Lou lazily polished the bar with a rag on a typical rainy, dreary day.

He thought back to his youth, to the experiences of high school, before he went into the service. The U.S. Army.

Although they asked him before enlisting in the military, while enlisting and during basic training, he never admitted to any drug use in high school. He had learned that people really don't want to hear the truth, they want to hear what they want to hear. They wanted to hear that he hadn't taken any drugs, so that's what he told them.

It was a time well before the myriad of precise drug tests. He remembers getting only one drug test his entire life, at a military training school, but it was so imprecise that it didn't register the marijuana he'd recently smoked.

While polishing the bar, he remembered a life altering realization he had while tripping on LSD. He had a lot of good times tripping. One was during an LSD trip at a friend's house, located next to the river, probably as a junior or senior in high school.

Taking the LSD, tripping freely as they were, he and his friend ended up on the beach down below the friend's house, in the middle of the night. He couldn't recall what the hell his friend was doing, but Lou sat down on the beach, cross legged, and meditated on the moment.

He saw himself clearly in the center of the universe, sitting on the beach, in the night, in the cold, by himself.

He came to realize that if he continued to sit there and not move, if he continued to sit there and not take any nourishment, if he sat there for long enough, he would be as a fire without being tended with fuel: He would die. If he sat there long enough, without fuel, without sustenance, he would expire.

He saw it organically, as if he were a glowing ember, and without further aid from either himself or from others, the heat, the internal life, would slowly grow less and less hot, becoming colder and colder, and he would expire, like a fire left untended.

In that moment he experienced his own death, understood what death was, and upon that realization, he got up and went out into the world. As he remembered the experience, he wasn't sure, but knowing his own nature, he probably went up to the friend's house and got himself something to eat.

Although Lou learned a few things from his days experimenting with drugs, he'd be the first to admit that not all lessons came easy.

Another time tripping on LSD wasn't so positive, at least for a few minutes.

He and two other fellows were standing around the basement of one of their houses, tripping on LSD, when Lou decided he'd try something he'd done before.

Once while high on marijuana, he'd tried hyperventilating. It had been fun. Simply put, one breathes deeply in and out about 10 times, and then holds the breath. It would create a "rush" that was dizzying and kind of fun.

He tried the same thing while on LSD, but the results were much different.

After breathing deeply in and out several times, Lou held his breath. Instead of getting dizzy, he fell to the floor.

He remembered the sensation was frightening and unsettling. While laying on the floor, helpless, an eternity passed by, typical of being on the strong hallucinogen LSD. As he lay on the floor, during what seemed like forever, he realized one startling concept: "What if I've permanently altered my brain with this dumb act," he thought to himself, "and I'll be forever mentally crippled?" He was scared, really scared.

Only with the passage of time, which seemed like forever, but really was only a few seconds, did he come out of the fit and regain his composure. His friends were amused by his little display. But Lou was shaken to the core, and never did anything so stupid again.

He treasured his mind, and wanted to live a full life. Crippling yourself while a teenager was not the optimum way to grow old and wise.

Drug experiences differ from person to person. Some people should never take drugs; others can be helped by drugs.

On the way home from the Club Festival, Linda knew something was up. Something was amiss in the appearance of the street around her apartment.

It was as if fate or kismet had caught up with her finally.

Along with a couple of strange, different vehicles, the street seemed quieter than normal for 3 a.m. You'd expect at least a little activity in the big city at that hour. But instead of a humming street, it was oddly quiet.

She always thought of her old, former friend Marcia, who went around the bend psychologically recently. Her friend, one she'd had since high school, had faced depression and anxiety after her husband took the children and left her. Then she lost her job. Then she started drinking. Then she started experimenting with artificial marijuana. In the end, Linda's friend went completely insane, insisting that a "spirit guide" was talking to her, giving her instructions on how to live. It was unnerving for Linda to listen to her friend's madness.

"I can hear my spirit guide," Linda's friend Marcia would say, looking up at the ceiling. Marcia also looked up towards the ceiling, crooked her neck, twisted her head and aimed her ear upwards. "I know you can't hear the spirit guide," Marcia told Linda, "it's talking to me."

Marcia Calibri's imagination was shifted into high gear.

"It's telling me all sorts of things," Marcia explained. "It's telling me to begin my own spiritual journey."

Linda sat across from her friend and feigned interest. Linda placed her elbows on the table, and then placed her chin in her hands, staring at her friend. Linda was filled with curiosity, certainly, but more by the sense that her friend had become a train wreck of an individual. It's hard not to stare at the scene of a catastrophe.

So it was only a few weeks after Linda had to call the cops on her friend that she noticed something funny about the way the street hummed that night she returned home.

The cops had told her there was nothing they could do to help Linda after Marcia begun leaving vaguely threatening phone messages. All they could say was, "Watch your back."

So "watch your back" she did. She turned it into a game, and tried not to get paranoid about the whole thing. But nonetheless, Linda had a streetwise attitude.

You see, after years of living in the city, Linda had become attuned to the woof and warp of the busy urban life. She could feel the vibrations of the city from below, around and above. It wasn't paranoia or fear, it was a sense of what was natural. It was like a hunter in the forest, understanding how the flora and fauna acted and reacted. It was as natural as that.

The strange cars, they attracted her attention in the past. This night, in one of the cars, a man sat in the passenger side, but no one sat on the driver's side.

"Where's the driver?" she asked herself.

"I'm gonna beat you like a rented mule, you bitch!" a strangely-dressed man yelled at Linda. "I'm gonna be your worst nightmare!"

Linda thought about what Lou had taught her about self defense, both psychologically and physically. It was time to combine the two, and use some of what Lou had been talking about. Time to test the theories.

All things being equal, she didn't see much of a percentage in encouraging a confrontation. Retreat in this case might be less honorable, but she'd be assured at least of a smaller chance of a beating or death. Plus, she couldn't be certain there wasn't another opponent hiding, waiting to come up from the batter's box and take a swing. Or a couple more hit men waiting for her. It's a nasty world; she felt like taking the smart route.

She let the whole world, and everything in it, flash before her mind. She considered as many of her options as possible, and began the process.

First, much like a football quarterback, she aimed to the right and headed left.

She bolted straight ahead, first off a few degrees to the right, then headed left. She flew by the guy on his right, before he could make a move.

By the time he could turn around to begin chasing her, she was a fading image in the process of becoming "long gone."

Although she thought the scene originally was going to involve her mentally defective friend Marcia, this wasn't the case. There was no conspiracy here; she was safe; safe on the city streets.

CHAPTER 21

Squint Eye sat quietly in his apartment, lost in memories, lost in the twisting tale of his life as a journalist.

"Where did it all begin?" he asked himself, as the sun slowly set in the West Hills of his hometown, Portland, Oregon.

It began with the permissiveness of both his parents and the wondrous public school system that, together in concert, raised him. That and the mass media, along with the influence of friends, equaled the sum of the parts of one each issue Squint Eye.

He had one distinct memory: That of receiving a new Merriam-Webster's Collegiate Dictionary for Christmas during his formative years. He thinks that he received at least a couple of the necessary items for any writer, with an updated version replacing an older one. He can't remember if he asked for such items, but received them he did.

He remembered receiving a penmanship award during fourth grade. He remembered doing some light reading of books, but mostly reading Mad magazine.

"Damned Mad magazine," he thought to himself. "Warped me, warped my sense of humor." He remembered the oddball cartoons, laced with contemporary wit and sophomoric humor.

He particularly remembered one of the many "Snappy Answers to Stupid Questions:" "Is that fish fresh?" a lady asked the grocer behind the counter at the meat market. "No, ma'am, it's well mannered," was the grocer's snappy response.

He collected Mad magazine and monster magazines with the

small allowance he received each week from his parents. His parents also subscribed to Life magazine. For Squint, his world was filled with words. Highlights magazine as a child, Reader's Digest in his Grandma's bathroom for reading, a world of words. He did some book reading in elementary school, mostly lightweight fare.

By the time he reached the 7th and 8th grades, he began exploring the real world of books, mostly science fiction. He enjoyed Robert Heinlein, Robert Silverberg and Ray Bradbury.

He started his writing career out simply enough. Where he found writing inspiration was in the pages of a national weekly magazine.

Hitching a ride to school with the neighbors across the street, he remembered waiting in their living room for the ride, and listening to classical music while the master of the house enjoyed his coffee and read The Wall Street Journal in his easy chair. Squint read recent copies of The New Yorker magazine, concentrating on three areas: The lengthy events calendar, the cartoons and the poetry.

It was the poetry that got him started writing.

In 9th grade, he started writing poetry. Crude stuff, nothing fancy, but he enjoyed the sensation of putting words together to form a poetic expression.

By the time he started 10th grade, known as "senior high school," he was ready to put his work to the test. During the first half of the year, he volunteered to be a writer for the newly-formed school literary magazine. It's here that he began a lifelong relationship with publishing and the printed word.

He wrote dozens of poems, and submitted a handful. He remembered the editor was rather harsh, and if the editor didn't like a poem, he'd placed "TBB" at the top of the page. "TBB" was short for "To Be Burned."

So it was early on, barely past age 16, that he learned to develop a thick skin when it came to criticism of his written work. He learned that editors were a tough lot, and that not everything he wrote was considered gold.

But it was also during that time that he heard about a city-wide poetry contest sponsored by the town's library. He entered, probably one of the few kids to do so. He earned first place in his age category. He remembered the prize was a silver dollar.

He stuck with the high school literary magazine, and saw a few of his poems published.

In his 11th grade, he took photography class.

In his last year of high school, he took the newspaper class offered, and wrote features for the high school newspaper. Literally. At that time, he didn't know any better than to hand write his features for the newspaper, and then have another student, likely a girl, transcribe the piece to typewritten for publication.

He got a taste of the unreal world of journalism. He remembered that the only thing he ever learned, except for unrestrained flowery writing, was the one adage the high school newspaper class teacher bestowed upon him: "When in doubt, throw it out." That meant that if he were writing something, and he wasn't sure about its veracity, to leave it out of the written piece.

He decided that a newspaperman is what he wanted to be.

So he signed up with the U.S. Air Force as a newspaper writer. He was supposed to have gone to a technical school for training, but instead was sent directly to his first assignment, with virtually no training in the field of journalism.

He learned by hard knocks.

Assigned his first story almost immediately, he began to write down the story longhand, much as he had done in high school. His editor, a crusty old master sergeant, came up behind him and watched him as he scribbled down the story, pen furiously scratching the paper.

"What are you doing, son?" the editor of the Air Force base

newspaper asked him.

"Putting the story together, sir," was young Squint's answer.

"Oh, no, that's not how you do it," the master sergeant replied. "You need to type the story directly from your notes, not waste time putting together some sort of rough draft. Get typing." It was then and there that he began to learn the craft of journalism.

He also took a series of on-the-job training sessions offered from a battery of booklets. He learned the rudiments of the business and the very basics, including the famous journalistic "inverted pyramid." The inverted pyramid, for those unacquainted with the phrase, means that the most important material must start at the top of the story, right in the beginning. The "lede" (journalism shorthand for "lead") of the story was the most important part, he learned, for two reasons. One, most basic to the reader, was giving the reader the vital part of the story right away. There wasn't time for flowery poetry or fancy words. Get right to the point. The other reason was more basic to the mechanics of publishing. If while putting the newspaper together, the editor was squeezed for space, he (for it was mostly male editors back in Squint's day) would simply chop the end of the story off to make it fit. If as a writer you'd followed the inverted pyramid lesson, less important details were placed at the end of article, and could be sacrificed.

He worked hard as a writer, learning the craft by experience. He interviewed retirees at the Air Force base, colonels in charge of squadrons, senior enlisted managers, lowly airmen worker bees, every type of individual. He learned right away a certain fact about being on the Air Force base newspaper, a fact that really would stay with him as a journalist all his life, and kept him wary of liars and those interested in only showing the good side. That fact was that he was always treated with kindness and courtesy, and it didn't take long for him to realize why. The reason? If whomever he was interviewing was good to him, he'd write a good story. If the person was not forthcoming, did not cooperate, then the story didn't turn out quite as good. It was a game that has been played between journalists and the general public for years.

He learned to take a nationally-released military story, and "localize it" by calling up a local source for at least one short quote. He worked from press releases and the like, and learned to type quickly. Squint was old enough to remember the days before computers. He worked at first on a manual typewriter. Within a few months the office received electric typewriters. The reporters would type the material, give it in triplicate to the editor, who would edit the material and forward a copy to typesetters. A second copy was given to the office's officer in charge. Such was the way in the day.

Human interest stories, sports stories, straight hard news, the young Squint learned to write it all. He became almost a writing machine. In fact, at one point in his brief military journalism career, instead of typing the story up with 8 ½ x 11 inch typing paper, again, in triplicate, with carbon paper between the pages, he was given something a clever editor had invented.

Clever goddamned editors. What young Squint was given was a large roll of paper, the size of an old fashioned coffee can. It was 8 inches wide, with three pages interspersed with carbon paper for the requisite triplicate copies. Squint was taught to place the paper in the typewriter carriage, and write like a madman until the story was finished. He then took a 12-inch ruler and ripped the story from the typewriter, and handed it in as written. In other words, the damned story could be feet long, but it mattered not, for the editor would divide it into roughly 8 ½ x 11 inch chunks for the typesetter. In this way, our young journalist became a writing machine, typing at a high rate of speed, doing "rewrites," which were, again, mostly press releases that needed a local quote or two to make them more relevant to the reading audience.

Much of what military writers on military newspapers did was to take orders from "on high" and make them more palatable for the masses of military enlisted and officers living and working both on and off the base. It was up to the military writer to take military times and turn them into a.m. and p.m. So something along the lines of "Air Force personnel will be at the flight line promptly at 1400 hours for inspection" would be changed to "Officers and enlisted men and women are requested to be at the flight line for a mandatory inspection at 2 p.m." It took the sting off the order, and, as the wording suggests, turned it into a request.

Of course, you still had to be there, but now it was less odious, in the eyes of both the officers giving the orders and military personnel having to take the orders. Or at least that was the wisdom.

That wasn't the only duty young Squint had to accomplish. The base newspaper was located within the Office of Information, which was also in charge of sending out pertinent press releases, and giving tours of the base to civilian organizations, including Boy Scouts, senior citizen groups and school children. Squint was, at age 19, standing in the front of the tour bus, microphone in hand, giving tours of the base. It was another life lesson that he was taught, another aspect to the military that gave him perspective and dimension.

He would have used some of the photography skills he had learned in high school, but in his case, at every Air Force base he served, there was always a military photographer who would accompany him on an assignment. He never once took a photo of the subject he was interviewing; that chore would come later, in civilian life, when it was part of the job to carry a camera with you to every assignment.

The Air Force's Office of Information was also in charge of what was known as "disaster preparedness," which meant that there were pages and pages of sample press releases prepared ahead of time, to be ready for any potential disaster on the base. Those disasters could range from the death of an airman to a nuclear disaster. To Squint, the modern equivalent would be risk management.

One thing that he did learn was a sense of humor about the whole world, a sort of satiric viewpoint that all journalists learn, a jaded view of the world. The unofficial byword within the Office of Information was, "First to go, last to know."

At least his recruiter did not lie: He was never issued a weapon on a permanent basis in the Air Force, and in fact failed the firing line test of the M-16 the two times he took it, in basic training and a few months before he was discharged.

"Don't worry, son," his recruiter said in his hometown interview, "they won't issue you a gun. For one thing, you'd be more dangerous with a gun than without it, and they have people who already carry guns. They're called the Army and the Marines."

He remembered his recruiter well. He also recalled once during basic training where the training instructor asked Squint who his recruiter was. Squint told the training instructor.

"I know that motherfucker!" the training instructor yelled at Squint. "He sent you here to fuck me up! Now get back in line!"

Instead of being issued a weapon, as a military journalist, Squint was issued a typewriter. If called up for an emergency evacuation to some foreign country, he was guaranteed a typewriter, not a gun, would be waiting for him on the flight line.

He stuck with the Office of Information, writing news articles for the base newspaper, giving tours to outside groups and scribing the occasional press release, until he got a little taste of being a radio disc jockey. He'd seen the base radio station operation one day, and was curious as hell. When asked if he was interested in going "on the air" by senior enlisted non-commissioned officers, he was eager to volunteer for any position. What he got was a bit more than he bargained for.

Out of the blue, he was told that he could not only become a radio DJ, he was unceremoniously named the radio station manager. He went from no experience on the air to running the base radio station from 8 a.m. to 5 p.m. Monday through Friday.

Shown the basics from the outgoing manager, an Army enlisted man, for his first day "on the air," he found out the hard way what radio work was all about. After the initial wonderment worn off, within an hour or two he realized that he was the only person there, and that to use the restroom, he'd have to put a long LP record cut on the turntable and run for the facilities.

After the first day, he began the process of finding enlisted personnel to come to the radio station to perform two-hour programs, playing music either brought in by the DJ or already part of the station's repertoire. Before long, he'd basically filled all the time slots, and found he had time to do some of the work of a radio station manager, including recording public service announcements.

But, of course, Squint had to take it too far. He'd found men and women to do radio shows for the whole day, so he spent considerable time at the base flight line café located within the same building as the base radio station. There he was secretly monitored by other members of the Office of Information, and one day was fired for goofing off. He returned to the Office of Information to continue his duties writing for the newspaper.

But he'd gotten a taste of radio broadcasting, and made efforts to switch his occupation within the Air Force from newspaper writer to radio and television broadcaster. He auditioned and was accepted into the Department of Defense Radio and Television Broadcast School.

The school accepted him with open arms, and he traveled to another military installation for schooling. The 10-week course for all members of the armed services also conducted a course for journalism, which Squint was originally meant to attend. For some reason, although promised and scheduled to attend the journalism course at the time of his enlistment, he went through what military officials called "on-the-job training."

Squint had been in the U.S. Air Force for a year and a half at that point in his military career, and was considered "permanent party." The majority of the men and women attending the Department of Defense Radio and Television Broadcast School were right out of basic training, and scared to death of anyone with a rank above them.

The radio and TV school was tough, with more than 100 varied areas that were either "pass" or "fail," and if students failed only one area, they were booted out of the school and sent back to whence they came. Squint watched as the students dropped like flies from the pressure of having to pass all the areas. It seemed that most of the older military personnel could not adjust to the rigors of broadcasting, and most dropped out.

To pass the radio portion of the education, there were numerous sections that must be tackled and passed. For radio, that included writing and producing public service announcements and doing a one-hour radio broadcast program. The TV area was more complex.

To pass the TV area of study, a soldier, marine, airman or sailor – and a few civilian types attached to the military – had to study and pass basic camera work, TV production, stage directing and more, including being able to put together a newscast and get in front of the camera. Squint did all these things, and passed the TV area handily.

He did have some difficulty with voice and diction, and took some nighttime remedial classes to get him up to speed.

When it came time to accomplish the radio section of study, Squint was told that the one-hour DJ program needed to include a diverse variety of music, including classical, country-western, popular and oldies. He thought he'd be a smart ass, and try to achieve that goal by making all the music basically rock 'n' roll. For the classical, he included Emerson, Lake and Palmer doing their version of Mussorgsky's Pictures at an Exhibition. For country-western, he did the Grateful Dead doing El Paso. His creativity was stretched, to the limits of his knowledge of rock music.

So was the patience of the Marine sergeant in charge of the radio section. After his show, Squint was called into the Marine sergeant's office.

"Airman," he said to Squint, who was standing tall before the man, "that was the worst fucking show I've ever heard here at the school. You failed the section, and will be sent back to your base."

Squint was shocked, but not disappointed. He knew he'd broken the rules, and was ready for his punishment.

Fortunately for him, military protocol saved his young ass. As it turned out, he already had orders for overseas, and to cancel those orders would be difficult. He was called into the office of the overall school commandant.

"Airman," the commandant said to young Squint, "this is your lucky day. With orders for your next assignment as a radio and TV broadcaster already in the pipeline, we are going to give you another chance to pass the DJ test."

Squint took the opportunity to learn from his mistakes, and did a much more mainstream radio program. He passed the DJ section, and all the other sections, including doing a TV broadcast. He then headed overseas to work in a television station.

Squint did well for the rest of the time in the military, and was asked to stay. He decided to get out while the getting was good. In fact, he got out of the military slightly early to begin college on the G.I. Bill.

He started college thinking he'd get a journalism degree, but it took only a couple of classes to realize that he'd learned all the basics while in the military. Getting an undergraduate degree in journalism would be a repeat of what he'd already learned. So he took a liberal arts degree with an emphasis on history and philosophy. Each year that passed after graduation only increased his confidence that he'd done the right thing. He'd learned something new, not something old.

During college he worked as an editor for a school publication, and also served as the public relations director for the student government.

After college, he took a few years off to try his hand at other occupations. He fulfilled a childhood dream of becoming a bicycle mechanic; he also worked as a radio advertising salesman and as a newspaper advertising salesman. He earned good money in all his endeavors, and enjoyed the time off from having to write.

By the time he was in his early 30s, he got back into the media rat race, and became at first a freelance writer, then a reporter, then an editor. He'd ply his trade as writer and editor well into his late 50s.

Squint had seen and done much in his life. Later, he became amazed that society was so kind to him, allowing him to switch jobs and do basically what he wanted. As a journalist and writer, the varied positions allowed him to deepen his knowledge of the field.

CHAPTER 22

Lou was probably out of his mind.

He had decided to invest heavily in a quantity of marijuana.

He was well past wanting to smoke the stuff himself, but he knew from his operatives at the Club Festival, mainly Linda Avery, Emily Lou Resnick and Randi Obvitz, that demand for weed was high.

It was also a fact of life that by the time a person had become desperate enough to buy from a stranger, they'd pay anything for any amount. It wasn't as if Lou had to try to rip off anyone; customers were willing to pay handsomely for marijuana.

He decided he wanted to make some money becoming a middleman for the sale of dope. So he made a series of telephone calls and ended up negotiating with a mid-level dealer who could offer a quantity buy of marijuana. Lou was not familiar with the current price of weed, but after a thorough indoctrination from the women at the club, he felt comfortable with the transaction he'd arranged.

The whole enchilada was accomplished over a period of two days.

First, he had to get a large quantity of cash together; checks, debit cards or credit cards were not going to work, too many ways to trace it back to responsible parties. He'd made a substantial withdrawal from his retirement savings account to be able to afford the deal.

"How would you like your cash, sir?" the bank teller asked Lou.

"Large bills," Lou said.

"Hundreds?" replied the teller.

"That'll be fine," Lou said.

The teller counted out the cash. Fifteen bills with Benjamin

Franklin's visage on them.

"Would you like an envelope?" the teller asked.

"Please."

Lou was instantly uncomfortable with carrying so much cash. Getting robbed was only one of the many possibilities. Humans being what they are, misplacing or losing the large wad was also possible. He preferred having his money in the bank. Having that much cash on his person made him nervous.

With the cash in hand, he was ready to complete the deal.

His waitress Randi Obvitz was going to be his main helper in the deal. She had a gram scale to help weigh the product, and promised to pick up small plastic bags in which to place the weed for sale. Then, they'd keep the product nearby the club, but not in the club, with all three women having access to a place for picking up the stuff. Whatever the circumstance, Lou did not want the drug dealing going down within the club. Keep the drug dealing separate from the club, and avoid legal entanglements.

The next day, as scheduled, he received a phone call from the dealer.

"Got the cash?" the man asked Lou.

"Of course," Lou said. "When and where?"

"Let's do it at your place, at noon," the dealer said. "I'll get the money from you, then go get the stuff."

"You're not gonna bring it with you?" Lou asked, nervously.

"No way," replied the dealer. "I'm not that stupid."

"OK, if that's the way you want it," Lou said. It'd been years since he actually made a drug deal, and he realized that everyone would be paranoid of being ripped off or set up by the cops.

The two met at noon at Lou's apartment in the Hollywood district of Northeast Portland. Lou handed the dealer the cash.

"I'll be back in one hour," the dealer said. "Just wait here."

It was the longest hour Lou had ever experienced in his life. There wasn't the kind of excitement he might have had in his youth, waiting to score weed with friends. Then it was an adventure. Now it was business, and it involved a lot of cash.

The dealer returned an hour and a half later.

"What took you?" Lou asked, as he let the dealer into his apartment.

"What's it to you?" the dealer replied. "I'm here."

The dealer entered the apartment and sat down on the old couch.

"Where's the stuff?" Lou asked.

"Don't you worry, I've got it," said the dealer. "What's your hurry, anyway?"

"No hurry," Lou said, trying to get a grip on himself. He didn't want to give the impression he was nervous – which he was.

"So how's business at the club?" the dealer asked.

"I've taken about all of your pussyfooting around I'm gonna take," Lou said, in no uncertain terms. The man was pissed, you could tell, and he wanted either the product or the money. At this point in the transaction, probably getting the money would suffice.

"I'll tell you what," the dealer said to Lou. "I'll get it to you when I'm damned good and ready."

"That so?" Lou gave the man a crooked look.

"That's so," said the dealer, in a rather matter-of-fact tone.

Lou didn't want to get physical with the guy, but he was about at the end of his rope. He was considering what to do next when the dealer broke out laughing.

"I'm fuckin' with you, man," the dealer said. "Chill. I've got the stuff.

"OK, cowboy," said the dealer, "here's the stuff," as he quickly whipped out a long, fat package the size of a submarine sandwich from inside his jacket, magically, as if out of nowhere.

"Excellent," said Lou.

"Let's keep the deal going," Lou said, as he examined the merchandise. The dealer got out a pipe and a cigarette lighter.

"I like what I see… and smell," Lou said. He'd opened the package, and the dank rank reek of the skunky weed began to permeate the residence. It had an unmistakable odor. Even without burning the damned stuff, it gave off a powerful and smelly signature.

The dealer got out some weed and placed part of a bud, about the size of an M&M candy, into the pipe. He lit the green material, taking a long drag. Then he passed the pipe to Lou.

Lou turned down the chance to take a puff of the sweet-smelling marijuana.

"No, thanks, really," he said. "God I love that stuff, it's great."

"So why don't you take a hit?" the dealer asked.

"I'm not into it anymore," Lou replied. "It's something that I used to do that I don't do anymore, like LSD."

"Gone soft on us, eh?" the dealer said. "You're not gonna get up on your high horse and start lecturing me about the negative effects of drugs, are you?"

"I'm no hypocrite," Lou said. "I used to smoke pot, and I don't have any objection to other people smoking it. I don't like the side effects."

The dealer put down the pipe after only two hits. He was plenty stoned on the high-quality bud and was cast adrift in a cloud world. The dealer got out of his stupor long enough to come up with an intelligent response.

"Like what?" the dealer said. "What kind of effects, man?"

Lou didn't really feel like having to explain his whole philosophy about drugs. It was complex. The dealer may be feeling good while under the influence, but Lou was feeling good, too. He was in good place in his mind. He was happy he wasn't so weak as to have to smoke the pot. It was also his philosophy, as espoused in the movie, Scarface, that in dealing drugs, you "Don't get high on your own supply." But there was more to it than that.

"Well," Lou said, "first of all there's the residual effect the day after. It's like having a hangover, except I call it getting 'burned out.'"

The dealer raised his eyebrows. He was familiar with getting "burned out," as Lou put it. It wasn't exactly like a hangover, in that there wasn't any painful headache or nausea. It was a feeling of being psychologically drained, emotionally numb, intellectually faded.

"I know you what you mean," the dealer said.

"There's also the fact," Lou continued, "that I did enough weed and acid back in the day to satisfy me. I certainly don't need to take any more chances with acid, that's a wild thing. But with pot, well, I'm OK with the way my mind works now. I don't need to cloud my decision-making process."

"But you're not against other people experimenting?" the dealer asked.

"That's true and not true," Lou said. "I think there are some people who shouldn't take psychoactive drugs. I couldn't really say who those people are, but I've seen guys whose minds were already unbalanced enough as it was. Drugs for them turned their minds into mush."

"Yeah, I know what you mean."

"There's also another type of person," Lou said, "who gets easily addicted to stuff, you know what I'm talkin' about, guys and gals who get hooked on other stuff like booze or porno. Those people are always gonna have to watch out they don't get hooked on something new. So pot probably isn't the best thing for them."

"I know, I know," the dealer said, reaching for the pipe again. "Are you sure you don't want a hit?"

"Nah, I'm good," Lou said.

The two sat there in silence for half a minute. The dealer's mind wasn't functioning as sharp as it could have been. Lou's mind was racing.

"Another thing," Lou said. "Getting high is also something to do on special occasions, not because it's offered out of the blue. I appreciate you offering me some, but I've got to keep my wits about me, and I've got more stuff to do today. If I got high right now, I'd be worthless for the rest of the day. And when the effects wear off, when I finally 'come down,' I tend to get sleepy. I need to be alert, there's a lot to do today."

"Sure, sure," said the dealer. "I understand." The dealer was tired of listening to Lou's excuses for not get stoned with him. It didn't matter to the dealer. "More for me," he thought to himself. The drug is expensive, and not altogether that easy to come upon, so it was OK that Lou didn't want to smoke it.

The dealer was curious about something.

"Hey," he said to Lou. "I heard tell that you're a Vietnam vet. Did you get to score some good weed when you were stationed in Southeast Asia?"

Lou looked at the dealer and wondered if it were wise to get into his military background with the man who dealt drugs. Satisfied there wasn't a risk, he opened up.

"First of all," Lou said, "I served in the theater of conflict, in Taiwan. I was attached to a U.S. Air Force base there as an Army supply grunt, for some reason. So although I got the ribbon for serving during a war and in the so-called theater of conflict, I didn't do the hard work the other guys did by fighting and dying in Vietnam."

The dealer shook his head up and down in affirmation, though his mind was so adrift that he really didn't completely understand what Lou meant. To the dealer, who had never served in the military, the distinction seemed hazy. It seemed to him that if you were in the military, you were in the military, and could be asked to kill someone at any moment, no matter who you were or where you were serving. He thought of it like someone in a basketball or baseball game, sitting on the bench waiting for his turn with the ball or at bat.

"Second," Lou went on, "Taiwan wasn't like Vietnam. The people there weren't living in the modern world, they were still living in the days when getting stoned meant getting liquored up on bourbon or vodka. That was their version of a good time.

"In fact," Lou said, "they shot heroin dealers. Execution by firing squad. I heard about it, and American military witnessed the executions. So scoring weed over there was a hassle. In fact," he stressed, "I scored weed only once in the 13 months I was stationed there. The situation was so desperate that dudes were getting high on cough medicine. They had parties where they got high on cough medicine, for the codeine, for God's sake."

The dealer was numb. The combination of the effects of the marijuana and Lou droning on and on about the Vietnam War, Taiwan and cough medicine had made him quite sleepy. He shook his head vigorously from side to side and blinked his eyes a few times to regain some semblance of consciousness and sobriety. It was time to leave. Time to get the hell out of there.

The dealer got out a plastic container, placed the smelly pipe in it and stuffed the whole affair in his front pocket.

"I'll see you," said the dealer to Lou. Lou's back was to him as he headed to the apartment door.

"If I could only get more folks like you lined up," the dealer said as he opened the door, "to buy this stuff. It's so hard to move weed in this town. Or anything. This town is so tight."

"I know what you mean," Lou said, as his parting words, and the door shut.

Linda's brother called one night while Linda was enjoying some time off from work. Her brother Joe lived in North Portland, across the city from Linda.

The two siblings did not get along. They were close as children, but as adults developed their own lives and friends, and had drifted apart. They only stayed in touch with each other out of family loyalty. Linda did not consider her brother a friend.

Her brother Joe began babbling about some problem at work. Joe was always having problems at work. He'd never been able to hold a job for longer than a year or so. At first the position Joe held was the greatest job in the world, but it didn't take but a few months before he became hypercritical of everyone he worked alongside. Within a few months he would develop an attitude about the job, and how he thought he could make it better.

Linda listened patiently as her brother went on and on about the strife, seemingly created in his own mind, about his latest workplace.

After 20 minutes of her brother's diatribe, Linda had enough. She then made a big mistake. She decided to give him some advice. He didn't take it so well.

"Don't argue with me," he said.

"OK, OK," she said, condescending to her brother. "I'm not arguing with you."

She realized once again that he was the type of person who didn't want to listen to anyone else's opinion, that he had it all figured out. He certainly didn't want any guff from her.

"Don't tell me what to do," he said. "I know what I'm doing."

So she kept her mouth shut from that point on. No need to give him any advice, good or not. He was going to do what he wanted, no matter what anyone said. She'd already had a taste of his attitude in earlier conversations. She would take the time to explain several salient points, but it didn't matter, she was wasting her time. He was going to do what he'd already decided in his mind.

He was the type to create the answer before he understood the question. He colored his world with his view of it, and no one could convince him otherwise. He was stubborn, set in his ways and full of himself. There's no stopping a man like that, and she began to realize it. She sat there brooding over his surly nature. Out the blue, she had to say something.

"I'll keep my opinions to myself," she snapped at him. "You seem to know what you're doing anyway."

"That's fine with me, dear sister," Joe said, and hung up the phone.

Linda sat in her apartment thinking about what had transpired. It seemed her brother was losing his mind. It was as if the whole world was losing its mind. Linda was nonplussed; she'd been through these episodes with her brother before. It'll all blow over after a few days. Or weeks. She was tired from arguing, and drifted off to sleep while sitting on her couch.

She was jolted awake by the phone ringing.

"Linda?" said the woman's voice.

"Yes," she said.

"This is Marcia Calibri."

There was a strain in Marcia's voice and she sounded agitated.

"Yes, Marcia," Linda said. "It's kind of late to call, don't you think?"

"I know, I know," Marcia said. "I had to talk with you. I tried to call earlier, but the line was busy, so I waited a while and called back."

"Oh," Linda said, "I was talking to my brother. What's going on, Marcia?"

"Linda, I need to talk to you."

"I heard you the first time," Linda said, beginning to realize that Marcia is no better mentally than she has been.

"Linda, Linda, I'm worried," Marcia said.

"Worried about what?"

"I'm worried about having an alibi," Marcia replied.

Linda was getting a bit worried.

"An alibi for what?" Linda asked.

"I want someone to die, and if they do, I don't want to get blamed for it."

Linda was really worried. Her old friend, who was now becoming more of pain in the neck than anything else, was going over the edge.

"Marcia," Linda said, "you're beginning to worry me. Tell me what's going on."

"I hate this man so much, I wish he were dead. But now I'm beginning to think that if he does die, I might get blamed for it."

Linda rolled her eyes upwards, not knowing what to think. She wished her old friend Marcia would go away and stop bothering her. Every once in a while, ever since Marcia went "around the bend" and moved to another state, she'd call with some sort of dramatic catastrophe, and Linda would have to salve her friend's upended emotional state.

At first Linda didn't mind talking to Marcia, but there was so little left of Marcia's mind, and though Linda wanted to help, it didn't seem like anything she did helped at all.

"Marcia," Linda told her, "I'm afraid there's not much I can do for you. Have you thought of seeking counseling?"

"Counseling?" Marcia asked. "I've already received counseling, a psychiatrist, and he's got me on some sort of combination of medications that don't seem to help."

"Well, you need to stick to it, girl," Linda said. "But I don't know what to say about your other issue. I don't think you need to worry so much about it. Just put the whole thing about your friend possibly dying and you getting blamed for it out of your mind. That's my advice."

"That's it?" Marcia said. "You haven't helped at all," Marcia's voice beginning to sound strained and excited. "I'm reaching out for help and that's all you have to say?"

"I'm sorry, Marcia," Linda said, "I don't know what else to tell you."

"Thanks for nothing," Marcia said, her voice trembling. "I'll keep my thoughts to myself from now on," and hung up the phone.

Now it was Linda who was upset. She'd tried to be patient with her friend, but there wasn't anything Linda could say to help. Linda sat in the near darkness and contemplated the situation.

CHAPTER 23

Another night at the Club Festival.

Linda Avery was busy hustling drinks to the thirsty men and women who had come to her establishment to get away from home and work, and to unwind in a relaxed atmosphere. She moved from bar to table and back again, filling drink orders, filling food orders. It was part of the gig; as the club's cigarette girl, she had learned to adapt to circumstances. Sometimes circumstances call for a cigarette girl to move her fanny and fetch some drinks. She also took orders for food.

The food at the club wasn't bad; the cook in the back, the old guy with the long grey hair, came up with dishes that were actually highly edible. He seemed to know what he was doing. He and the other cooks who worked there had a commitment to quality food. At least no one had dropped dead from food poisoning. Linda also knew it was the law that food be at least available at a place where liquor was served. The Oregon Liquor Control Commission saw to that.

Linda found it amusing that within the OLCC name was the concept of "liquor control," when there were so many who couldn't control their liquor at all. People who look forward to that one drink that gets their day started on the right note.

Sloppy drunk men and women were the bane of her existence. She put up with it as best as possible. Of course, if someone got out of hand, there was always Lou around to give the offender a gentle push out the door.

"Hit the bricks, meathead!" would be the goodbye received.

Linda kept an eye out for anything unusual, anything out of the ordinary. She knew her boss Lou would be appreciative of any information regarding a nefarious scheme or diabolical plot. She only wished that Lou would take her idea of planting listening devices under each table to spy on customers. He rejected that idea without thinking about it.

"Lou," she said the day she brought up the listening devices, "I've got another great idea."

"Oh, yeah?" he answered, interested in hearing more. He liked Linda well enough, as well as he could. He was cold-hearted, having been through the mill with a ton of women. He respected women, but he didn't have the luck with any of them.

Before Linda could tell him her idea, his mind fixated on a phone call he'd received recently from an ex-girlfriend.

The ex-girlfriend, now there's a handy thought. In this case the woman was a bit of a chatterbox under normal circumstances. Due to her psychological makeup she would be either down in the dumps or chipper as a baby robin, depending on what life had handed her in the preceding few hours or days.

She called to tell him that she had sex with a fellow who gave her HIV/AIDS, and that the same man had ripped off her laptop computer.

"Are you gonna be alright?" Lou asked the ex-girlfriend. "Are you gonna be OK?"

"Yeah, yeah," she slurred. He couldn't tell if she was on or off her medications; the effects were similar. The drugs she took were supposed to be anti-depressant, but it was always hard to tell if they had any real effect. On the drug she was loose as a goose, but not necessarily euphoric. Without the drugs she might have been tearful, might have been giddy; there was no telling.

Anyway, the call seemed odd and the excuse as flimsy as the day was long. He was used to giving the big kiss-off to women, but to be on the receiving end of some obviously made-up story was disturbing to him. It was as if Lou were privy to a sort of role reversal; that is, getting the flimflam, the lousy excuse, the premeditated sidestep.

"Lou?" Linda asked. "Are you still with me?"

Lou snapped out of his daydream, and shook his head to clear it.

"Yeah, I'm here," he said. "What were you saying, babe?"

"I've got a great idea," she said. "Instead of trying to save the salmon on the Columbia River, why not give up on the whole deal, and dam the river every 10 or 20 miles? There's no way we're gonna save that damned fish anyway, and I'm sure we could use the hydropower."

Lou listened absently to his cigarette girl's banter, but returned to his daydreaming. He sometimes felt as if he was living his life mostly in memories.

"Yeah, that's a great idea," he said, absently.

"Lou," she said, "are you OK?"

"Yeah, yeah," he said back, lazily. "I'm peachy."

He drifted back into the state of ennui that was occupying his dull mind. He thought about the other women in his life, how he knew so many good women, and how they'd all slipped through his fingers. He wondered if he'd ever find a wife. Find a wife again, that is.

Linda wandered away, realizing Lou was not in the mood to listen to her. She also had customers to take care of.

A regular customer she'd seen several times looked as if he might need something more than a well-made cocktail.

"I don't suppose there's anything else I can get you, sir?" she asked the gentleman.

"Can it, sister, I get that kind of chit-chat all the time from the hookers," he said to her, exhausted, worn out from the day. "I've heard enough of that line of bullshit to last a lifetime."

"OK, big guy," Linda said, knowing when she was out of line. "I get it. Give it a break. Anything else, stud?"

"Enough of your hard time," he replied, and turned his attention to his drink, giving the cigarette girl the brush off. She was used to the brush off.

She was out on the tiles, hittin' the bricks, when another customer caught her attention.

"Just the lady I was lookin' for," said the regular customer, another jackass with his eye wandering and his checkbook ripe for the plundering.

"I suppose you need the time of day," she said to her newfound friend. "Is that right, buster?"

"You're right on time," he said, laughing, enjoying his own pun and the night in general. He was happy to have come to the Club Festival, it seemed like a safe place to rest, to kick back and survey the scene in P Town, as the locals call it.

"Scuze me, sorry," said one impatient customer as he cut through the crowd at the club. It was a Friday night, everything and everybody was hot, pulsing and ready for action. It was the place to be. If you were a low life, slow life or the underbelly of society. No one of any particular fame or fortune came here. It was a last resort before making it to the coast or way inland to the desert.

"Sorry, sorry," as another desperate customer practically dove through the writhing flesh in the club.

"Get off of me, you hog!" yelled a customer in the back. One second later, an altercation broke out between two customers.

"You queer bait motherfucker!" were the last words spoken before fisticuffs broke out. Punches were thrown, avoided and returned. So few punches landed that it was like some sort of Hollywood movie fight scene, where the actors are missing each other on purpose.

Lou moved quickly to break up the fight.

"Hey, fellas, let's relax, OK?" he said as he stepped in between them. It was a dicey maneuver, but a chance he had to take. After all, it was his place of business. The last thing he wanted was a knockdown drag out between two drunken customers.

Lou's intervention did the trick. One of the two men sat back down. The other, worn out and tired, shuffled out the backdoor to the street.

Another fine night, indeed, at the Club Festival.

Within a minute of all the excitement, the atmosphere was back to its usual.

Linda had picked up a bit of news about her old nemesis Tail Gunner. It seemed he may have gone from bad to worse.

"Tell me what's shaking?" Linda asked the customer with the news on Tail Gunner. He worked in the same liquor distributing company as Tail Gunner.

"I'll tell you," the man said, "but it's not good news."

"Shoot," Linda said, impatient to hear about it.

"Well, it seems Gunnar's in trouble with the law," he said. "Seems as if he's been driving around in his own private vehicle, and in the middle of traffic, he lays on the horn heavy, for, like, ten seconds. It scares the hell out of other drivers, maybe causing accidents. He does it for the hell of it. A friend of a friend works at the Portland Police Bureau, and she got to see the report.

"Seems ol' Gunnar was blasting his horn a couple of days ago," the man continued, "and was caught by an off-duty police officer driving his own private vehicle. I guess a warrant was issued, and Gunnar got some sort of summons through the mail to report to traffic court. He could lose his license, I don't know."

"That crazy butthole," Linda said. "I don't get him. What motivates a man like that? What gives him joy?"

"I think he gets joy of out watching other people suffer," the man said. "He's one odd bird."

"Thanks for the skinny, fella," Linda said, and went back to work.

Linda happened to wander by her boss, Lou.

"Hey, Lou."

There was nothing coming from the man. He was lost in a total mental flow, thinking about the infinite possibilities.

"I've never seen the devil," he said, aloud. Linda was walking away, but somehow heard her boss's mutterings.

"What'd you say, boss?" Linda said as she turned around.

"I said," Lou began by straightening up in his chair, as if to pontificate. "I said I've never seen the devil, but I'd like to. I'd like to see him come up through the floorboards, grab me by the lapels and pull me down into hell."

"That's nice," Linda said, dryly. She wasn't going to patronize the man any more than possible. No reason to add to his misery by giving credence to his inane ramblings. At least, that's what the cigarette girl was thinking at the time. She might have taken more of a compassionate view if the mood struck her, but the mood didn't strike her, so she was apathetic to the whole thing.

"Lou, are you losing it?"

Lou was stunned for a moment, stunned by what he had uttered, stunned by what the cigarette girl had said. Stunned from the whole thing appearing and disappearing in front of his eyes. His drift was heavy, so very heavy, that it was hard to extricate himself from his own ennui. He was stuck, plain stuck right on the spot.

He shook his head vigorously from side to side, shaking some sense into his noggin. He woke up long enough to realize where he was and what he was supposed to be doing. He looked directly at Linda, grasped the situation and engaged once again in the game of life.

"I'm here, babe, I'm here," he said. "Ol' Lou's on top of it."

"You're not acting 'on top of it,' boss," Linda said, the

consternating look on her face showing the concern and sympathy.

"You must be suffering," she said to him, trying to cut through the bullshit and get his attention.

"What?" Lou looked at Linda with a puzzled countenance.

"I said, 'You must be suffering,' you heard me."

"No, I didn't, smart ass," Lou said.

"Well?"

"Well, what?" Lou said.

"Lou, you aren't connecting, are you?"

"No, I guess I'm not. So leave me the hell alone."

Linda decided it was time to give up on Lou and carry on with whatever she usually does at that time of the night. That would be paying attention to the drunks and drunkards and drinkers, by the dozen, without constraint and without another thought from that feeble brain of hers.

CHAPTER 24

One thing that kept the slightly illegal – and isn't being slightly illegal like being slightly pregnant? – activities from getting onto the law enforcement radar was collusion and cooperation between certain bar owners in Portland. No one knew about it except for those bars that offered illegal services or substances, and a few well-paid off cops and members of the local sheriff's office.

The only vices allowed by these select few men and women were agreed upon ahead of time, and to keep the whole thing under wraps, those previously agreed upon activities were strictly adhered to by all parties.

First of all, no selling of heroin or methamphetamine. All the players involved knew that trusting people with addictions to either of those substances was asking for trouble. Heroin addicts, as meth addicts, will do anything to keep up the habit. If those addicts weren't functional human beings with jobs, it meant they had to rob, steal, cheat and defraud.

Second, if there was to be flesh peddling – better known as prostitution – there was no toleration for using under-aged women. Lou Brodsky at the Club Festival didn't like the idea of having prostitution come into his venue, but he knew that most of the other clubs in the bund offered that vice. It didn't matter to him, he had his way of operating.

Third and last was gambling. Whatever the race track or off-track betting operations didn't offer, most of the time at these bars and clubs you could get in on all sorts of interesting action. Illegal cock or dog fighting, football games, TV shows and Presidential elections. That was another thing Lou didn't like at his club, but as with prostitution, he'd send those curious to another bar or club for that action.

Every once in a while key members of the bars and clubs involved in these illegal activities would meet, often with a member of law enforcement on hand to give out advice.

At the latest meeting, held at the Club Festival early one morning, the de facto president of the combine – a man known as "Jerry" – was trying to figure out if someone in the organization was feeding information to the press. A small mention in the city's biggest alternative newspaper gave passing notice of a growing crime organization in Portland, carrying on a tradition of accepted vice in the otherwise staid quintessential American city.

Linda happened to show early at the club – it was her day off – to pick up her check. She and Lou had a burgeoning friendship, so he had nothing to hide from her. Anyway, although she hadn't been around for a long time, she had been good to Lou, helping him keep customers in line at the club. She knew as much as Lou about the illegal activity there, being one of the marijuana dealers, and had her share of experience with street trash and thugs.

"Jerry," Lou said, "it's not a big deal. Who reads that goddamned rag anyway?"

"Don't try to ignore me," he said, visibly upset by the situation. "I don't like to be ignored."

Everybody looked around at each other. The routine meeting had turned into something volatile. The apple cart had turned over, spilling the goods onto the street. Everybody was suspicious of one another.

"Everybody stay calm," said Jerry. He thought by getting the upper hand, he could control the outcome of this situation; at this junction, that's what was needed. Someone to take charge, to give the proceedings momentum, instead of stalling and heading into chaos, which it would be doing in only seconds, if not given a new direction.

"So now we gotta find out who's the rat," he said. "We gotta find out which one squealed, 'cause it's obvious to a blind man that we got a squealer."

"Shit, you're right!" a couple of participants added, nearly in unison.

"You bet I'm right!" he yelled back.

Now the shit hit the fan.

The spotlight was pointed right at Linda. She was the new one. She was the one no one knew. She was the only stranger that couldn't be accounted for. Jerry and a couple of the bar owners turned their heads toward where Linda was seated; Jerry gave her an icy stare.

"Don't look at me," she looked up at the crowd – which included one fierce-looking woman – with all of them ready to take off her head.

"Don't think for a minute…" she said.

But it didn't matter. The group was in a mean mood, and was ready to hang someone, and Linda appeared to be the likely suspect. Several of them stood up and began to converge on her.

A shot rang out.

It was Lou.

He was brandishing his .38, and had taken a shot straight into the air. A stream of dust came trickling down from a hole in the ceiling above his head. A rotating ceiling fan nearby carried the white dust spray into the atmosphere at the Club Festival. The barroom was suddenly quiet. Everyone, frozen in position, starred at Lou.

"Well, now that I've gotten everybody's attention," he said, quickly taking hold of the situation, "let's see if we can get some sanity into these proceedings!"

That broke the spell. The angry mob acted like a balloon taking a dart – quickly deflated. Anyone standing sat down in their seats.

Lou slowly lowered his weapon, stuck it back in his pocket, turned around and walked out. Linda followed close behind.

"Scuze me," she said as she squeezed past three of the men who were threatening her. Lou was headed to the front door with Linda in pursuit.

"Lou!" she yelled at him. "Wait a minute!"

By the time the two hit the street outside the club, everything seemed normal. No one had been walking by the club when the gunshot rang out, and no one had heard it. That was partially due to the excellent acoustics at the club, but also that it was early morning, and the gunshot could have sounded like a car backfiring.

"Thanks for having my back, Lou," she said, the cold morning air causing her breath to be visible.

"You're welcome, sweetie," he said. "Those boys sure get testy, no?"

"What's up with all that?" she asked.

"They'll all wacky," he said, "totally wacky. But you get used it after a while. That's the nature of the business. You've got to be a little crazy to be in this business."

"Well, anyway, thanks again. I 'preciate it."

"Don't mention it," he said, getting out a cigarette. "You'd better get out of here. Take off."

"Thanks, Lou," she said, and was gone.

Linda Avery, cigarette girl, once again was safe and sound.

Safe from danger. Sound in the mind.

The next day, while having a bite to eat in the food court at Portland's oldest shopping mall, the Lloyd Center, she thought about what she'd learned about hospitals.

Linda remembered what she'd learned about the inner workings of hospitals almost entirely though her nurse friend Beverley Beech.

She enjoyed visiting Bev at the hospital were Bev worked, and finding out how a hospital functioned. The gathering of that knowledge seemed to give her a sense of calm. Maybe it was because life for her, and life for most Americans, started and ended in hospitals, with many trips to them in between.

To Linda, hospitals and the people who operate hospitals were mysterious and interesting. Because she'd been paying attention to details, over a period of time they became less mysterious but not less interesting.

She began to realize that a hospital was a business, sure, but more like a family business. The nurses, doctors and staff were there to help make people better, certainly, but Linda found out it was the turf of those who actually worked there; those employees were there to help each other as much as to help patients. She discovered a profound sense of territory and ownership, and that each person who worked there did so with the knowledge that every other staff person was there to back them up if the going got tough.

Linda knew that hospitals had rules and regulations, called protocols, and when a patient entered a hospital, that patient was under the exclusive care of the personnel working there. There was nothing insidious or nefarious about a hospital, but much like the military, the police and the Mafia, those coming into a hospital were considered "civilians," and as such were given a structure with which to adhere.

Understanding this basic notion was what separated a confused, casual observer from a mature, enlightened participant. Know the rules, know the regulations and you could get along easily with hospital staff. Try to bend or break the rules and you were immediately placed under scrutiny. Linda wasn't sure, but it seemed to her that nearly everything that happened in a hospital was recorded somewhere for future reference. Troublemakers and those prone to argue with hospital staff were noted, if not on paper, then in the minds of hospital personnel.

Linda developed a personal philosophy about hospitals, not as much to manipulate the nurses and doctors, but to rather make sure her feelings and thoughts could be considered seriously if there were any need. There were ways to get along with the staff in such a way as to be able to receive maximum consideration.

Like any business, a hospital is filled with individuals with idiosyncrasies and quirks. The more experienced, older doctors and nurses were wise to anyone trying to pull a fast one. Those hospital staff with less experience generally had to look to those above them for guidance. Those simple facts made getting along with everyone easier.

Another interesting discovery Linda made about hospitals is that, like any business, the people who worked there around the clock, the male and female nurses, worked in shifts. Linda watched and listened carefully to Bev explain some of the ins and outs of the business of a hospital.

"One thing that most people don't realize," Bev told Linda one day in the hospital cafeteria, "is that we operate in shifts, usually simple eight-hour shifts. The way I try to explain it to friends is that if a family member wants information from a nurse attending a loved one, all they have to do is ask. Be direct. Be persistent.

"But," Bev continued, "if someone from the outside is trying to get information about a patient, and they run into a brick wall, my advice is to call back in a few hours. Chances are good they'll get a different person, working the next shift, and that person may be more forthcoming with information. It's all a matter of attitude."

Linda loved learning about how hospitals worked, and felt truly blessed that her friend Bev let her in on the secrets and inner workings of these vital institutions.

Each of us has an accumulation of experiences that create the person as a whole.

Randi Obvitz was familiar with another facet of modern life: racism. She'd seen it up close as a young black woman growing up in New Jersey. She wasn't old enough to remember the civil rights marches of the 1960s, but had older relatives who'd lived through the ordeal, a trial by fire.

She dreamt of a country where race did not matter, where gender did not matter, where all that mattered was what you could contribute to society. She believed in the Constitution, in freedom of choice, in the right to life, liberty and the pursuit of happiness. It was no accident that sooner or later she'd want to defend her rights. It was no accident that one night she and one of the customers at the Club Festival would get into a lively discussion bordering on the subject.

"Thank you, sir," Randi said as she finished delivering the hamburger and beer.

"You don't have to call me 'sir,' young lady," the man replied.

"You don't have to call me 'young lady,'" Randi said.

"What exactly am I supposed to call you?" The man was beginning to sound angry with the banter between him and his waitress. "Do you want to call you a 'liberated black woman'?"

Randi thought about the question and placed a hand on her hip. She gave the man the most serious look she could.

"I am liberated. I am black. I am a woman. I guess you've got those parts right. Now if you could just mean what you say, instead of patronizing me."

"I am the patron," he said, with a big grin.

"You know what I mean, sir."

"I told you not to call me sir."

"I'm sorry, buddy, but it's just the props," she said, then correcting herself. "I mean proper respect. You are the customer, after all."

"I guess what we're doing here is defining our roles," he said, smiling. He was no longer angry, more curious than anything else. The waitress had given him something to think about.

"I'm glad you brought up the subject," Randi said. "I appreciate the opportunity to express myself freely. That's OK with you, isn't it, honey?"

"Now it's 'honey,' is it? I'd like to say I like a woman who's got something going on upstairs other than shopping and the beauty parlor."

Randi felt that the conversation was deteriorating rapidly. She decided to cut it off before either one of them said something more than mildly offensive.

"I've got work to do," she said. "Is there anything else I can do for you?"

"No, thanks, honey, I've got everything I need." He hastily began chowing down on his burger.

Randi walked to the back, not sure what had happened, if anything, with her latest customer. She retrieved the customer's order from the food line, and made sure he was being charged correctly for everything. He struck Randi as the kind of customer who would complain, and loudly, about any discrepancy in the bill.

"Liberated black woman," she thought to herself. "We have come a long way, baby."

"I don't understand what you're talking about!"

An argument between Emily Lou Resnick and the aged cook in the back had, like the food, gotten a little heated up.

"I'm just saying," said the cook, his long grey hair done up in a ponytail, "that in a few generations, people will be wondering what the hell we were thinking of believing in God."

"I don't understand how you can say that," Emily Lou gave back. "It doesn't make any sense. How can something that's so much of our culture disappear like that? It won't ever happen. There will always be a belief in God."

"Don't count on it. I can tell you that attitudes have already changed, in the last couple of generations. Look at the number of people not attending church, you read about it all the time, how certain churches are going downhill because the aging parishioners are dying off, and no one is replacing them."

"Oh, I heard about that," Emily Lou said, "but there are people taking their places, young people who believe in God and church."

"Yeah, yeah, I'm sure of it. But the numbers are dwindling. Unless of course you watch TV, where the audiences are packed into auditoriums."

"You're egging me on," she said. "I'm trying to have a rational conversation here, and all you do is bait me. I don't think I like talking with you."

"You must," the cook said. "Otherwise you wouldn't be standing there giving me such a hard time over something so trivial."

"I don't consider the belief in God a trivial matter."

"Well, for once we're in agreement. The belief in God has never been trivial. Look at all the people who have fought and died and killed over the belief in their God."

Emily Lou glared at the cook. She was, like the soup, about to boil over.

"You are such a jerk!" With that final comment, Emily Lou turned abruptly around and walked away from the discussion.

Randi stopped Emily Lou as she stormed out of the kitchen area.

"I overheard you two," Randi said. "Quite the heated discussion, no?"

"I'm not interested in talking anymore about the subject of God, church or anything related."

"OK, OK," Randi said. She stood as Emily Lou took off for parts unknown. Randi was thinking to herself that it was possible Emily Lou had exited the premises and was on her way to church to pray.

"That's not fair," Randi thought to herself. "I shouldn't prejudge the woman. Maybe she's not a rabid God believer. I don't even know her."

Randi finished looking over the bill for her customer, and went back out to see if all of her customers, including him, were happy. That was her job.

CHAPTER 25

Now Linda remembered why she didn't like smoking weed.

It's too disorienting, and she knew it. It made her anxious. It made her go spiraling into herself, become paranoid, withdrawn.

But, she had to share a toke with the tall, strange man. She was fascinated by his chiseled good looks and his height. Wicked tall, as they'd say. Still, she was making a big mistake hanging out with a man who buys marijuana from a cigarette girl.

"Take another drag, sweetie," he purred.

"I'm good," she answered back, barely able to talk, a combination of dry mouth and of having the drug coursing through her veins.

"Man, this stuff sells itself," he said. He proceeded to smoke the rest of the marijuana cigarette, also known as a joint, until it was down to what is called a roach; at that point he handed the disheveled remnant back to Linda for her disposal.

She didn't care how much of the joint he smoked. She was suddenly extremely tired of hanging out with the good-looking stud. She wished to hell she'd never offered to test it with him. She'd taken him to the available apartment above the Club Festival. "Never fraternize with the customer," she thought to herself. "First rule of trafficking."

It was late in the day, around 9 p.m. Linda took a break from her work selling cigarettes and sundries to enable her to sell the marijuana to the man, something she might not have done normally. But it seemed like something she could pull off and not have a problem. The fact that she was smoking dope during her work shift was not usual, but she felt she could handle the effects of the pot. She'd maintained her cool previously under much more stressful circumstances; at work she was queen bee.

Suddenly, the stranger made a violent move toward Linda. He grabbed her from behind, putting his left arm around her throat.

"Stop!" she yelled.

"Shut up, bitch," he growled back, shoving his right hand over her mouth.

"St…" she tried to yell, fighting the large man.

But the struggle was for nothing.

Soon she'd begin to fold, and he'd have his way with her. He shoved her to the floor, holding her by her throat with one hand while peeling down her pants and underpants with the other hand, in one continuous tug, to expose her lower half. She was stunned with fear. He let go of her throat.

"Lay there, baby, and don't say a word."

Dumbstruck with intense fear, she could only watch as he pulled down his pants in preparation for the act of rape.

When it was all done, he was filled with shame.

"I'm sorry," he said, pulling up his pants. "I'm sorry."

Linda pulled on her underwear and pants, and stood up. She looked her attacker straight in the eyes.

"You're not sorry, you bastard," she said to him, her voice shaking.

"I am, baby, I am," he repeated. "Believe me, I'm really sorry."

But he wasn't sorry for any good reason. He wasn't sorry he raped her. He was sorry he might get arrested for the crime. He was sorry she was alive and a firsthand witness to his sexual brutality. He remembered an old school buddy telling him once, "It's only illegal if you get caught."

As he finished pulling up his pants, his mind was abuzz with activity. Once the sexual act was over, he was transformed from a seething sexual beast to a calculating killing predator.

He realized in his manipulating mind there could be in his reality only one thing to do.

He'd have to kill the cigarette girl.

Sure, someone probably saw him at the Club Festival, whispering to her as he asked about getting the weed, but since he was a transient anyway, taking off for another city would be easy. His only choice was to eliminate the only witness, the victim, of his heinous crime. He could show no mercy, no compassion if he were to continue roaming the streets and taking advantage of the weak, the infirmed, the sick. His mind was made.

It was either him or her.

A loud racket all of a sudden came from the street.

When Linda turned around to see what the noise was, he reached into his pocket.

"Quick and easy," he said to himself, "quick and easy."

When Linda turned back around, the man was holding a knife in front of her face. She knew that the time was now, or there may not be another time. Another time for her.

He lived in a black and white world, no more, no less. The man knew what he knew. Everything else was superfluous. In his world, he was king. He thought of the world as his own, not meant for anyone's enjoyment but his. He was the physical and spiritual reminder to all other human beings of madness, pure and simple, filled with evil, filled with passion and avarice and device. Full of the qualities buried deep, qualities that drive men mad, that makes them first crazy and then insane.

The stranger symbolized the end of all that is good and right, and the beginning of the evil and the wrong. Seeing this powerful evil clearly, about to go into action, Linda knew she had no choice than to take matters into her own hands.

She knew she could wield power as well as any man. It wasn't for her to prove, but when the time was right, she would prove herself.

"I'm my own woman," she'd tell anybody. "I'm a cowgirl riding the desert." She was a cowboy in her own way, now more than ever before. She took life one day at a time, one step at a time. She seemed to be on top of her game. It would be time to prove that image.

"Look out for the rough stuff," he said, and took a brutal slash with the knife.

Linda's reaction was quick. She lithely stepped back just enough for the man's knife to miss. Then she went on the offensive.

Her left arm quickly rotated to the right and up, catching her assailant's arm with the knife in it, and the knife flew out of his hand.

With her right arm, she took the heel of her hand and jammed it into the underside of his nose, shoving the man's nose into his brain. She felt the cartilage move, sliding up and inside the skull. It knocked him out instantly. Whether her assailant died or not was of little concern to Linda. She knew it was either her life or his death.

Linda was in shock, medical shock.

She'd never done anything like that before, but had seen it done previously as visuals to modern media. It was part of our violent culture, the martial arts films, the Dirty Harry films, cowboys, gangsters, men with power and a willingness to wield that power on a wholesale basis.

But still, the sight of the man lying motionless on the floor was enough to make anyone feel a bit queasy. Blood had begun running from the front of his face.

"I think I'm going to vomit," she said, aloud. She lurched forward, heading to what she hoped was the bathroom.

She tripped over an old cardboard box, hurled herself into the wall, and was knocked out like a light. The whole incident, with her rape, near death and then his instant demise, was more than she could handle emotionally or physiologically. It had wiped her out, drained her thoroughly and left her with no energy in reserve; you could have knocked her over with a feather.

Linda woke up a couple hours later and found herself sprawled out on the floor. Although it was dark, there was enough light coming into the room from the neon lights on the street for her to see the outline of the man who attacked her. Barely visible was a shiny pool of blood around the man's head. The man she had to kill.

Linda was momentarily stunned, waking from a deep sleep to find herself living a horrific nightmare.

Then the whole horrible ordeal began to seep back into her mind. The rape. The attack by her rapist. Her killing her attacker.

She began to shake uncontrollably, and broke down and cried. She cried for a total of two minutes, and then began to get a grip on the situation. She sat up.

"I've killed a man," she thought to herself. It was a shocking self-revelation. She thought back to the time she saved Tail Gunner's life from the fire, and the whole play of her life unfolded in front of her. She saved a man's life; then she took a man's life.

She began to shake uncontrollably again and vomited onto the floor. After she emptied the contents of her stomach, she wiped her mouth with the sleeve of her left arm. With the sleeve of her right arm she wiped the tears from her eyes.

She sat for another minute, drained of energy but filled with tension and anxiety.

"It's over," she said to herself. "It's all over."

Her eyes rolled back into her skull as she fell backwards and passed out again. This time she slept until the middle of the morning of the following day. She awoke, looked around the place and remembered what had happened.

She dusted herself off and got up. It was time to deal with the situation.

She would tell the cops the whole story, that's for sure. No reason to hold back this time with the truth. Besides, the dead man acted like the type who'd have a criminal record.

Before leaving the fetid apartment, now filled with the malodorous stench of old marijuana and fresh vomit, she thought about the situation. She thought about the incident and she thought about the man who was dead. If he had family, no one cared anymore about his existence, she was sure of that. Friends? Yeah, right, a man like that probably had no friends. That left the only people with some reasonable connection to this wayfarer, the legal authorities. She asked herself, would they care that another despicable criminal haunting the city was now dead? No, they wouldn't. It would be the opposite, that they'd like the fact. Would the authorities care who killed the killer? No, that's not important, she hoped.

Not much time to act, she thought, looking at the man who had raped her. The blood was pooled all about his head. He was as motionless as a slab of beef. Linda once again started to become sick to her stomach, thinking of the man who attacked her. She realized he was most certainly dead. He was dead.

"Man," she thought, "this place really stinks."

It was time to call the cops.

First she'd tell Lou. He may have some handy advice. She left the scene of the crime and went downstairs to the club. Apparently no one had heard the rape and struggle in the apartment the night before.

No one saw as Linda entered the club from a rear staircase. As she wove her way through the club, she was in a trance, noticing nothing. She knew she probably didn't smell great, but that was her last concern. As quickly as she could, she found Lou.

Lou could see by her condition she'd been through something traumatic. She sat down in his office and sobbed out the whole story.

When she was done, she felt relieved. Lou called in one of the waitresses, Randi Obvitz, and told her to bring a cold, wet towel and a couple of glasses of water.

"I wondered where you'd gotten to last night," Lou said. "I was kind of worried when you didn't come back to work. I saw you leave with a guy, but I didn't think anything of it. I thought you'd gotten lucky, or something like that. I really let you down, didn't I?"

"No, Lou, don't say that. You're a great guy. I'm an adult. I should be able to take care of myself. I didn't. I let some asshole take advantage of me. Then I killed him. He's still up there in the apartment. I've got to call the cops. What am I supposed to tell them?"

"Tell them the truth," Lou told the shaken cigarette girl. "Don't try making anything up, because if they take you in for interrogation, they'll trip you up with your own lies," the bar boss continued to counsel. Randi brought the towel and the drinks, and left.

"A stack of lies," she said, in return, with an understanding wink. "It's pretty obvious that I can't lie my way out of this, isn't it, Lou?"

"No, Linda," he said. "Play it straight this time."

Lou thought about what he said, and then amended his statement to Linda.

"There is one thing I'd like you to avoid."

"What's that Lou?"

"You probably need to avoid telling the cops you were selling pot to the guy. That's what was going on, wasn't it?" If Lou was correct in his assumption, Linda was selling some of the pot that he had purchased in bulk and was providing the staff at the Club Festival to sell.

"You're right, Lou, I was selling some of the pot you fronted me. So what am I supposed to tell the cops?"

"You can tell them anything you want," he said, "but whatever it is, you need to stick to it. Let's put our heads together and come up with a reason."

Linda took a drink of water, and then wiped her face with the towel.

"I got it, Lou!"

"Lay it on me."

"I'll say that it was his pot. I'll say he wanted to smoke a joint with me, and like an idiot I agreed. It won't matter, because all there's gonna be is a roach in the ashtray, sitting up in the apartment." Linda opened her purse, took out the small baggie of pot she was going to sell to the stranger, and handed it to Lou.

"You'll probably have to weigh it again before you sell it, to see how much is still there."

"Perfect," Lou said. "Now we've got our bases covered."

She used the phone in the coat checkroom to make the call to the police. She reported the attack, in brief, and the fact that as far as she could tell, the man who attacked her was dead.

The cop on the other end of the telephone line told her to stay put, they'd send a squad car down there right away.

Although she was no longer in the same room as the dead man, in her mind she could still see his limp, ragged body lying on the floor of the stinking apartment. That vision would linger for a few years, and come back to haunt her in dreams. She'd replay the sorry scenario time and time again in her dreams, each time vividly. For the first year, she'd wake up in a sweat, bolt upright in her bed. She remembered right before waking crying out for help, in a mumbled way, half asleep, half awake.

Not that she really had bad dreams generally. Nothing too wild. She was afraid of heights, so in her dreams she always seemed to be getting into a rickety elevator to the very top of a very skinny building. She finally guessed she was trying to work some therapy on herself, introduce herself enough to the experience, and get over it. She also dreamed of floating or flying, dreams that were joyous.

But one thing she'd admit. She didn't have horrific dreams. Though she may have talked tough, and had seen plenty of terrible images both real and created on the screen, she was not a person prone to violence. But she had seen the blood and guts and the spray of blood in real life.

Yet, she didn't have bloody, crazed killing dreams. Her dreams were pleasant for the most part. She got to visit with people she never thought of, people from high school and the like.

She also remembered having dreams of going from restaurant to restaurant in the downtown area, up stairs, into rooms filled with laughter and food and drink and all manner of people, like some sort of Charles Dickens scene. There would be a plate of food offered to her, and a drink, and everyone there was a complete stranger, yet everybody was ultra-glad to see her, glad to be alive and enjoying the moment.

Dreams only had an effect on her if there was something memorable in the dream, and if she could recall that memory right after awaking. If it was scary, then the day might start out tense and frosty. If it were gratifying or happy, well, that would have a positive effect on Linda's psyche.

She also realized that after you're dead, there's not going to be any more dreaming. It'll be all over. So sleep, necessary as it is, also provides the benefit of being able to enjoy and appreciate the dream state.

Only a control freak like Linda would fall asleep worried that her dreams might take her to places she doesn't want to go. Well, that's the gamble of the dream, baby, and the gamble of life.

Born and bred in the great Pacific Northwest, alongside the mighty Columbia River, Linda was smart enough to understand what it took to get along in this world, what it took to carve out a niche for yourself among the populace.

For her, an upbringing in a small town, with easy access to the big city, reaped many benefits. Bucolic, pastoral days along the river or out in the country, with occasional bus rides to see movies along cinema and theater row on Broadway in Portland.

An easy childhood, excepting the terror of the stepfather, the yelling and screaming and horrid sounds. It was nice. If you were Frankenstein's monster.

Lou Brodsky, thankfully, was no Frankenstein's monster. He truly cared for his cigarette girl, in the same way a father cared for his son or daughter. He'd enjoyed getting to know Linda over the past few months, and felt that they had created an honest rapport between themselves.

He was as concerned for Linda's safety as he could be. He realized that having her lie to the cops about the marijuana wasn't the best strategy, but he had to be honest with her. It was a matter of survival. He knew he was breaking the law providing pot to his staff to sell.

"I hope you understand that everything I'm doing is for your best interest," he told her.

"I understand, Lou."

CHAPTER 26

"Let me do the thinkin' for both of us, honey," Lou told Linda, while they waited for the cops to show up.

"Sure, Lou, anything you say," she said back.

Unfortunately, Lou's thinking never had been that clear in the first place. When God was handing out brains, Lou thought God said, "trains," and said, "No thanks, I'm not going anywhere."

But anything would be helpful to the cigarette girl.

Linda had gotten herself in a jam, and needed the help of a strong, willing man. Lou had been a confidant, friend, almost a father and thankfully never a lover, so she could count on him for sober counsel. He told her to be straight with the cops, that being honest would keep her from getting in over her head, that everything would work out.

"It's easier to remember the truth," Lou told Linda. "It's so much easier to remember the truth, that's hard to forget. But a lie, that's made up, and it's hard to remember anything made up, even an hour after you made it up.

"That's how the cops trip up suspects," Lou continued to explain to Linda. "The truth is easy to remember. For some people with a photographic memory, the truth is burned into the mind. But a lie, that's fabricated, and the mind has a harder time recalling a fictional story."

Linda listened attentively to what Lou had to say.

"You don't want to lie to the cops," he said. "They'll record everything you say, and use it against you later on in an interrogation. I've seen it done on TV, and though TV's got a bunch of lying crap on it, I'm certain that the cops work every angle to get to the truth.

"Besides," said Lou, "they're supposed to be on the side of the good guys, so don't lie and become an instant bad guy. Be a good guy, not a bad guy."

Lou's advice was like some sort of "Truth, Justice and the American Way" speech you'd hear at a lecture at the Elks club. But Lou knew that at this moment, the best advice he could give to Linda was the straight poop, no bullshit.

Then it struck him. He realized again he hadn't thought about Linda and her attacker smoking the marijuana.

"Oh," he said. "Everything I said is true, but there is the matter of the pot. That's the only thing you'll have to make up. But that'll be easy. Stick to the story that it was the strange dude who wanted to smoke with you, not the other way around. Got it?"

"I got it, Lou. In other words, tell the truth for everything except why we were smoking the pot. We were smoking it because he wanted to get me high, that's the only reason we were up in the apartment."

"Right. Keep that one fabrication in the forefront of your mind, and don't stray from that story."

"I'll do my best."

"You'd better do better than that. I'm not thinking only of your hide, but of my own skin. We've both got something to conceal."

A police patrol car pulled up in front of the Club Festival. The lone officer in the vehicle parked the car and came into the bar. By then Linda was sitting in the main barroom, with Lou behind the bar.

"I'm lookin' for Linda Avery," the officer said to Lou as he entered the bar.

"She's right over there," Lou said, pointing to Linda sitting at a table by herself.

"Ma'am, please come with me," he said. The two went out to the car, and then to the police station. At the police station, Linda gave her story to another officer, who then disappeared into the bowels of the police station.

Of equal if not more importance than the death of the unknown man was Linda's accusation that he raped her. The police response to that part of the story was immediate and swift: They began the process of having her medically examined.

Linda gave the officer the address of the place where the death occurred. The police would begin their investigation.

Linda was then taken to a local hospital, where a nurse administered a test for rape, along with a medical examination. Linda knew the truth, but the authorities had to have the scientific, objective facts. There was no way around it, no matter how embarrassing or demeaning it was to the victim.

The proof was there.

"Wait here a minute," the nurse said after the examination. Linda took the time alone to go over in her mind what she was going to say to the police. Within a minute, a police officer came into the room.

"Looks like we're done here, ma'am. I'm going to take you back to the station now. Are you OK?"

Linda didn't look or feel particularly OK.

"I'm fine," she said. "Let's get this over with."

She had many of her own questions, but was not ready to ask anyone anything. She was still gathering her thoughts.

One thought that popped into her mind was getting an attorney. But then she thought that if she obtained a lawyer, that would be proof that she had something to hide.

"I've got nothing to hide," she said to herself. "I can do this. I know I can."

Returning to the police station, before questioning, the cops needed Linda's cooperation. An officer had taken down some information at the hospital during the physical examination, but there was more information required. Assigned to the case was Portland Police Bureau Detective Tom O'Malley.

"I'm sorry, ma'am," said O'Malley, "but you'll have to come to the crime scene with us."

"Do I have to?"

"Yes, I'm afraid it's necessary in this case. Please, come along with me."

Reluctantly Linda accompanied O'Malley and another officer to the building that housed the Club Festival, and to the apartment above where the incident had occurred.

By the time she arrived with O'Malley and the uniformed police officer, another police car with two officers was already at the scene. The body of the dead man had been loaded into an emergency vehicle by the time Linda and O'Malley arrived.

"You'd better wait here in the car," the uniformed cop who accompanied O'Malley said to her. "We don't need you contaminating the scene."

After waiting in the squad car for about 20 minutes, the officer came back down to retrieve Linda.

O'Malley and the police officer escorted Linda up to the apartment room. Yellow police tape was placed across the door; the three of them ducked under the tape and went into the room.

Blood was still pooled on the floor, looking more like thin black pudding than blood.

"So this is where is happened?" O'Malley queried Linda.

"Yes, but I don't want to be here."

"OK, OK," O'Malley said. "I need you to confirm that it was this apartment. Can you please tell me where you were when the man attacked you, and where you were when you…" he hesitated, trying to think of the right word. "Where the man died."

Linda tried her best to describe in detail where and when

everything happened. She was getting nauseated describing the incident all over again.

"Can we go now? I can answer all your questions back at the police station. This place stinks, and brings back bad memories."

"OK, little lady, let's go."

When they got back to the police station, it became perfectly clear to Linda that Detective O'Malley had an agenda right from the start. His line of questioning seemed to imply that somehow she was guilty of something, whether it be murder or manslaughter.

What was most galling about the detective's smarmy attitude was that Linda had been raped and nearly killed, yet he seemed inured to the issue. It was as if he didn't care one iota about Linda Avery and her devastating run-in. His callous attitude was an outward sign of his inward disdain for women in general.

O'Malley decided the minute he met Linda that she was up to no good, and that he was going to make it rough on her. He was going to question everything she had to say about the death of the man, and do his best to put her in jail for a very long time.

By the time O'Malley was finished with Linda's story, it might be game over for the cigarette girl.

Looking back, Linda remembered the good advice she got from her friend Lou. Good advice she did take. Be honest, he said. The cops are on your side, he said.

Well, Lou may have been streetwise, but he was also a wiseass, and had himself more than one run-in with the law. He'd always escaped prosecution.

Between high school and entering the military, Lou had a run-in with the law that could have put the kibosh on his military career.

One night he and a couple of buddies went driving around, drinking cheap wine and playing loud music. He was young, wild and free. The evening was filled with revelry and celebration.

By 2 a.m. the buddy who owned the car in which they'd been carousing had passed out in the backseat. That left Lou and another fellow to drive. Lou's friend had ingested some sort of pill that made him loopy and unable to figure out the four-speed on-the-floor stick shift. At one point, his friend took the car nearly over an embankment, high centering the car at its edge.

The young men were lucky enough to have some Good Samaritan drive by at 2:30 a.m., hook up a winch and pull them back onto the street. That should have been a sign, a signal, an omen. It was time to give up on the driving and park the car.

But, no, with youth comes inexperience and with that inexperience comes no sense at all. The two continued to drive around. Lou's friend had been grinding gears all night, and Lou had enough.

"Let me take over," he told his friend. Lou got behind the wheel of the car, and off they went.

But cruising around town at nearly 3 in the morning meant they were conspicuous. As they drove through town, they drove by a police car parked along the boulevard. Lou didn't think anything about it.

Until he saw the flashing lights.

The cop pulled the car over.

Luckily, Lou had stopped drinking hours before, and all the cop could cite him for was driving on the wrong side of road and without the headlights on. Unfamiliar with the car, Lou had forgotten to turn the headlights on when he got behind the wheel.

The one buddy passed out in the back woke up with a surly attitude. As the cops pulled him out of the vehicle, he took a swing at one of the officers. Lou watched his buddy go down hard as the cops took him down to the ground. Lou remembered the sound of flesh grinding into gravel.

The three ended up in the county jail that morning, and woke up in prison garb.

Lou remembered the finality of the jail, how in the movies the bars were always thin looking and placed far apart. That wasn't the case. The bars were stout, and there was hardly any room to get your hand through them. It was apparent he was in a place where escape was impossible.

He also remembered the other inmates, some of whom were spending some considerable time there. He remembered one exchange between a couple of the inmates.

"Let's throw up our breakfast," one said to the other.

"Yeah, that sounds like fun," replied his cell mate.

It was obvious there wasn't much excitement in the jail. It wasn't a place Lou ever wanted to return, and he never did.

He got off with a fine, which he was able to pay, and there was no mention of the incident as he entered the Army several weeks later.

But Lou was a softy. He'd lived life to its fullest, and had no real complaints. The way he saw it, the problems a person had usually were the problems a person created. So though he'd been arrested, he understood it was like a game. Play by the rules, and everything goes well. Break the rules and you pay a price.

You see, the law's like any other institution: There are some good guys, some OK guys and then there are the guys who are out to get something for themselves by being on a criminal's payroll.

Detective O'Malley of the Third Precinct was a little bit of all of them.

Corrupt cops are like fleas: If you find one, you know there are more of them hiding somewhere. O'Malley wasn't the only corrupt cop on the force, that was for sure. He happened to be the vilest, the most underhanded one interrogating Linda. His attitude from the beginning was that she must be guilty of something. He was determined to make her crack, to get some sort of confession out of her.

In the case of O'Malley, and for that matter, in any case, one thing that Linda had learned in life was being able to put yourself in the shoes of the other person. Placing yourself inside the perspective of the person with whom you are dealing is the best way to understand from where that person is coming.

That ability comes in many forms.

First, there's the ability to empathize with individuals, to look at an issue from their perspective, to see life with their eyes. It's not hard to do.

Another important aspect of placing yourself in the other person's shoes is not taking anything for granted, and not assuming anything. Don't assume that the person you are dealing with is in the same mental condition as yourself. You may feel grand, or you may feel anxious. That's not necessarily how the other person feels, although they may feel grand or anxious. Also consider that they might be physically sick, emotionally drained or on edge from a nagging spouse or haranguing supervisor.

There is so much to consider when dealing with another human being, it's best to expect the unexpected, to never assume and to take nothing for granted.

A lesson from a professional salesman is good here. When "cold calling" a prospective client or a client on a contact roster it's best when first speaking to the person to ask, "Am I calling at a good time?" or "Am I interrupting anything?" This is the optimum way of placing yourself in the other person's shoes. You may have scheduled a time to make sales calls, but it doesn't mean that the person at the other end of the line is ready for a conversation. They may be busy; they may have recently barfed into a trash container; they may be having sex. Anything and everything is possible in the world.

At the police station, Linda was placed in an interrogation room. She sat there for an hour while those involved in the investigation pored over the data collected so far. An autopsy on the body was being made that instant. The crime scene had been scoured.

The girl who sold cigarettes at a local bar sat quietly, nervously in the interrogation room. Inside the room was a table and three chairs. The space featured one of those long two-way mirrors that detectives and police officers use to observe suspects being grilled.

The room was deathly silent. Not even the noise from the hallway or the street seeped in. It was so quiet that Linda could hear her stomach grumbling.

She thought she was a tough gal. But being left alone in the interrogation room for over an hour began to grate on her nerves. She was thirsty. She had to pee. Her butt was getting numb.

Finally, the detective in charge of the investigation waltzed into the room.

"Sorry to keep you waiting, Miss Avery," he said, slamming the door behind him. "It's been a busy morning."

"That's OK, I've got nothing better to do than sit here," she snidely responded.

"Let's get one thing straight, missy," he shot back. "This business with the dead man is no laughing matter, and I take my job pretty God damn seriously."

"Sorry," she said. "I've been sitting here so long…"

"Screw her," O'Malley thought. "The man who's dead will be sitting in his grave for a lot longer."

As he stood behind Linda, O'Malley finally got the chance to inspect his suspect. He could smell baby powder, or some womanly scent, which emanated from her body. O'Malley was proud of the fact that his olfactory glands worked well after all these years. Not smoking cigarettes, and being sensitive to one of the basic sensations of the human body, those were his keys to making the sense of smell pay off. He'd worked on it. He knew that the nose could distinguish between thousands of odors and scents, and that a good number of them were neurologically hotwired into the brain and its memory.

"I got the police report, but I want to hear the whole story from you. Let's go over it again," he said, with a hint of impatience. "Start from the top."

CHAPTER 27

Linda asked herself: "Where do I start? How do I explain the whole seedy affair? I'll do what Lou told me to do, tell the truth."

"Well, detective, it all happened like this…"

Linda then began to unwind the story, intricate in its details, like the guts of a fine watch, with each detail painfully told. The initial meeting at the club. The customer offering to smoke marijuana with her. The two of them going to the apartment above the club to smoke. The rape. Then he got a knife out and was about to kill her when she took action. Shoved the palm of her hand into his nose and killed. In self defense.

She'd kept her cool during the interview process. It was easy to tell the story, except for the part about the marijuana. She knew she was lying about that, but she wanted to protect Lou from any investigation. He'd been so good to her. He deserved that much at least.

"That's quite a story, lady," O'Malley said, in a gruff tone. "I don't know if I believe it."

"It's the truth," she responded, calmly and self-assuredly, yet with a twinge of insecurity over the lie about the pot.

"I'm sure it is," O'Malley dryly replied. "You didn't leave any details out, did you? I want you to take your time in describing the whole incident. Leave no detail out."

"No, it's all there, nothing more, nothing less."

"OK, OK," the cop said. "So you went up to the apartment to smoke some pot. Why there?"

"Why there?"

"Yeah, why go there? Why not to your place or his place or to an automobile?"

"You're kidding, right?"

"No, ma'am, I'm not kidding."

"The guy was a stranger. I didn't want to go to my place. I certainly didn't want to go to his place. And I'm not interested in sitting in some stranger's car to smoke pot, out in open. It seemed like a logical thing to do."

"So what's up with this apartment? Who is the person who rents the apartment, anyway?"

Linda hesitated for a moment. He was rattling her with his zeroing in on the marijuana. "Did he suspect something?" she thought to herself.

"You must know who rents the apartment. I mean, where did you get the key?"

Linda didn't want to implicate Lou, but at this point, it seemed the truth was the only way to go. She instinctively knew that any subterfuge would result in some hole in her story.

"The owner of the Club Festival lets employees use the apartment in case of an emergency, like if we need some place to crash after a long night at work and we don't feel like trying to get home. If I ask Lou for the key to the apartment, he'll give it to me, no questions asked."

"I see," said O'Malley. "So who is this 'Lou'? What's his last name?"

"I think it's Brodsky," Linda said. "I'm not positive. All I know is he is my boss at the club, and that he lets some of us employees use the upstairs apartment for emergencies and the like."

"Smoking pot is an emergency?"

"Well, I didn't exactly tell him why I needed the key. I asked for it and he gave it to me. He's a great guy."

"I'm sure he is. I'm sure he's a peach of a guy."

"What do you mean by that?" Linda asked.

"Oh, nothing." O'Malley was doing his best to shake up Linda and see if her story would come apart. For all O'Malley knew, Linda and the club owner were up to something.

"So this 'Lou' didn't know the fellow who accompanied you up to the apartment?"

"No, he didn't meet him formally. He might have seen him in the club, but that was it. He didn't know the guy."

O'Malley would have to check out that part of the story later. When he did, he found that the cigarette girl had been telling the truth, that Brodsky lent out the apartment out to anyone who needed to use it in an emergency. He also found out that Linda was telling the truth about Brodsky not knowing the dead man.

"You know that smoking marijuana is illegal in the state of Oregon, don't you?"

"Yes," Linda said. "I know that. But I want to be honest with you, and tell you everything that happened."

In his mind, something didn't fit about her story, but he couldn't put his finger on it. Something was off. There was a silence, a long silence while O'Malley paced the room, circling the table, circling the cigarette girl.

"Now," the cop said, "you wouldn't be holding anything back on me, would you?"

"What the hell are you talking about?" Linda shot back. "Listen. I called you guys to report the crime. Immediately. I told you where to find the body. I could have done none of that, I could have dumped the body into the river, and no one would have been the wiser. Instead, I admit to defending myself against a rapist, and you bully me to cough up more details."

O'Malley was not amused.

"Listen, lady," he returned. "There's a little matter of a dead body, and I want to make sure I understand how this man died."

"I'm doing the best that I can," she said, beginning to get impatient.

"Do better," was all he could say.

Linda began to suffer from shock. The rape, the killing, then the medical examination. The whole process was physically and emotionally numbing. Being placed under such scrutiny, under the microscope, so to speak, for so long was extremely stressful.

The cigarette girl was tough, alright, mighty tough. This would either make her tougher or break her.

"I'll be right back," O'Malley said. As he left the room, he slammed the door. Linda jumped in her seat. She was left alone in the interrogation room. She had some time to think.

She began to realize that if her story didn't wash, if there was some extenuating circumstance, if she couldn't prove her innocence, the least she might be charged with would be manslaughter, not self defense. Manslaughter was a felony that would place Linda behind bars for years. Not a pretty scenario.

She began to think of her life, placing it all in perspective. If she got out of this situation without facing prison, would she do anything differently? Would she live her life any differently?

She began to think about her dreams and aspirations for life.

Out the blue, she began to think of Squint Eye. She remembered a short conversation she had with the man. She daydreamed while her interrogator was out of the room, and she was alone.

"It looks like a downpour out there tonight," she said, as Squint got his hat and coat on for his usual walk home in the middle of the night. Actually, more like the early morning hours, right before closing.

"Yep," he said, straightening out his coat, adjusting the collar. "Just another lousy day in paradise."

"Aren't you afraid of some of the characters who are out this time of night?" she asked.

"No, not at all," he said, with no bravado. "It's up to guys like me to patrol the street and keep an eye out for the bad guys."

"Really?" she replied.

"The way I look at it," Squint said, "the more good guys are out there on the streets, the fewer bad guys. The good guys reduce the odds are against some creep taking advantage of the innocent."

"Good attitude," she said, as Squint headed out the door.

She recalled that conversation while waiting for O'Malley to return for more of his interrogation.

It began to dawn on her: Maybe she was falling for Squint, maybe she was after all attracted to the man with the funny name. She made a promise to herself.

"If I ever get out of this thing," she thought to herself, "I'm gonna ask Squint out for a date."

O'Malley wanted more from the cigarette girl. Much more. He had some burning questions.

One of the police officers had discovered a wad of hundred-dollar bills in the dead man's jacket. He passed on the information to O'Malley, who was curious as hell.

"That's a lot money," he said to the officer. "Our suspect didn't mention anything about a big wad of cash."

"Tom," the officer said, "it's obvious she didn't go through his pockets, because first of all the wad of cash was still there, and second, she never mentioned anything about it."

O'Malley was puzzled. He knew something about the Club Festival and its owner, Lou Brodsky. He knew, but didn't know for sure, that the whole club was dirty, and that criminal activity was carried out there constantly. But he'd never got the goods on Brodsky and his gang.

One thing he did know: That his blond cigarette girl, although she appeared none too bright, was no liar. Everything added up well enough, and if she was anything but on the level, why didn't she frisk the dead man and pilfer his wad?

But to the cop mind, there wasn't anything akin to being able to grill someone during a stressful time. Things come out of people's mouths, wild things, under those conditions.

It's like in the rest of the world. At a job interview. During an interview with a newspaper reporter. Talking to the cops. It's always the same: If given a chance, people tend to say more than they need to. Job interview, newspaper interview, murder investigation, all are basically the same. People get nervous, sweaty, jumpy. The interviewer asks a few questions, then falls silent. All you have to do is shut up and the guy or gal in the hot seat will fill in the empty space, the void, the quiet, with talk. Unnecessary talk.

You've already told the basic story, then the interviewer stops talking. Then it's off to the races. The nervous Nelly starts yammering and jabbering about everything under the sun. Opinions. Wild ideas. It's all downhill from there.

As he paced around the room, the cigarette girl became more and more nervous.

The fact that she had to pee didn't help.

"Can I use the facilities?" she asked O'Malley.

"Sure, in a minute, sweetie," he said, coyly.

After what seemed an eternity, O'Malley told Linda she could use the restroom. A female officer escorted her to the ladies' room.

The hard-boiled cop took the time to consider what he'd been able to extract from Linda.

She was clever, in her own way, but not clever enough to fool a cop. He felt that she was telling the truth, but it was his duty, under oath, to do his best to chase down the details, to get at the heart of the matter.

Linda was not able to fill in the details. Her intersection with the dead man was brief, very brief, and gave no clue as to what he was really up to. The wad of hundred dollar bills, adding up to over $2,000, was a mystery. The man's ID was fake, so all they had to go by were fingerprints. The FBI fingerprint files came up blank. Dead end.

"Where do I go from here?" O'Malley thought to himself.

The answer was all of a sudden pretty obvious.

Grill her hard one more time, then he'd have to cut her loose.

The cigarette girl strolled into the interrogation room, with an empty bladder and a chipper attitude.

Immediately after she returned to her seat, O'Malley leaned on the table, trying to look as menacing as possible.

"You knew him, didn't you?" he practically screamed at her.

But it was too late in the game for his interrogation techniques to be of any use. The girl had given all she could, she had no more to give.

"What?" she retorted. "I never saw him before in my life, I told you that!"

"Don't lie!" he bellowed. "You must have known something was up!"

"Get off my case!" she returned, giving him a steeled look that would melt, well, steel.

Forced to make a decision between life and death, she had made the only choice.

"What was I supposed to do?" she'd ask. "Take the punishment and die? Would you do that? Lie down and take it? No frickin' way."

"What you're telling me is one thing," the lieutenant told the nervous woman, "but what you're broadcasting from your body language is an entirely different cup of soup," he added, mixing his metaphors.

"I'm not guilty of anything but defending myself," Linda proclaimed, and lifted her head and jutted her jaw out in defiance. She was innocent, and she knew it.

"I did it in self defense," she stressed.

"We'll see about that," O'Malley hissed.

It was back to the grind, the slow burn to get the subject nervous enough either to start making mistakes in their statement or to end up blurting out the truth.

"OK, sweetie," he said. "Let's go over the whole thing again."

It was as if she were already on trial, the way O'Malley was acting. He'd loom over Linda, scowling, intimidating as hell.

"Tell the truth," he told her, sternly. "It's always easier to tell the truth. Give it to me straight, lady."

"I'll try," barely audibly she responded.

"Try, hell!" he shouted, "You'll DO IT!"

Linda leaped out of her seat.

"Jesus," she cried out. "I can hear you!"

"Listen," he said. "I'm determined to get to the bottom of this case. For whatever reason, you seem to be hiding something. Do you take me for a fool? Don't you know I'm clever enough to realize your story stinks? It stinks!"

He'd driven Linda to the point of tears. She broke down and started sobbing.

"Oh, that's great, turn on the water works and you think I'll go easy on you! There's a dead man and I want to know why he's dead!"

"I've told you," she said. "I've told everyone I've talked to that there wasn't a choice. It was either him or me!"

"That's a load of hogwash, and you know it!"

"If you're so sure I've done something wrong, why don't you arrest me and charge me with murder! That's what you want to do, I know it!"

"Oh, cut the crap!"

O'Malley stormed out of the interrogation room. Within a few minutes, a female officer came into the room.

"Are you alright?" she asked.

"Yeah, I'm alright," Linda said. "That O'Malley is a bastard! He's convinced I'm guilty of something, but I'm innocent!"

The female officer sat down in front of Linda.

"Tell me," she said, "have you ever been in this sort of trouble before?"

"No, I've never been in this sort of trouble."

"You know," she said. "We have a report that you recently were involved in some sort of incident at a local motel."

Linda took a deep breath. The incident she was referring to was the trouble at the Fleece Motel, where Tail Gunner nearly died in the fire.

"Yeah," Linda said, "I was involved in that incident, I'll admit it. But I wasn't doing anything wrong. In point of fact, I helped save a man's life."

"The officers' report was rather sketchy," the female officer said. "It looks like you're telling the truth, and that no one got hurt at the motel. Are you sure there's not something you want to tell me?"

"I've got nothing to hide," Linda said. "I've told the truth and I don't have anything more to say. I know you've read me my rights, and I have rights. Doesn't it say something that I haven't gotten a lawyer involved? Doesn't that show you people that I'm innocent, that I have done my level best to cooperate with all of you?"

"You're right," the officer said. "I guess we've gone about as far as we can."

The female officer got up from the chair, and was about to exit the room.

"When can I leave?" Linda asked.

"It'll be soon, I'm sure."

"How soon?"

"That's up to O'Malley. He's not quite through with you."

The officer left the room.

Linda sat there and wondered when the cops would be finished with her. She wanted to get on with her life. She wanted the entire horrible incident to go away.

"What more can I do?" she asked herself. "What more can I say to convince these fuckers that I'm innocent, that I'm the victim?"

O'Malley came back into the interrogation room.

"Well, is there anything more to add to your statement?"

"No, I've told you all I can."

"So there's nothing more to add?"

"What else can I say?"

"Let's go over the story one more time."

"One more time? Haven't you gotten everything out of me that you possibly can?"

"I don't know," O'Malley said, grinning. "Humor me. Tell me once again what happened."

After another half hour of intense grilling, O'Malley could see that there was nothing more he could do, nothing more he could get out of her. He was fed up with the cigarette girl, and felt that if she was guilty of anything, he wasn't going to get it out of her this way. He made a decision.

"Get the hell out of here," he barked at her.

"I can go now? Are you sure you don't want to ask me to go over the story for the umpteenth time?"

"You are one snotty broad," he said. "I said get the hell out of here, and I mean it!"

"Thanks for nothing," she replied, with a snarl.

Linda got up, gave him a nasty stare and left the room. Once out of his sight, she relaxed, her muscles sagging from the release of tension.

It was all over. For now.

CPSIA information can be obtained at www.ICGtesting.com
Printed in the USA
BVOW022002050513

319842BV00001B/46/P

9 781612 962030